SPIRIT OF ONE

BY
KEN McKOWEN

Publishing Syndicate
PO Box 607
Orangevale CA 95662
www.PublishingSyndicate.com

SPIRIT OF ONE

BY
KEN McKOWEN

Copyright 2012 Ken McKowen
All Rights Reserved

Cover and Book Design: Publishing Syndicate
Back Cover Illustration by Collette Munk

Published by

Publishing Syndicate
PO Box 607
Orangevale, California 95662

www.PublishingSyndicate.com

Print Edition
ISBN 978-0-9850602-0-6

Epub
ISBN 978-0-982-4654-9-3

Mobi
ISBN 978-1-938778-48-3

Library of Congress Contol Number
2012930981

PROLOGUE

In the Ancient Age before the times of prophets and oracles, villagefellows and peculiar creatures alike kept silently and intently to themselves, living simple lives free from worries and ignorant of fear. Nature sheltered them, never allowing the driving, icy winds from the north to blow down upon their lands. Only seasonal rains, warm and gentle, washed across their fertile fields, replenishing wells and ponds that irrigated life from the rich, dark soils of sand and loam. Change was little, but when change came, it came as quiet words passed from one villagefellow to another, moving as slowly as the ancient ice masses that ground their way toward the Great Sea to the west.

Throughout these ancient times traders were few and adventure travelers rarely encountered. So when the annual autumn trading time brought with it hushed talk and mumbled confusion about a massive and powerful army marching from the western Great Sea's edge to the high mountain eastlands, it was greeted with bewilderment by some and amusement by others.

It was told that a new and dangerous leader had emerged from the Eastern Bottomworld desolation. Furtively in the beginning, then blatantly as his successes mounted, he quickly consolidated power, stealing soldiers, treasures and influence from others less ruthless and less deceitful than he. The word stories focused upon this single and lone general whose name was said to be Aa-Tanox.

In the beginning of Aa-Tanox's rule, he set forth his Principles of Tanox. The Principles were simple in thought and harsh in reality, as they allowed Aa-Tanox and his descendants, power over all who lived and all of the lands they inhabited. Of this the far distant villagefellows initially knew little and cared much less because Aa-

Tanox, after time, had diverted the energies of his great army and slaves to the building of a massive black stone edifice to honor his own greatness.

When at last the time of Aa-Tanox was brought to closure, his eldest son Ba-Tanox assumed control of the empire and its great black castle. As with his father, the edifice became Ba-Tanox's monument to himself and was henceforth known as the Castle Krog. It served as the heart of his ever-expanding empire, an empire whose menacing destruction began quickly to cast its shadowed Principles far and wide. Ba-Tanox was the first to enlist the services of demons and wizards as they emerged from the withering fires of blackness and evil and began to test their dark powers upon the earth and its unwary inhabitants. It was his growing enclave of personal dark wizards and sorcerers who led his soldiers against the ways and lives of the villagefellows in faraway lands, with forays into homes to kill the men and kidnap their women and children as slave workers for his ever-expanding empire.

Succeeding generational leaders of the family Tanox followed in the ever-deepening and darkening footstep memories of Ba-Tanox. They continued to draw upon the Bottomworld powers. Yet, after the passing of nearly two dozen generations of the Family Tanox, and long after the original Principles had become distorted by age and many times redefined by changing interpretations, the darkness of Tanox suddenly lurched outward once again. Its renewed and much pervasive drive sought to suffocate the bright and shining light of truth that lay far beyond the Eastern Mountain edifice that marked the elusive and changing boundaries of the Tanox domain.

During the reign of Qa-Tanox, the most powerful sorcerer from the deepest depths of the Bottomworld, the most evil and magical creature of darkness ever to emerge, chose to serve this new master. The Grand Black Sorcerer created a partnership with the family Tanox, a partnership that rested on a trust as tenuous as the continuing existence of the known world. It was a partnership that was solidified and strengthened by the discovery of a massive gemstone of misunderstood power. The Fire Ruby of Molock stood all-powerful upon a pedestal in the bowels below the Castle Krog.

During the seventh nexus of their ancient times, and upon

the death of his father, Ra-Tanox assumed control of the empire. His demonic Grand Black Sorcerer continued to serve, leading the Tanox armies of doom. His victims were mostly simple villagefellows who cowered before the black knowledge of the Principles, though none understood why. Those who chose to listen to the stories of the ancient talltalists and wishtongues often misinterpreted the vague and wispy fabric of their whispered word stories, always foreseeing the worst and preparing for nothing. Even the distant Eastern Mountain dwellers began to feel their lives and memories slipping nearer to ending forever.

    No mountain cave dweller nor lowly villagefellow had yet succeeded in winning even the smallest of battles against the great armies of Ra-Tanox. Those few who did challenge, perished. None yet possessed the power of knowledge required to guide their visions and successfully penetrate the darkness in order to release the ancient light of freedom. As the gray-horsed armies of Ra-Tanox and his Grand Black Sorcerer raided closer to the remote settlements near the Eastern Mountains, a single and unlikely cave dweller stepped forward.

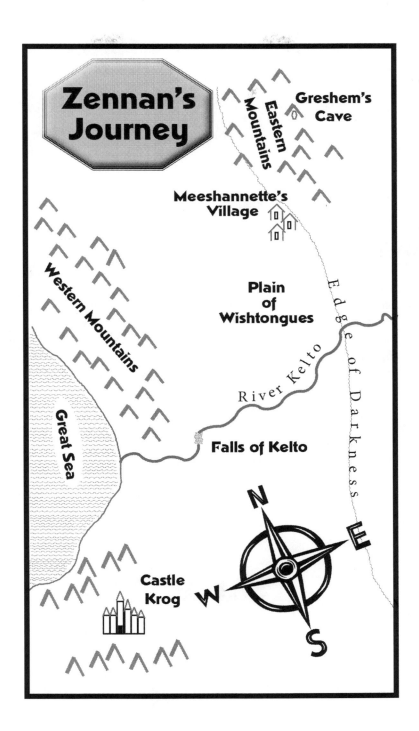

CHAPTER ONE

A lone candle's flame splintered the blackness, dancing its golden rays across the ancient limestone columns. The orange glow from a warming fire pilfered further slices of midnight from the cavern's interior, silhouetting two lone figures crouched before its embers. Their muffled voices added a magical and melodious resonance to the silence of water dripping ever slowly from the ceiling's ancient stalactite forest.

"Yet you continue to believe that such thoughts, merely by your thinking them to be right, powerfully right, will change the course of destiny, our destiny? It is with regret that I must remind you that your naiveté far exceeds the bounds of common ignorance."

"Greshem, your own ignorance and failure to clear your mind of the Principles' evil blasphemy is precipitously more dangerous than any ignorance you misjudgingly perceive in me. We are the only ones remaining who can pull ourselves back from the brink of our self-imposed end."

"You, Zennan, are the one who remains isolated in ignorance, insulated from the masses who suffer at the hands of the Principles," said Greshem as he stood to his full and towering height. Still squatting, Zennan reached for a short stick and stirred the coals of his fire, sending a shower of embers swirling upward, mushrooming outward as they kissed the jagged limestone ceiling.

Greshem's voice grew lower, its normally melodious sing-song conspicuously absent, anger welling to the surface. "You are the one who in your ignorance of reality constantly speaks of change. Yet you remain here in near secrecy, studying and practicing ancient and dead talltalists' rites and repeating their babble, refusing to venture beyond the beginning of the end of light and sever the bonds that are strangling us into oblivion."

Slowly, Zennan stood to face Greshem. His youthful face snapped taut with anger, his mind sharpened by Greshem's intentional antagonism. He extended his muscle-sculpted arm and pointed directly at the old man's broad and wrinkled forehead. Greshem pushed the long gray and white strands of braided hair back from his face, but before he could speak further, Zennan continued the movement of his arm, bringing his finger to touch the side of his own head. "In here, Greshem, in here lies the answer to ending the loss of our present and our past to the Principles of which you know little and understand less," he said.

Greshem's voice returned to its melodious base tone as he leaned over and tapped his own index finger upon Zennan's smooth forehead. "No, in here lie half-truths, vaguely understood notions, and unfortunately, the principles of a real-life ignorant, an untested being fit only to live in a cave, isolated by the misinformed banterings of ancient talltalists. Your mind remains void of any concept, beyond that of foolish mystical rites, of how we might save our once strong and proud civilization," Greshem said,

"You, Greshem, are a non-believer, a hypocritical old man, devoid of hope, lacking confidence in the ability . . ."

"In the ability of good to defeat evil?" Greshem interrupted.

"Yes," Zennan answered. "In the ability of good to cast aside evil and extend light back into the darkness that descends closer upon us with each sunrise."

Greshem turned and took several steps back into the shadows behind the nearest of the floor's limestone stalagmites. He pulled the fur cape up closer to his neck to ward off the sudden wisp of outside frigid air that further cooled the cave's already damp cold.

"You have buried your head in far too many old manuscripts and listened to the fantasies proffered from the withered minds of equally withered talltalists, themselves lost in the unrealities of life and destiny," Greshem said.

"Is it wrong to believe, Greshem, is it dangerously wrong to believe that I can save our world, bring change to lives made pitiful because of how the bloody Principles have directed and controlled our lives?" Zennan asked as he again stirred the coals of his fire, shivering away the cold.

"No, Zennan, you are right. We must believe in the possibility of change, because without change, our world, as pitiful and cowered as it has become during the past millenniums, will surely die. Yet it is in the interest of sanity that we believe in that which is believable, believe in that which can be understood, believe in that which is attainable." His voice trailed off into silence.

Greshem removed his fur cape and tossed it to Zennan who seized the flowing garment with his huge hands. "Here, my cold blooded friend. Perhaps this can protect you from the icy fingers of winter that squeeze the heat from your bones and slows your thinking," he said, his voice tumbling out in melodious sing-song mockery.

"You fear the reality that faces our people, my friend. You fear a reality that you don't understand, Greshem. You prefer, as far too many old ones have preferred, to spin your own fantasies about gods and demons, to accept the Principles' version of truth, rather than cast out their blasphemy with the power of knowledge, defeat the brutal outside force that remains the continuing reality of our domination," Zennan said. He bent down and moved another log into the fire before looking back at Greshem. "You remain here, lingering in your own comfortable ignorance as the Principles continue their total destruction of us, lingering here until the youngest of the mountains rises from the great and ancient seas." Again, he stirred the fire before continuing with words that he had held deep inside his mind since his coming of age. "You continue to do nothing although the encroaching Principles have yet to control us physically with their power and mastery, awaiting and accepting our weak thoughts that bind our minds in submissive acquiescence"

An unwelcomed gust of frigid air rushed the cavern's interior nearly extinguishing the flickering candle, while twisting the fire's smoke and embers upward. A pained moan accompanied the frigid air as Pipman stumbled inside, snow swirling around his half-frozen body. Greshem rushed to the wounded warrior and supported the weight of his body as unconsciousness wrestled control of Pipman's remaining mind. Greshem gently knelt, lowering the limp body to the ground.

Anguish spread across Zennan's face as he realized the labored, sporadic breathing that his last living brother valiantly forced from his body was only moments away from ceasing for eternity. Zennan looked down upon Greshem who still supported Pipman's head and placed Greshem's fur cape over the great barrel chest of this valiant warrior. The beginning of eternity came mercilessly soon to the once strong and brave warrior.

"Your brother has finally escaped the Principles' chains," Greshem said, his eyes cast upward, looking deep into Zennan's mind.

"Yes, but he has escaped in the same futile manner as my younger brother Tomman, and as my father and his father before him," Zennan whispered, more to himself and to his dead ancestors than to his long-time friend and confidant, Greshem.

Suddenly, in the ancient ways of warrior solace, Zennan's voice rose, filling the cavern with its deep resonant pitch. "They will pay for this. They will pay for this, my brother. This shall be their last transgression against my families, against my people, against me. I swear on your cold, warrior's body, their blood will darken the greatest seas, fill the deepest valleys. We will end the crimson reign of the Principles."

Greshem stood and placed his hand on Zennan's shoulder. "I can feel your energy, your anger for the death of your brother, dear friend," Greshem said. "I can feel your need for revenge. But to charge the open mouth of the lion will result in your merely filling a small portion of his cavernous and empty belly. You will not kill the lion king, but only increase his insatiable appetite for our peoples' blood."

"My long and selfless friend, I am disappointed that you bestow such honor upon the Principles by placing them in a class with lions," Zennan said. "As for me, I would much prefer being a hearty meal for a lion king than entertain thoughts of continuing to live as cattle fodder for the Principles' grist."

Greshem lowered his head and spoke softly. "Shall we perform the ancient requiem for the departing warrior spirit of Pipman?"

"You know my feelings about such ceremony, Greshem."

"Your brother did not feel as you."

"Do as you please to honor my brother's spirit," Zennan said. "I shall honor him in my own way. I shall honor my brother tonight, then depart at first light and seek what must be sought to avenge my brother's death."

"So, you have decided to forego your life of self-imposed isolation and seek the mouth of the lion with only the storied lies of the talltalists as your weapon? I shall pray the ancient words for you," Greshem said.

"I hope to your God, my friend, that she listens to the power of your prayers and pleadings and grants me a miracle."

"Whether or not my God chooses to ignore or to hear my prayers and pleadings, I fear it will take much more than simple prayers and a magnanimous miracle granted by her for you to return to us alive, let alone triumphant. I fear that just as the moth seeking safety is attracted to the candle's light, that you too shall be swallowed by the beginning of the end of light surely as the waiting nighthawk swallows the unwary and blinded moth."

"I fear neither the lion nor the nighthawk, dear Greshem. The talltalists' visions have filled me with the strength and power of their enlightenment, a strength and power far beyond that possessed by simple muscle and sinew," Zennan revealed. "I will depart the darkness of my cave before first light and seek the vision that will free our people and make us safe and proud once again, Greshem."

"I wish you well, but wish also that I could travel with you, providing light where your eyes can't see and company when lonely seas of blackness fill the harbors of your mind." Greshem bowed to his young protégé.

Zennan acknowledged the honor of the old leader of his people and responded with a correct and polite head nod. Greshem bid his friend good leave.

CHAPTER TWO

Dawn broke cold and dry, the night's storm lying quiet and pure upon the deep snowpack of winter. The vast and frozen white sea impatiently awaited spring's warming sunshine that would initiate its long and tumultuous trek to its final destination a hundred distances to the west. Zennan had planned that four days of travel would bring him to the edge of the frozen white sea and near to the beginning of the end of light. Like spring's melting snow and its meandering streams, Zennan did not think about his route, but strode ever onward seeking only the easiest passage, the trail of least resistance.

On his third moonrise, the night before the day of his planned arrival at the beginning of the end of light, Zennan slept fitfully, his mind alive with dreams, dreams preaching death, a disturbing contradiction for one so intently dedicated to ending the Principles' millennia-long regime of terror. The contradictions did not remain contained in Zennan's sleeping subconscious mind, but flowered in his consciousness, further confusing, further heightening his resolve.

The wizard who appeared that night, was he imagined or real, was he proffering answers or precipitating confusion? A blue light, its focus tight, its border surrounded by jagged bolts of lightning, bright and thin, penetrating and translucent, emerged from the place where light no longer shines. From the center of the blue light came forward the wizard, powerful in his presence, confusing in his message, calming, yet terrifying.

Zennan looked above the smoldering flickers of light that danced from his warming fire. Fully awake now, his conscious mind overpowered his subconscious need for sleep, his reality a dream, his dream reality. The vision before him, the wizard of blue light, his voice a warbling hollow baritone, spread his arms out, up, and then brought both of his index fingers to bear, aimed to penetrate deep within Zennan's mind's eye.

"You grow impatient in your journey," the wizard sang. "Lest you become careless, it is best that you travel the day only in your dreams, leaving your trodden journey to the starlight vistas that patiently await your coming." The wizard lowered his arms to his side, his long and leathery hands disappearing into the flowing folds of his midnight blue robe.

"You have been long in coming, my friend," Zennan said, his eyes squinted in a vain attempt to shield his vision from the emanating blue lightning that rimmed and silhouetted the wizard's deceptively languid body. "Yet you speak words that are hardly meant to inspire hope in even the most ardent and intent of warrior venturers."

"I make my presence seen only when hope is more than a fleeting spasm in one's mind, my friend. You have traveled far in your life, often on paths that others of less character would have fallen from, tumbling forever, deep into the abyss of ignorance."

"Your point, Wizard? Already you begin to bore me with your timeless teasing and useless riddles and ramblings."

"Such insolence from a man in your vulnerable state should be suppressed."

"Insolence as you term it has served me well, Wizard, keeping me from wastefully pursuing endeavors meant more for the winnowed, worthless and mindless leftovers who now inhabit our land," Zennan said. He reached to his side, chose a small, half-rotted limb of scraggly pinus and tossed it on the fire. Sparks flew skyward, swirled by the twisting winds that accompanied the wizard's presence. "You do not serve me well, wizard, with your weak assurances and mealy worded vocatives that are better served to those with mental palates more accustomed to yellow fat and mush meal."

"I have come freely offering my guidance for your adventure," the wizard said.

"I have heard the talltalist's stories of your powers. I did not believe all of them when I was a child. Nor do I believe them now," Zennan mused, his voice again momentarily taking on a slightly melodic tone as he continued. "Using the trickery of light is well known and often practiced among your kind, but I believe there to be little else that your perceived magical powers can accomplish."

"Even the wisdom of ages possessed by the most ancient of your talltalists did not foresee all that was around them. Much they knew, that is true. You were wise to live among them." The wizard raised his head upward toward the blackness of night, closed his eyes, but only for a moment, then continued. "But even your talltalists do not possess the wisdom of all ages. Before them, there were others of equally mindful tales, and before those, still others."

Zennan turned his back to the wizard and slowly strode several steps away into the darkening blackness untouched by the fingers of light cast from his warming fire.

There was no sound, no movement, but instantly the wizard was again standing before Zennan, his blue halo glowing even brighter now. Zennan tried to suppress his surprise.

"You possess tricks that surpass any I have ever before witnessed of man or talltalist."

"Others pretend. I do not present myself before you with falsehoods."

Zennan again turned away from the wizard and stepped back to the edge of his fire. He used his foot and moved a small, half-burned limb back into the consuming flames. Again, as before, the Wizard's image had moved before him.

"You will stop your trickery and tell me what it is you desire, and if there is nothing that you want of me, what is it that I may expect of you?" Zennan asked, with all signs of pleasantness banished from his voice.

The wizard, silent, stared at Zennan for an eternity. His hands slithered out of the slits that served as pockets in his long, flowing robe, and he folded his arms across his chest. The wizard spoke slowly, his voice firm. "What I want of you is your life," he said.

Zennan quickly drew back from the wizard. He wasn't frightened; in his own mind there was no reason to be. He turned his head to the side, eyeing the wizard cautiously. "If it is my life that you seek," Zennan asked, "what has stopped you from slaying my pitiful being with your supremely magical powers?"

Suddenly, the wizard pulled his arms apart and again raised them skyward. "You misunderstand me, which I find not totally unexpected. It is not your life's blood that I seek. It is your life, your willingness to dedicate your entire being to discovering the truth that lies beyond the beginning of the end of light. Your mind must travel beyond the minds of even your most learned talltalists, beyond the great void created by the Principles."

Zennan stood in self-imposed silence for several moments, shrugging his robe up over his shoulders to ward off the cold. Snowflakes were falling once more, even as the full moon shone through the scattering of clouds that drifted across the late winter sky.

"I grow weary of hearing your riddles," Zennan said, plaintively. "If I continue to open my ears to your ranting and bellowing, I shall never enjoy the success of my quest."

"I have yet to bellow, and I will offer but one last warning."

"Offer? Or will you force my ears to be burdened by your words?" Zennan asked.

"The state of your ears is not my concern, my friend. It is your mind that more concerns me. If your mind remains open you will begin to understand that which you will encounter on your quest, some of which is real, some of which is but a facade that exacts a terrible toll from all those who allow themselves to remain under the control of the darkness that pervades all light."

"Then such shall be my fate should I choose to allow such darkness to control my thoughts, a goal that I shall never entertain, my blue friend," Zennan answered, his words drifting into nothingness as his thoughts entered the domain of darkness, and the wizard faded into obscurity.

* * *

Already, the first rays of the morning sun pushed through lingering clouds, clouds swirled by the winds that emerged from beyond the wizard's presence. In the distant darkness lightning cracked, its flashes focusing their energies on the tallest of the tall mountains to the west. Zennan gathered his meager belongings, traveling light, depending on his skills and his learned mind to secure him food and shelter each evening. As his feet left their lengthening trail of prints in the powdery soft pillow of snow, Zennan once again brought the preceding night's dreams to the forefront of this mind. Wizards? Magic? Blue lights and lightning bolts? Were they real or merely lingering afterthoughts of a stormy night's dreaming?

Soon his thoughts were interrupted. A distant lightning bolt appeared, not crashing down from the sky, but emanating directly from the volcanic mouth of the far western mountain. Zennan watched, amused, concerned, as it seared distant trees and evaporated snow along its path. As the powerful bolt of light approached him, it suddenly exploded just to the front of his chosen path. From the resulting smoke and fire, Zennan's dream Wizard appeared once again.

"Wizard, I felt you in my dreams last night."

"Your dreams are more real than your mind sometimes wishes them to be," the Wizard said.

"And what, I pray you to tell, shall I expect to glean from your words of mysterious confusion, Wizard?"

"You Zennan, you are still but a feather, soft and flexible, warmed by the sun, cooled by the snow, fluttered by the breeze, driven by the wind. You must allow your single feather to become many. Only then will your strength be adequate. As with the eagle, only then will you soar with the strength and wisdom needed to venture safely beyond the beginning of the end of light, where darkness claims the brightest of suns." The wizard raised his hands to the sky, his robe immediately ablaze in blue-edged crimson fire. A sudden blinding flash sent the blue lightning bolt shooting to a thousand distances skyward, arcing through the whimsical winter clouds that remained, then tracing off in a slow, but direct flight, returning to the mountain from whence it had come. The wizard remained before Zennan.

Zennan watched, amused, yet vaguely aware of a change deep within himself, a change he did not know, did not understand. "So, great wizardly one, how would you propose that I proceed on my journey?" Zennan asked, brushing several newly fallen snowflakes from his brow.

"You possess the fleeting gift of youth, Zennan, which will serve you well, while it shall also serve as your greatest enemy," the wizard offered. He then waited patiently as Zennan furled his eyebrows, annoyed at this apparent condemnation of his youth.

With a sweep of his arm, Zennan commanded, "Wizard, be gone from my presence. Your words are riddled with insult, your proffered assistance designed more to confuse and confound than to educate and illuminate."

The wizard bowed low, the bottom of his long and flowing, midnight blue robe billowing out gently from his clawed feet, settling back in a cloud of sparkling dust. He raised his eyes from their downward cast and again looked directly at Zennan. "Your brother, your father, your grandfather before him . . ."

"You knew my brother? My father?" Anger-laced confusion shot through Zennan's voice, although the wizard did not noticeably react to the interruption.

"But of course. And his father and even his grandfather before him."

"And is this advice you offer me, your indecipherable riddles and insults, the same advice you offered to them?" Zennan asked, the anger still welling up inside him.

"It is."

"They died, my brother just days ago."

"So they did. But they died, not because of the knowledge that I imparted to them, which was much as I offer to you, but how they listened, perceived, understood or ignored what I offered," the wizard explained, watching Zennan for a reaction. There was none, so he continued, "You must go among the Principles and understand them, a task not easily learned nor quickly accomplished. Listen to their commoners, hear their leaders, their prophets, their enemies. Each has much to say, and all will present circumstances, but each will behold differing interpretations and conclusions. Some will lie. Most will remain truthful, but their truth is always a perceived truth, a truth seldom perceived by all."

"Certainly they cannot be as confusing as you have been and continue to be."

"You have only begun to enter the world of confusion. It is a troubled and confused empire, shrouded in darkness and deceit, wallowing in evil. While most remain strong in their commitment to do good, unwittingly, far too many often do so only at the expense of good."

Zennan closed his eyes for a moment, then slowly opened them again, in reality hoping that the wizard would be gone, along with his past night's encounter with confusion and contradiction, all merely a continuation of his dream. As light reentered his darkened sight, the wizard remained before him, still surrounded by the blue glow emanating from the center of his being. But, as before, Zennan felt an unexplained surge of change move through himself.

"I shall take my leave, now, wizard," Zennan said, finally. "And I will pass among the people at the end of the beginning of light and learn both of their strengths and of their weaknesses. When finally I know my enemies as I know myself, then, and only then, will I be able to lead my people from the most awesome and debilitating control of the Principles," Zennan said, the words coming from the changes he continued to feel deep within himself.

"Well said, my friend." The wizard eyed Zennan with renewed interest. "And how will you go," he quizzed.

"I will go with the wind, choosing not to fight that which is unwinnable. I will grow in strength, my feathers becoming many, my wisdom great. I shall use the wind to my favor, much as the pilot uses his sail to gain the power of the wind, yet steers his boat where he wishes, not where the wind and sea should dictate."

"It pleasures me to hear that you have come so far so quickly," the wizard complemented.

"Yet I am still standing here talking to my dream," Zennan said. "I believe I will again be off on my journey."

The wizard motioned Zennan away. "Go then, and do not return until you have secured the secrets of the Principles."

"Will I see you again, Wizard?"

"You will see all that chooses to make itself visible." And the wizard was gone.

* * *

More days passed beneath Zennan's feet since he had entertained his dream wizard, the distance to the end of the beginning of light being far greater than he had thought. He passed only a few villages, their inhabitants secretive, suspicious and wishing to remain invisible. They shuffled about their hovels, most of which were indistinguishable from any other. Those few that were set apart were significantly more spacious and surrounded by low earthen barriers. Zennan, uncertain whether these creatures who inhabited the fringes of the beginning of the end of light were yet settled and civil, trudged on, seeking more definitive signs of the knowledge he sought, knowledge that would ensure success in his long and arduous adventure. And, as he trudged onward, little worth noticing passed his searching eyes.

On the dawn of Zennan's fortnight of his meandering passage, he drew himself to the upper edge of a great mountain ledge that cast its shadow tall over the wide and deep valley below. From his outpost, huddled among jagged rocks and dried gray-green, xerophytic vegetation that clung tenaciously to life in this harsh and unforgiving land, Zennan carefully eyed the vision below. From the faded images of three packed-earthen trails that spoked into the center of this villageplace, it appeared that this was a possible gathering land for far distant peoples. He decided that before venturing forth he would sit for a time and observe all that could be observed.

As the morning sun climbed higher and warmed Zennan's chilled body, a brown, shifting haze formed over the cityplace. It appeared to magically attach itself to the upper edges of the mountains just steps below him, spreading outward in a mantel of unknown that reached to the distant ends of his vision. Even during the bright afternoon light the cityplace appeared dark and gloomy as a few slow-moving inhabitants ventured forth, oozing only the vaguest signs of life from within their bodies. As the sun continued its endless track across the landscape toward the far side of the valley, a few wispy clouds cast shadows upon Zennan, momentarily shading his eyes from the sun's blinding rays. Beside him, in the lengthening shadows, a few small bristly-haired creatures appeared from their rock-encrusted sanctuaries to sample the sparse brown grasses that struggled upward from the smallest collections of wind-blown soil. Zennan momentarily diverted his attention to these strange creatures and watched their peculiar behavior.

As time passed, so passed Zennan's vision from the frolicking, feeding bristle-haired creatures, to the darkening abyss below. While the setting sun's rays still lighted his high mountain viewpoint, below, the deep valley's engulfing shadowed darkness was growingly punctuated by sparkling speckles of yellow and white lights. Then green and amber flickerings joined the growing carnival, casting their unworldly colors upon the face of the hovel-like structures. Zennan squinted, his concentration focused on the nearly imperceptible movements far below.

Behind Zennan a branch snapped, its sound too loud for the small and now departed bristle-haired creatures. His body froze. The sound was near, very near. As thoughts raced through his mind about how he should respond to this potential and unknown threat, another small branch cracked, this time to his right and closer than the first. His body remained stiffened, his mind liquid in thought searching for pragmatic answers for confronting this potential threat. Zennan feared no man in his homeland, but now he was a trespasser in a land where reason did not necessarily dictate one's thoughts or actions. His heart pounded, adrenaline surged through his being. Fear gripped his reflexes, although it was not fear of death, but fear of the potential for failing to free his people from suppression and darkness. For Zennan, it indeed was a very foreign experience not being in control. Now, his focus centered upon springing to physical confrontation with his potential aggressors.

"You appear nervous, stranger," came a soft and tiny whisper from behind him and to his right.

Zennan froze his intentions.

"Strangers are seldom seen here and never welcome," continued an equally soft second voice, punctuated by the snap from another cracking branch from behind and to his left.

As Zennan slowly turned his head to follow his eyes that strained hard right to see what creatures these were that dared approach him from behind, he thought to speak slowly and softly so as not to alarm and provoke them into a premature and unnecessary attack.

"Who is so daring as to stalk me in this darkened land of strangers?" Zennan asked.

"You have evidently traveled great distance, for it is you who is the stranger," the first voice said.

"Perhaps you are requiring personal assurances that we mean

you no harm," the second voice chirped, its last word punctuated by the small but sharply accentuated crack of yet another brittle ground twig.

Zennan, his mind and body coiled for aggression, maintained his strained readiness as he continued slowly to turn, remaining in his crouch, until finally he faced his two transgressors. What he saw renewed his confidence that he would not fail in his mission. Zennan roared with laughter. "I see that I need not fear the two of you." He belly-laughed at the two unarmed fat and bespectacled furry creatures with pointed ears and large, thick and rosy lips who stood but waist tall before him. "Why should I not crush you from my thoughts so that I may continue onward with my pursuits?" he asked them, knowing that he would do no such thing unless attacked.

"Why did you fear us so before you turned to face us," the first voice asked.

"Fear of the unknown was the reason," the second voice answered before Zennan could fix upon an appropriate response befitting both his self-stature and the situation.

"So, perhaps it would be to all our advantage if you learned from us rather than attempt to destroy us," the first creature said.

"Because, although our appearance is now obvious, our powers remain mysterious and unknown to you, stranger," the second creature added.

Zennan laughed once again. "Such is the wisdom of little creatures? To threaten me with the loss of unknown knowledge should I choose to eliminate two such inconsequential beings?" Zennan asked, stating a question that he really didn't expect nor did he need answered. Zennan stood to his great height, towering tall above the two creatures. "Be gone from my sight," he bellowed. "Be gone before I change my thinking about why you two should be allowed to continue drawing air into your puny lungs."

"Ooh, you choose the way of darkness?" the first creature asked.

"Others have traveled your chosen path and succumbed to that which they did not understand," the second creature explained. He then quickly and nimbly moved to stand near his friend.

Zennan drew silent for a moment, the words and wisdom from the wizard fracturing his desire to quickly and permanently end this seemingly meaningless and trite conversation. As desire grew to intent that merely awaited his final decision to act, swirling blackness engulfed the soft glow of the moon that was rising above the shadow of the mountain to his front. Zennan became cognizant of this dark and ominous sign that certainly foretold of an evil of a level which he could not predict. He glimpsed down at the two creatures as they muttered words to one another, words unintelligible to himself. He interrupted their increasingly intense and animated exchange.

"If your evil words have summoned these black clouds, I certainly do not fear them any more than I fear the consequences of removing the life that flickers within your two feeble bodies," Zennan announced, turning slightly sideways to these potential adversaries. He slowly and deliberately took up his attacking stance by spreading his feet apart just slightly wider than his broad shoulders. It was his show of a threat that he had no intention of carrying out.

The two creatures quickly exchanged a few last mutterings before the first creature stepped forward two paces, once again alerting Zennan's sense of self-preservation. "Your mission to free yourself and your people from the bonds of the Principles will fail," the creature announced matter-of-factly as he peered deeply and directly into Zennan's eyes.

Stunned by this announced knowledge of his mission, Zennan stood speechless.

"Oh, yes," the second creature interjected. "We are well educated in the ways of your people. Others have come before you, their quests always the same, and sadly, their failures forever destined to be repeated."

Zennan again raised his eyes toward the rising moon. Any small and remnant desire for bringing harm to these creatures subsided within him for reasons he did not fully understand. So then, too, did the black clouds dissipate that had for a moment shrouded the moon, once again allowing its golden glow to feather across the darkening landscape. With more thought, Zennan saw that his options were indeed limited, so he made his decision, allowing the powers of fate to intervene in his quest.

"I have decided to allow no harm to come to you two creatures," Zennan said, but quickly added, "However, for the protection that

I offer, you two will lead me to your living abodes where I may eat my fill and be relieved of my weariness."

The two creatures standing before him merely glanced at one another for a moment, then looked back up at the giant who towered above them.

Zennan felt strong and secure in his direction. Fate was before him, offering its hand and he was not going to allow the moment to pass. "After I have eaten my fill and closed my eyes for a time, you will guide me through the intricacies of this strange world that lies at the edge of the beginning of the end of light," Zennan said.

"Tis a lofty crown you have mistakenly placed upon you own head," the first creature said.

"Manners and good sense your mother failed to teach you, tis obvious," the second creature added.

Zennan stared hard at these two strange creatures who dared mock his words and disobey his command. Indifference and irreverence were not generally responses garnered by his presence. Perhaps, he thought, these two insufferable creatures were in some magically mystical manner associated with his dream wizard. He couldn't take a chance that might prove costly. Obviously, these two creatures feared not his size, nor his strength, nor the reality that within moments he could crush life from both their beings.

"Ooh, his mind twirls in confusion and concern," the first creature chided.

"A decision is near on the appropriate action to pursue, that I can see," the second creature added, scratching at his scraggly but manicured beard, mimicking his friend who was doing the same at that same moment. "Face," he moaned almost as an afterthought.

"Ah, of course," the first creature concurred. "Bravado and bravery beneath a facade."

"Moronic," creature two howled. "Creates much too much distress and much too much suffering."

"And for far too many, it is well beyond their minds that are so small," the first creature added.

Zennan stood in disbelief, his interest now focused only on what these two were saying. "You two are as confused and misdirected as others who opposed my undertaking of this epic journey," he said.

"Please, Zennan, do not perceive debated discourse as misguided confusion. There does truly exist much for you to learn in your journey to the end of the beginning of light, if your effort is not to be in vain," creature two said.

"While I should be surprised that you have in some unknown way assimilated my name into your vocabulary of nonsensical babbles," Zennan muttered in frustration, "I am quickly learning that I should only become amazed if there are thoughts that I am indeed capable of keeping from you. Since you two seem capable of tapping my inner being with your small yet invasive minds, I will simply allow you to counsel me as and when I should request." Zennan's face transformed from arrogance to askance.

"Oh no, you misunderstand once more," creature two said, sympathy oozing softly from his voice.

"We do not read your mind, only your intentions," creature one said. "But together we predict that you will follow us into the valley below."

"Face, remember face," creature two chided.

Creature one looked quizzically at his friend, but frustration quickly replaced his short moment of confusion. "Ah yes, so utterly time wasting and always a nuisance," he said.

"Yet so very necessary for those who still dwell in darkness."

"So it is," creature one said, nodding slowly.

Zennan looked away from his two antagonists pretending to ignore their petty patterings while he adjusted the shoulder strap of his carryall sack.

"We will travel together, providing that you two agree to speak to no one without first informing me of the reasons and content of your intended exchange," Zennan demanded.

The creatures giggled, or at least that is the reaction that Zennan perceived as these two creatures before him again exchanged mumbled ramblings.

"He still fails to understand," creature one said.

"Nor does he comprehend," creature two offered, "though such response is hardly to be unexpected so early in our journey."

Both creatures ignored Zennan.

"Shall we be off?" creature one asked.

"Wait just a moment, here," Zennan suddenly demanded, taking several quick steps toward the creatures. "You two act as though

I am someone insignificant who will simply allow your continued disrespectful actions."

"Hmmm," mouthed the first creature.

"You're right, of course," creature two said.

"Face?" creature one asked, knowing that it was so.

"Face," creature two confirmed to his friend, then turned back to face Zennan. "We must apologize for our perceived disrespect before you."

"Who are you," Zennan suddenly demanded, mostly out of frustration.

"Why should such intimate knowledge be of concern to you?" creature one queried.

Zennan hesitated for a moment, letting his thoughts meander. "If we are to spend our coming days together, I must know how best to call you, at least by something other than how I am most inclined to address you."

"Very well," creature one agreed. "I am One."

"And I am One, too," creature two offered.

Zennan smiled for the first time in a very long while. "So you will be known then as Wun and Wuntu," Zennan misinterpreted. "And now, we shall be off."

"After you, Wun," Wuntu said, bowing and bringing his arm across his body and pointing the way down the dark, nearly obscure trail.

"Oh, no, after you. I insist," Wun countered, also bowing at his waist.

Zennan's patience had vanished. "Be done with your irrelevant and repetitive ramblings and lead on, Wun and Wuntu, creatures of darkness," Zennan ordered, unable to conceal the suddenly rekindled coldness and concern that laced his words.

Wun and Wuntu shrugged off Zennan's attitude knowing that he was incapable of completely understanding their roles, but that he also must maintain face, even and especially among those he would soon encounter in the world at the beginning of the end of light. As the late evening's darkness turned to night's blackness, the two furry creatures trotted off, side by side. Zennan fell in behind them. The night's travel distance to the first of the villages below proved deceptively greater than he initially perceived.

CHAPTER THREE

Overcast shadows and misty banks of shifting fog darkened the sun during the day and blackened the moon each night it was destined to shine. A shrouding gloom had descended upon the world since the celebration of the northern hemisphere's winter solstice. Deep within the great walls of the Castle Krog, home of the Principles, the belching Inferno of the Family Tanox warmed the withered winter air within its dank walls. The rulers of these great lands, for forgotten millenniums the masters of all creatures and peoples who drew breath from the world's bounties, had controlled the fabled and powerful guardian Fire Ruby of Molock. It by its very nature of creation was a part of the adjacent inferno that belched forth from the deepest bowels of the underground nether world, nurturing its presence, harvesting its evil darkness.

Beyond the time when the longest memories had faded to emptiness and the ancestral stories had evolved into mystical tales of whim and fancy, the Principles had been in place. Casting their powerful domination to lands where the beginning of the end of light quickly danced into obscurity, only the tiniest few living creatures managed to escape the will and wile of the Principles. Those few outers who had remained living beyond the bounds of the Principles' sphere of control only temporarily evaded their destined fate. Ultimately most were discovered and toyed with in humorous games of chance or eliminated during the impassioned anger of the ever-searching, testing, grasping tentacles of the family Tanox, minders of the Principles. In a time unremembered, the Principles had morphed from philosophical commands designed to control, into their own disembodied evil being.

The anger of Tanox, as it was understood, came not from reaction to fetes of honor or heroic ventures attempted by warriors of the outcast folks of lowly rank and minimal abilities. The Family Tanox feared not such weak feinted attempts at breaking the shackles of their black and evil power. A few outers had tried, and they had died horribly while listening to the crushing laughter of the Principles, as their last breaths of life were forced from their helpless bodies. The evil of the Principles came from deep within the minds of the Family Tanox members who thought truly controlled the power of the millennium. Yet even they and their newly born generations had failed to fully understand and control the power they so indiscreetly directed.

Within the Great Hall the coronation of the newest leader of the Castle Krog and its lands of darkness, minder of the Principles, had entered the final hours of the Feast of Thirteen Moons. The crowning feast had been set upon the great table's ebony surface before Ra-Tanox, the only son of Qa-Tanox, the recently deceased 17th master of the ancient lineage of the Tanox mastership family. Now that the father of Ra-Tanox had passed into the great abyss of the nether world's belching inferno, the time of Ra-Tanox had finally descended upon the inhabitants of the Castle Krog and upon all those of the ancient and untracked lands hiding at the ends of the most distant darkness. In this final hour of feast, the newly crowned leader of darkness assumed the role that he had cherished jealously and pursued unrelentingly since becoming old enough to know and understand his right of accession upon the patriarch's death.

The great castle's intricately carved gray and black quartzite walls towered upward into the dark sky. Its dozens of spun minarets were controlled by sirocco troops, the most decorated and allegiant soldiers of their new master, Ra-Tanox, the 18th and destined to become the most ruthless leader yet of the great family Tanox. The castle's walls, massive stone edifices that stretched the distance of a day's travel, surrounded the darkness of the master's cityplace. Here, in the towers of habitation, were the places where those cityfellows whose families had remained in favor with the past leaders of the family of Tanox now lived. At the very center of the cityplace stood the bastion towers of the Great Palace of Tanox, a black crystalline massive that loomed its darkness over the lands and lives of all those who cowered before it.

Along the gray-cobbled grounds surrounding the Great Palace, the cityfellows of the castle had gathered, their presence assumed, therefore their presence mandatory. They stood shivering in self-imposed silence as newly formed rainsnow drizzled its icy dampness from the angry skies above, down upon their lightly clad bodies. Inside, Ra-Tanox, adorned in his flowing robes of ebony silk and raven feathers, and with his thick, gray-black hair streaming down his back, stood upon the towering dais and raised his arms. Immediately, an even more ominous quiet swept across the faces of the masses who sat before him in the Hall of Greatness, those cityfellows both willing and allowed to partake of his benevolence during this, the final stage of the year-long Feast of Thirteen Moons, the ancient ceremony of transition.

Whisper quiet it was when the voice of Ra-Tanox sounded softly, forcing even those close to him to strain to hear the sound of his great and powerful words. "You stand before me, my faithful and dedicated legions, as I once stood before my father, accepting his word as that of the most powerful of Principles." Slowly, his voice began to rise in volume and force until its power shook the very foundations of the castle, cascading its deepest fears before the minds' eyes of those who stood before him and stabbing deeply into the hearts and minds of those who stood outside the Great Palace in the Grand Courtyard. "There is a land that exists beyond the Castle Krog, beyond where the beginning of the end of light no longer exists," he continued as a sudden and damp coldness pervaded the Hall of Greatness. Ra-Tanox, immediately aware of the intrusion, ignored the sign. "While my father before me chose not to extend the Empire of Tanox beyond its ancient and present boundaries, I have chosen to bring forth the unbridled power from the depths of the nether world. Calling forth the Principles, with their greatest power of powers within my grasp, I shall destroy those who dare oppose me, crush life from those who dare question my destiny."

Again, a rush of coldness infiltrated the Hall of Greatness, this time its strength was powerful enough to ignite the masses into hushed whispers about this strange and never-before experienced phenomena. Ra-Tanox, too, felt the rush of cold. Looking upward, he bellowed, "Who dares question the power of my crown? Let him step forward and stand before the vision of my eyes." As quickly as it appeared the intruding coldness succumbed to the heat of the Inferno of Tanox as the power of the nether world belched forth, forcing the intruding invader from the Castle Krog. Ra-Tanox returned his attention to the masses who filled the Hall of Greatness in his honor.

As the celebration wound toward closure, Ra-Tanox retired to the Black Crystal Cavern where he partook of drink squeezed from the crimson berries of Nador. Surrounding him, the Black Crystal Cavern appeared as a great castle within a castle, its towering black translucent walls and spires disappearing into the inky heights above. Languishing on the great bed of thorns, enjoying his moment of aloneness with the power of the nether world at his whim and control, he dreamed of the future when all quivered at the mention of his name and cowered in his presence.

At Ra-Tanox's beckoning call, the Grand Black Sorcerer strode through the crystalline doors, chanting his discordant melodies of Ra-Tanox.

"Master of evil, chancellor of death,
your command I eagerly await
For all that is cold, all that is black
consumes my future as is my fate."

Ra-Tanox ignored the Grand Black Sorcerer, who continued his chanting, and stared deeply into his ebony goblet filled with the Nador elixir. What had caught his eye in the crimson drink's reflection was a shimmering silver and gold image possessing the brightness of a thousand lights shooting outward from within its ghostly body. Repulsed by the alien sight, Ra-Tanox flung the goblet, smashing it against the chamber's crystalline wall. From the shattered goblet a flash of blue light momentarily illuminated the Black Crystal Chamber, releasing with it a chilled stream of wind that swirled up from the crystal shards and its spilled elixir, then swept through the room.

"There is an evil that lurks within the walls of Krog, threatening my power, belittling my authority," Ra-Tanox shrieked. He rose from the bed shedding himself of his silken ebony robe, revealing the black tattoos, their swirling designs covering his slender, pale and thin white body. "From where, sorcerer, do these infringements upon my being, upon my power originate?" he demanded to know.

The sorcerer's eyes grew large in awe of the power that flashed before him "From the deepest of the enclaves that lie beyond the beginning of the end of light, oh Great One," the sorcerer opined. He entered a trance, his eyes closed, yet open as they witnessed what was not meant to be seen. The Grand Black Sorcerer lurched forward, his ardor transformed, now readying his attack upon this foreign coldness with his magical chant, even as Ra-Tanox continued to shriek his anger.

"Remove this madness from my presence, sorcerer, or I shall serve your head to the masses during a special festival in your honor," Ra-Tanox threatened.

The sorcerer stood silent, his eyes now closed tight. Gathering his ancient powers and focusing them upon the circling wind, his voice finally boomed its mighty echo from the crystalline walls as he chant-commanded the intruder to be gone from the Castle Krog:

> *"From within the great walls of Krog*
> *made invincible by ancient command,*
> *I beckon forth the almighty powers*
> *from the darkest abyss of our land,*
> *Cast out and destroy this invader*
> *who dares shun Ra-Tanox the Great,*
> *Again make pure the Castle Krog and*
> *destroy this wind as is its blackest fate,*
> *Madness are they, invaders of Krog*
> *their message screaming in pain,*
> *Challenge the power of Ra-Tanox*
> *your intrusion now burns in vain."*

Cautiously, once again the sorcerer opened his eyes, relieved to see the ruler's sanctuary free from intrusion.

"And why is it these puny and impotent beings can suddenly

dare to invade the sanctity of my domain, Sorcerer?" Ra-Tanox demanded, moving across the smooth, crystal floor to where he poured a new goblet full of the crimson liqueur. "What say you, Sorcerer?"

Again, the sorcerer closed his eyes letting his words come slowly. They followed closely the image of his earlier vision. "In a land far to the east there exists a being. Lost in the antiquity of time, he was born of a union destined to occur only once upon each millennium change. It was a union whose fate will bring change to the world, an end to the reign of Tanox."

"Blasphemous heresy! How dare you question the omnipotent power of the family Tanox, of me, Ra-Tanox, the greatest of our great ones?"

"It is not I who belittles your position and questions your power, oh Great One."

Ra-Tanox grew more arrogant. "And what say you, how shall this being's armies conquer the omnipotent power of Ra-Tanox and cast out the Principles?"

Again, the sorcerer closed his eyes. "Oh, great Ra-Tanox, I see no massive armies marching before us; I see only one being, a man of marginal stature, even among his own kind. Yet, a man of extraordinary vision." The sorcerer emerged from his trance-like vision. His eyes opened wide, troubled, not by what he saw, but more by the strange feelings his vision had stirred to life deep within his being.

"No armies? Then what is it I should fear? One man, against my castle? Against my power?" Ra-Tanox cried in boisterous relief. "He will die like those who came before him, his life crushed from him beneath my laughter."

"The invader, Great One, he comes with wisdom, and wisdom alone."

"Wisdom? What great power is held in wisdom without an army to follow the path of that wisdom?" Ra-Tanox asked. He drank deeply from the goblet, then slammed it to the table before him, ranting at his sorcerer. "Be gone old wise one, be gone from my view. And when this commoner of such professed greatness and powerful wisdom happens through our gates, bring him to me, shackled in a manner that befits any soul so bold as to challenge my reign."

An involuntary shiver flowed through the sorcerer's body, its effects lasting only a second, but its memory lingering on deep within the departing wise one.

Ra-Tanox watched his sorcerer leave his chambers, and then returned to his bed of thorns where he lay down, dropping into restless sleep.

CHAPTER FOUR

Sound sleep had escaped Zennan as unknown images cascaded their parade through his mind. He continued his journey, making the dark descent into the valley below along a steep and treacherous path. The faded facade of the ancient trail meandered through the scrag rocks that gave way to scrub brush that in turn evolved into gentle trees, their listless branches hanging lightly, casting dark shadows through the moon-illuminated blackness across their path. The twisted trees were many, straining their tenacious tentacles, seeking sustenance and survival at the very edges of rocky cliffs that offered an environment of hostility rather than hospitality. In Zennan's view these feeble attempts at life were wrought with disease, much the same as his own people; too weak to gain any level of physical supremacy over their lives, too void of wisdom to understand their own pointless and pitiful situation.

Wun moved before Zennan, following the wind as it flowed easily over the rocks and around twisted and dwarfed trees. Wuntu followed behind, keeping within sight of Zennan, guarding the rear, keeping at bay the spirits of evil that already lurked among the blackest shadows. As the trio entered the first of the peripheral hovels in the valley of darkness, some still showing the flickering shafts of candlelight through tattered curtains and broken windows, Wun cautioned care to Zennan whose occasional arrogance still served as master over his fully understanding the power of knowledge.

Voices, muffled soft by the wind, amplified only slightly by the hard surface of the maze of stone walls and hard-sided hovels, brought Zennan to cautious stillness, listening for the slightest intimations of pending danger. He stooped behind the breastwork adjacent to one of the unlighted hovels. The voices, their words still made unrecognizable by bending winds, were none-the-less growling louder, closer, more menacing for Zennan who still knew nothing of those he was destined to confront. Zennan looked around commanding his eyes to penetrate the darkness, expecting to see his two companions. They were nowhere within his limited view in the blackness of night. Still, before him, ominously, the voices grew louder. Behind Zennan a quick and low-pitched squeak caught his attention. A voice, its texture rough, yet absent of malice, addressed the hulking intruder.

"The night wanderers are to be avoided. You are welcome to join my family in our humble refuge," said the voice, softly.

Still hearing the voices before him grow stronger, the tenor of the words growing increasingly discernible, increasingly menacing, Zennan turned to face that who welcomed him. He slowly, ever so slowly, shuffled his body toward the welcoming voice, finally passing through the opened oval door, a door crafted by careful hands from woven strands of bark stripped from the twisted trees. Once inside the darkened hovel the door closed and a wooden bar thudded into place, effectively locking the entry secure. The hiss of slow and regular breathing surrounded Zennan.

Zennan's eyes strained to focus on the faintest of images that the glowing embers in the fireplace were only now beginning to illuminate. "I am called Zennan. What are you called?" he asked.

"Zennan, hmmmm. Such an unusual name. One that I have never before heard. I am called Faro and around you are the members of my family." The short, yet huskily strong family leader stepped from the deeper shadows, allowing the flickering light of the fire's glowing orange coals to reflect his features, finally giving Zennan a sense of who these folks might be. The short and stocky host wore a green and fuzzy cape about his shoulders and a heavy apron around his front, an apron cut from the skin of an animal, probably to protect his flax-woolen breeches from lowly trade work such as a stableman, Zennan thought.

"The dangerous ones have passed for now. You must be hungry. Please, join us for our evening meal," Faro offered as he lighted the wall-mounted oil lantern. He motioned toward the corner of the small home. The taller of three sons, each of whom appeared as an image of their father, lighted another of the wall-mounted oil lanterns.

Still cautious, Zennan quickly surveyed these strangers and their even stranger home. The hovel's interior had no apparent seams between the meeting joints of the floor, walls, ceiling and window openings. Each blended from one to the next, the transformation from one material and one color into the next occurring smoothly, yet immediately. Emerging from the wall above the orifice that served as a fireplace, a large, vertically rectangular sheet of black ebony, a portrait perhaps, seemed to pulsate life. Or maybe it was just his imagination, Zennan thought. He slowly began to relax as his hosts returned to their food preparation chores.

"My friends and I are grateful for your hospitality," Zennan said as he removed his overgarment, welcoming the warmth of the hearth.

Faro looked quizzically at Zennan. "Your friends?" he asked.

"Well, yes, Wun and Wuntu," he said, his eyes searching but not seeing his two companions. "They must be beyond your entry. I will allow them inside, if you, sir, are not opposed to their presence."

"There was no one but you, traveler. I welcomed you inside because of the danger that approached and your apparent inability to recognize it," Faro said. "You were alone, or, were it different, I would have offered my humble roof and my mealpot to your friends, also."

Zennan, although not overly attached to his traveling companions, was becoming more and more convinced of their importance to the success of his adventure quest. He wasn't entirely certain from where these feelings and thoughts originated, but unmistakably they grew stronger deep inside his being.

"Even three of your kind would not be safe encountering the night wanderers of Ra-Tanox. Beyond the dictated hour of curfew there is no escape from their evil," Faro offered, making it sound as more of a condolence.

The tallest of Faro's offspring stepped to the closed door. "I will seek your companions," he said and quickly slipped outside. He returned in a matter of seconds. "Your friends are not within the nearby outside darkness."

"But they must be. We stood together just moments before

your father spoke his words of welcome to me. They certainly would have followed me inside," Zennan said, confused. He started for the door himself. "I must look. They could not have gone far."

Faro stepped between Zennan and the door. "It is pointless to wander the outside before daylight washes away the darkness of night," he said. "Your friends, if they are still outside, have not been discovered by the night wanderers. The night remains quiet, so your friends are quite safe, as long as their concealment remains complete."

"I see," Zennan said, reluctantly abiding by the wishes of his keeper of temporary sanctuary. Faro's youngest and smallest son took Zennan's overgarment and carefully hung it from a hook that emerged from the wall's smooth surface near the door.

A loud crash on the outside door startled Faro. His sons moved quickly away from the table, melting into the dark corner shadows as each lantern's faint light flickered dead. Zennan remained calm, yet he made ready to move quickly if needed as he watched Faro creep forward and place his ear against the door.

"It is probably my two traveling companions," Zennan said.

"Ssshhh," Faro hissed, his warning sound simultaneously echoed by his three sons.

From outside the door a faint tapping begin slowly and increased with frequency, quickly filling the room with its soft sound vibrations. Slowly, Faro raised the wooden bar across the doorway. The tapping became more rapid, yet its sound did not increase in volume. Faro cracked the door ever so slightly, and the outside blackness flooded into the room. Two small, yellow glowing circles broke through the blackness. Faro whispered through the crack.

"You should not be here," he cautioned the outsider. "A new traveler has unexpectedly joined with us tonight." Faro motioned for his second son to re-light the lanterns.

"I too have traveled great distance for three days at the beckoning of One," the blackness said. "I must see the traveler and warn him of treachery that awaits should he enter the great walls of the Castle Krog."

Zennan heard the voice of the yellow eyes speak its warning. He was becoming uncomfortable discovering another stranger aware of his presence, let alone of his quest. Zennan stood and went to the door, pulling it open in spite of Faro's objections.

"Please, let this messenger from the bottomworld join us. I am becoming weary of secrecy, especially when it seems that all know my business better than me," Zennan announced. "My curiosity abounds at how one maintains a sense of urgent secrecy in this world of darkness. Please enter and entertain me with your name and your reasons for interest and knowledge of my quest."

Yellow Eyes entered Faro's hovel, the creature's face dissolving into blackness beneath his dark and heavy hooded robe. "Your mockery is expected when confronted with the unknown," the visitor said, softly. "One advised me of your impetuous arrogance, your need for dominance even when confronted with powers beyond your experience and comprehension."

Zennan focused on the glowing yellow eyes buried deep within the hood, trying to see a face that could not be seen. "You relate knowledge that could have come only from Wun or Wuntu," he said. "Apparently my traveling companions have spoken with you."

Yellow Eyes looked blankly through the darkness of his hood. "I have spoken with no strangers. I share my thoughts with you only, and with my friend, Faro, since this is his home and to do anything less would shame our mutual trust."

"Who are you?" Zennan asked.

"Who I am is less important than what I am, and what I am is less important to you at this time than the assistance I am able to provide you. Others came before you, others who carried your zeal, your ambition." The yellow-eyed visitor stopped and stared deeply into Zennan's eyes, beyond the boundaries of his bright blue pupils that before this time had always reflected outward others' probing, intruding visions. The stare of the yellow eyes penetrated the reflections, passing deep into Zennan's inner mind. Zennan could feel the mind intruder's invasion, yet he was powerless to prevent the thievery of his deepest thoughts. Finally, Yellow Eyes lowered his head, once again returning Zennan's mind to its own thoughts.

"But you are different from those who came before you," Yellow Eyes said. "You have something that none before you possessed."

"Must all who inhabit this land of darkness speak in riddles?" Zennan asked.

"The riddles of the ancient language mirror the riddles of life."

"And the riddles of life are without answer. Again, I ask, what are you called?" Zennan insisted.

Yellow Eyes once more stared into Zennan's mind. "You have much to learn, but you are the one," he said.

Zennan turned back to Faro. "You, Faro, who is this hooded stranger you welcome into your home?"

Yellow Eyes nodded to Faro and Faro understood. "He is known as a wishtongue," Faro offered.

"A wishtongue?" Zennan exclaimed in surprise. The melodic flow returned to his speech. "The talltalists spoke often of wishtongues, but always as myth, much as they uttered their words of gods and demons, spirits and beguilers."

"Ah, but when the myth stands before you, offering what may be offered, how shall you receive the offer?" the wishtongue asked, the cast of his yellow eyes again retreating into the darkness of his hood.

Zennan thought for a moment, knowing what he wanted to ask, but uncertain whether to pose his question in the way of an ancient cryptic verse. He chose not the way of talltalists, wizards and wishtongues, instead desiring no misunderstanding, yet expecting a reply subject to many interpretations. "You came with a warning, a warning to tread cautiously among the walls of this place you call the Castle Krog? I ask only that you allow me information to assure safe passage on my journey to the beginning of the end of light."

"Already, your aura has betrayed your presence and your planned entry into the valley of blackness controlled by Ra-Tanox and his Grand Black Sorcerer."

"And, Wishtongue, does this betrayal mark my end as near, or shall I continue onward?" Zennan asked.

"Life begets life; death is forever the giver of life. The dangers that await your presence are nothing more than what should be expected," the wishtongue offered.

Zennan merely looked at the wishtongue, not knowing how to respond.

"You have little to fear, yet fear is what will propel your journey to its conclusion."

"And will the conclusion of my journey be met with success?" Zennan queried.

"Success is always sought, yet a single success is but one step closer to your journey's eternal end."

Faro interrupted. "My two guests must be in need of nourishment," he offered. "Please, my daughter will serve you what humble offerings we have to share."

From a darkened corner of the hovel where the entrance to a small room had gone unnoticed by the usually vigilant Zennan, a young, raven-haired woman, much taller than her brothers and father, and extraordinarily beautiful, momentarily stopped the speech of Faro. Zennan watched her move across the room to the fireplace pot that steamed its aroma throughout the small home. She chose a large, carved wooden mug from the mantel and carefully poured it full of a clear liquid from an earthen jug chosen from among several jugs sitting inside a small shelf next to the fireplace. She carried the mug across the room and set it before the wishtongue, rightly assuming him to be the elder of the two visitors. Her eyes were instantly drawn to the second stranger and, in turn, her eyes were quickly set upon by Zennan's own. The wishtongue accepted the mug, but did not begin to drink. The daughter's vision remained locked with Zennan's, but rather than lower her eyes in embarrassed deference as Zennan would have expected of the young and eligible females he knew in his own land, she simply nodded to him, smiling ever so slightly.

Zennan was immediately infatuated with this young beauty. "You, Faro, do you have any more surprises as pleasant as this daughter you have kept hidden from your visitors?" Zennan asked.

Faro, with the concerned eye of a protective father, looked at his daughter. She acknowledged her father's concern and returned to the shadows where she filled another mug for their second guest. When she set the grog before Zennan, their eyes again locked and the slightest of smiles once again curved the young woman's lips.

"And to what name does your daughter answer, Faro?" Zennan asked.

Faro bowed his head in apology. "I have failed as a proper host to introduce all of my family," Faro admitted. "But you must understand my concern for the safety of my own when a stranger is invited suddenly into my home during the dark of night."

"I do understand, Faro, and if you choose to keep secret from my eyes such a fair daughter, I shall understand the mind of a concerned and protective father."

"I do not fear either you or the yellow-eyed wishtongue, nor do I believe that you are a danger to my children," Faro said. He motioned for his sons to come forward. "May I present to you my eldest son, Cerro, my middle son Parro and my youngest and most impetuous son, Raffo."

Zennan waited for his strange host to complete the last introduction. Faro remained silent.

"Have you not forgotten your daughter?" Zennan asked.

Faro looked toward his daughter, who pretended to ignore the words of the stranger. "The females of our village are not included in such introductions," he said.

"There is much I must learn before I will understand your ways. In my land, our elder females are often family leaders," Zennan said.

"You indeed are a stranger with strange ways." Faro rubbed his forehead with his leathery hand. Slowly he looked at his daughter, then back at Zennan. He spoke slowly, caringly. "My daughter, who possesses the beauty and fire of her mother and a zest for adventure that certainly she did not capture from any known ancestor, her name is Meeshannette," Faro explained to his two guests.

"A name as beautiful as the young woman who wears it," Zennan offered. As he stared, Meeshannette ignored his complement, although her ever-slight smile reappeared. She quickly disappeared into the dark recess of the back room.

"If you would permit me," Faro said, interrupting Zennan's thoughts. He walked to the fireplace mantel. Zennan's mind was quickly transformed into silent confusion, as the wishtongue patiently watched. Faro carefully withdrew a hand-sized cross of ironwood from an iridescent shell-inlaid holding box that suddenly emerged from the wall above the mantel. Next, Faro held the cross in his extended right hand, while with his left hand's index finger he touched the broth steaming in the black iron pot suspended over the fireplace's orange-hot coals. Each of his sons in turn came forward and stood before their father, all bent slightly forward at their waists. Faro touched the cross upon each of their foreheads. He then raised his broth-wetted finger skyward and chanted in a dialect unfamiliar to Zennan. A moment later Faro's chant was finished and he returned the cross to its holder. Meeshannette once again entered the room and dipped broth with a long-handled ladle, filling the bowls of her father, each brother, and larger bowls for Zennan and the wishtongue. She set them on the square wooden table as everyone except Zennan took their places along the benches.

Zennan, still unsure of the significance of Faro's magical incantation, and his eyes once again fixed upon Meeshannette, watched her as the others, including the wishtongue, quickly began slurping from their meal bowls. Meeshannette returned to the pot and filled herself a bowl, but rather than sitting at the table, she sat at a small bench, placing her bowl upon a narrow wooden shelf that appeared from the wall. Zennan sat and began to eat, but he wondered about these people's strange eating ceremony. Not wishing to show ignorance, which might be interpreted as an insult, Zennan phrased his query carefully.

"Your thanking ceremony is one with which I am not familiar, but one which obviously pleases your greatest God, who must, in his infinite glory and power, provide adequately for your needs and comforts," he said.

The wishtongue momentarily raised his eyes from the focused attention on his meal, but said nothing. Faro and his sons did not even raise their eyes in response, but continued eating heartily. Meeshannette, careful to see that her father's eyes remained downward cast, chanced a glance at Zennan, but knew that if she spoke her father would deal harshly with her upon these strangers' departures.

Zennan looked at each of his hosts in turn, and in turn each ignored him. Such was not the case when his eyes turned once again toward Meeshannette. "Meeshannette, your meal is also one with which I am not familiar," Zennan said. "Surely this broth of wild taste brings your father and brothers the strength of the bear that bravely parted with its life so that you may properly sustain and strengthen your own living selves."

Now, Faro and his sons stopped eating and looked at their guest stranger in anguished concern. Even Meeshannette looked surprised, yet fascination tinged her inner thoughts. The wishtongue spoke before any of the family might hurl insults or insinuations.

"You have much to learn on your journey, stranger from the eastern lands of faded light. The god who gives life to the people of this village does not remove the life of animals in order to sustain the lives of their masters, just as he does not require sacrifice from these people's lowly existence to support his own living," the wish-tongue explained.

Zennan was confused. "You do not eat of wild flesh? How then do you maintain the strength of your bodies?"

Faro and his sons continued their disbelieving stares at Zennan.

"While we certainly have not attained your physical size, our chosen sustenance provides the strength and stamina needed to maintain all which we have," Meeshannette offered.

Faro flashed a look at Meeshannette that sent her respectfully back to her own business of consuming the meal she had prepared. Still, Faro chose not to make eye contact with Zennan, but noisily slurped another spoonful of the soup.

Zennan remained confused, and although the taste of the soup was acceptable to him, it now seemed to lack the filling body of such meals prepared in his homeland. "Surely without the muscle and sinew, the heart and brains of animals, and preferably animals of the wild, rather than beasts domesticated to subservience, your bodies will wither just as grass dies in summer and trees lose their strength each autumn," Zennan suggested.

Finally, Faro spoke, slowly and confidently, although he still did not look up from the food before him. "Do not the trees regain their leaves and grow larger and stronger each spring? Do not the grasses, even in their death, sustain and build the bodies of many wild animals?" he asked.

"Yet it is the wolf and lion that feed upon the weak and defenseless grass feeders," Zennan interrupted.

Now Faro looked up, his eyes locking with those of Zennan. "But nearly always it is only the weak and injured grass feeders that become food for the carnivorous beasts, leaving the strongest and wiliest to live and create new life. And certainly, the peaceful grazers significantly outnumber the eaters of meat," Faro said, pausing for a second, enjoying Zennan's contemplative reaction. "What will become of the wolf and lion when one day the grass-feeding beasts of numbers, the wisest and strongest that have successfully escaped the jaws of death and have flourished and passed their abilities on to their offspring for countless seasons, decide that their task of providing sustenance for these meat feeders has been completed?"

Zennan sat thoughtfully for several minutes, slowly and unconsciously stirring a smoothly-carved wooden spoon through the bowl of soup. Finally, he looked directly at Faro. "You have made a point that is strong. I would like to be around at such time, because since the very beginnings of remembered and recorded time, it has been those possessing the most strength and speed, the sharpest teeth and longest claws who have controlled these lands of darkness. I have much to contemplate on my journey." Zennan and his host returned to eating in silence.

As he swallowed the last of the meal, Zennan felt a sudden coldness run through his veins. He looked up and his sight was met by the yellow glow of the wishtongue's eyes.

Locked with Zennan's icy stare, the wishtongue temporarily ceased his consumption and continued with his earlier interrupted explanation. "The Grand Black Sorcerer, whose evil permeates the castle proper with his mere presence, will stalk your moves, haunt your thoughts, blur your vision. His soul is black, his heart dead, his mind with but one purpose, a purpose dictated by the evil of Ra-Tanox, the most evil of the evil, the perpetrator of the Principles."

A breeze, cold and black, swept through the walls of the hovel, though no door was open nor a single window cracked. Faro shivered, while Zennan merely became more aware of his surroundings, his mind focused, his vision penetrating the shadows, his ears alert for both noises and the sounds of silence, each possessing its own evil.

The wishtongue smelled the air. "You would be wise to leave soon, well before the morning sun rises above the horizon," he warned.

Zennan, too, sensed the change. "May I call upon you for knowledge when knowledge is needed?" he asked.

"My future is as clouded as yours is destined, my friend. I do not deny destiny, nor do I attempt to change that which is destined. For what may befall you, nothing may be done. But be consoled by your fate and whatever shall become of you and your world," the wishtongue said. He returned his mind silently to the attention of the remainder of his soup, motioning that Zennan should do the same.

Meeshannette reappeared, this time holding the handle of the steaming iron soup pot. As she once again ladled Zennan's empty bowl full, they allowed their eyes to lock, but only for the briefest of moments as Meeshannette glanced toward her father's down-turned head. She felt this stranger's instant infatuation with her, but she also knew that her father wished to betroth her to Peldo, the eldest and widowed son of his oldest friend, Lelothe, the villagefellow horsestabler. Meeshannette, while not wishing to dishonor her father's best-intentioned wishes for her welfare and happiness, found no interest in a man nearly twice her age who searched for a mother for the two young children of his deceased wife. And Peldo had, unhappily for Meeshannette, with his and her father's insistence and encouragement, settled upon her as his replacement wife.

"Eat heartily, my friends," Faro said, then take rest as best you can for the sun comes early."

CHAPTER FIVE

Moments later as best Zennan could comprehend, Faro shook his shoulder, awakening him from the deepest sleep he had enjoyed since entering these strange lands.

"I fear it is best that you and the wishtongue continue on your journeys, for no good may come of your presence here," Faro offered. He hesitated for a moment of contemplation. "Even now the first scattering of the new day's light can be sensed behind our mountains. Your journey will fare better if you have a beast to sit upon for your upward path to the Castle Krog." Faro looked at his daughter who was wearing her long woolen work skirt and standing near the fireplace as she coaxed the previous night's fire back to life. "Go to the stable of Peldo and bring a horse for our guest," he commanded.

Meeshannette's father was always creating reasons for sending her to the stable where Peldo labored. Meeshannette attempted to avoid the trips, but seldom were her arguments strong enough to overcome her father's wishes.

"Wouldn't it be good for Cerro to go? He would be better able to choose an animal possessing the strength and character best suited to Zennan's needs," she queried. As usual, her father simply ignored her words, his indication that she should indeed follow his wishes. After a short moment of quiet and wistful hoping, Meeshannette bowed her head in acknowledgment of her father's wishes. She removed her pocketed apron from around her waist, pulled a light cloth across her shoulders and walked to the door. Stopping for a second, she looked back over her shoulder at Zennan and smiled. "It is near the end of the village where I must walk. I will return with the strongest of animals and wish you well on your adventure," she said, then quickly turned and left on her task before her father could reprimand her for such impertinent and misplaced speech.

Zennan understood the need for his most immediate departure. He had no desire to bring down the wrath of this savage one called Ra-Tanox, nor that of his sorcerer of darkness, upon these hapless people of peace. Zennan smiled at his host and nodded understanding. Faro took on a look of relief and nodded to his youngest son, Raffo. The youngster quickly got up from the bench and gathered mugs for everyone and filled them to their brims with a dark brown and bitter-tasting grog. Together they drank in speechless somberness, awaiting the return of Meeshannette. The wishtongue was the first to finish his, and with only a nod, bid farewell. He quickly and quietly slipped outside, greeted by the silence of the very first rays of the day's coming light.

* * *

The soldiers of Ra-Tanox, the sirocco troops of the Castle Krog, sat atop powerful gray steeds surveying their creation, a desolate land stretching to beyond the ends of their collective visions. Two dozen riders sidled apart as the Grand Black Sorcerer, his magnificent white horse beneath him, trotted to the top of the view knoll. His eyes closed, he scanned the horizon, sense-hunting for the invader who had entered the land of his proclaimed master, Ra-Tanox. Moments lapsed until he opened his eyes facing toward the hovel village in the valley below. Slowly, ever so slowly, he raised his arm and pointed to the village.

"A power lurks at the very edge of the beginning of the end of light," the Grand Black Sorcerer proclaimed through a voice that came from deep within his bowels. "A power that drinks of the gifts of Ra-Tanox, but knows not of allegiance to the master of all that lives and dies." The Grand Black Sorcerer lowered his arm and nudged his white stallion forward toward the distant image of hovels in the valley below. His soldiers fell into a single line behind him, their gray steeds kicking clouds of dust before them, obscuring their image, yet transforming their presence into one mighty beast, descending upon those of little hope.

Upon reaching the outer hovels of the village, the Grand Black Sorcerer reined his great steed to a halt. His sirocco troop followers spread into lines extending equally from both of his flanks. The sorcerer closed his eyes so he could better see to his front through the soon-to-come glow of the rising sun. Now he could clearly view what a bitter wind it was that had visited desolation upon this land of Ra-Tanox. Yet, his vision remained partially blurred by a power he could not comprehend, a power not familiar to him. The sorcerer once again opened his eyes, allowing them to shift left then right, following the two lines of his flanking, mounted troops. He raised his hand to his forehead to shield the growing reddish rays of the rising sun from his eyes, at the same time signaling for his left flank soldiers to move into the village. Slowly the dozen gray steeds, guided by their riders and led by the sorcerer's lieutenant, trotted down the path that meandered to the center of the small village.

In single file they passed the smaller, perimeter hovels as the inhabitants remained inside, cringing in corners, cowering in cellars. The lieutenant rider smiled when he saw a caped and hooded figure move slowly across the path a distance in front of their travel, then disappear behind a small line of hovels that shared a common exterior sidewall. The pace of the horses increased as the lieutenant rode to where the stranger so brazenly dared show himself before the army of Ra-Tanox. He pulled his horse's reins back hard stopping his great gray steed just after he passed the corner of the hovel nearest to the path. The hooded stranger should have been visible, but nothing living moved within the lieutenant's sight.

The lieutenant hissed his anger. "Who dares trifle with the army of Ra-Tanox?" he bellowed. He quickly motioned for half of his sirocco troops to circle around to the front of the line of hovels while he and the remaining troops galloped down the back, expecting to pincer the stranger between them. As they charged around the final hovel and turned hard left to meet their counterpart troop of stampeding soldiers approaching from the opposite side, a small cloud of white smoke exploded in front of the lieutenant. Inside the cloud two powerful yellow lights cast their beams toward him. The lieutenant's horse skidded to a halt, causing the soldiers following fast behind him to do the same. In the confusion most of the lieutenant's remaining troops charged hard around the corner adding to the unplanned chaos. The lieutenant finally brought his mount under control and turned the beast in a circle attempting to spy the escaping stranger. He was not to be seen.

Moments later the Grand Black Sorcerer, bringing the remainder of his mounted sirocco soldiers with him, rounded the corner. His scowl, aimed directly at his incompetent lieutenant, cowered the officer into groveling submission.

"The stranger was powered by a magic greater than ours," the lieutenant uttered in self-defense.

The sorcerer's horse reared high, then settled back down. "You allowed him to escape? I would have thought better of your skills," he growled, the menace in his voice unmistakable.

"But, most masterful magical one, his power was too great. He simply vanished in a cloud of smoke," the lieutenant pleaded, hoping the sorcerer would absolve him of his misdeed.

The sorcerer looked beyond the lieutenant where the wisps of smoke still clung. Faintly, he could see two yellow eyes within the white cloud looking upon him. The yellow quickly faded to nothingness leaving only the last wispy remnants of lingering smoke. "Ah, I see," the sorcerer mused, turning his attention back to his lieutenant, his ire now rested. "It should worry you not that success evaded your best efforts. Wishtongues are not beasts easily imprisoned by such simple plans and meager forces."

"A wishtongue?" the lieutenant asked, his confusion complete. "Are they simply not evil beasts of ancient proverbs?"

The sorcerer looked at his still-cowering lieutenant, but did not answer his question. Instead, his attention was drawn to a sudden cold wind that blew through his soldiers, whirling the remaining white smoke, then quickly whisking it away to the west. As the wind passed, the sorcerer felt a slight shudder ripple through his being, but he simply shivered it off. His horse reared nervously, as did those of his soldiers, then quickly settled down into an anxious, circling prance.

"Enough of this. We travel onward and leave this village to the no-lifes who inhabit this pit of formless mass," the sorcerer cried. He reined his mount backward for a moment, feeling once again the presence of a power that he did not yet fully understand, but knew was near, though its source was not yet understood, neither in its form, nor in his mind. The Grand Black Sorcerer spurred his great white beast forward toward the end of the hovel village. The lieutenant signaled his subordinate gray-steeded sirocco soldiers to follow.

Before the sorcerer's eyes, leading a saddled horse away from a small and pitiful stable, walked a young hovel woman of unquestionable beauty, the possessor, he immediately sensed, of this unconsummated power that swirled about him. As he swept down upon her, Meeshannette at only the last moment became aware of the great white steed that filled the sky above her. She leaped backward from the path of the black-cloaked rider, but as the great beast galloped by, she suddenly found herself snatched upward, held in an arm of unmistakable strength. She screamed in surprise, not in fear, for fear had not yet registered in her mind. Finally, realizing her position, Meeshannette struggled against this madman who had taken her, but to no avail.

The lieutenant passing nearest to the stable ran his horse at the gawking villagefellow stableman. Peldo, reduced to a fear-cringed and crying creature, scampered quickly back into the confining safety of his trade structure.

The Grand Black Sorcerer knew that the prize in hand would be adequate to momentarily appease the appetite of Ra-Tanox. He reined his white beast toward the wide and barren winter pasture beyond the hovel village, catching the meandering path that would lead him on the shortest roadway return to the Castle Krog.

Peldo, slowly, cautiously, poked his body beyond the walls of his stable and saw, through the blurring tears of his fear, only the distant dust of the departing kidnappers. Assured now of his own safety, he emerged from his cocoon and raced to the hovel of Faro, his father's oldest friend.

* * *

Zennan lowered his mug for the last time, having toasted the recently departed wishtongue. As the early morning's first light cascaded through the thin curtains that draped the windows, he had for the first time a complete and lighted view of the interior of Faro's neatly modest hovel. Above the fireplace, what he viewed earlier in the night as a black opaque slab of some decorative order, came into focus. As the beams of sun illuminated its translucent black surface, an image, feint at first, but quickly growing strong and beautiful, appeared from deep within its surface. A young woman, her hair long and raven in color, her face angelic, appeared before him. Her life-like appearance at first startled, then for some unknown reason soothed Zennan's fear of the destiny that awaited discovery.

"Who is this one of such great beauty who magically appears before me?" Zennan asked.

Faro's head sagged low, and immediately he was comforted by his sons. "Sadly," Faro finally said, "this is my wife and the mother of my four children."

"Why is your wife, who shared generously her beauty with your youngest daughter, not here among us?"

Faro stood silently and began to weep softly. Finally his eldest son stood forward.

"My mother was kidnapped by the soldiers of the Castle Krog," Raffo said.

"And in what ways did you attempt to free her from the chains of this apparent master of evil?" Zennan inquired.

"Since the earliest of our storytimes, when any of the family Tanox chose to steal the females from our hovel villages, we were to never again see them," Raffo said, anger flaring in his young eyes for the first time since Zennan's coming. "The gray-steeded soldiers of Qa-Tanox descended upon our village just weeks after Meeshannette was born. They stole my mother while she tended our family's sheep."

"Qa-Tanox? Tell me more about he who carries this strange and evil name of which you have spoken."

"You indeed have traveled from a very far distance, stranger, if you have not heard of the family Tanox nor heard the name Tanox uttered." Faro said. He eyed Zennan carefully. "Perhaps you come from the ancient and evil world that is far to the east, far beyond the beginning of the end of light?"

Now it was Zennan's turn to eye the old man carefully. Feeling that he could trust this man Faro and his sons, yet not wishing to reveal too much, lest this Ra-Tanox of whom these people spoke of in hushed whispers of fear, learn of Faro's knowledge and force it from him. Zennan chose his words carefully and spoke them slowly. "For a millennium my people have been outsiders to this land. But once, before the black shards of evil pierced our hearts, my great ancestors lived among these magnificent mountains and wondrous valleys. This is where their ashes became one with the Earth Mother that gave birth to them." Zennan waited a moment, looking for a reaction from Faro and his sons. None came. They merely stared blankly and silently at this mysterious stranger who stood before them.

Again, Zennan's voice became melodic in tone. "I search to discover that which my elders say is undiscoverable, but that which our talltalists speak of as truth. I search for the knowledge that my friend and mentor, Greshem, predicts is unattainable; I search for all that I must find to reach my destiny."

Faro motioned to his middle son to tend to the fire that was beginning to smolder into smoke in the fireplace, then turned his attention back to Zennan. "Your task appears befuddling. For what purpose do you propose to serve by your actions, should success be your fate?"

"I shall attain the purposes of my people, so long held prisoners in lands which are not our own," Zennan replied.

"If you are indeed prisoners, surely the only power capable of holding you is that of the family Tanox, yet his name and that of his family, is not in your mind?" Faro mused aloud.

"Perhaps his evil is of such power that it overshadows the spread of his name," offered Zennan, thinking that maybe he had discovered the force that imprisoned his people.

"Ra-Tanox is not one to be associated with modest obscurity," Raffo, the youngest son, interjected. "He is an evil who forever perpetuates evil. Alas, even before the death of Qa-Tanox the Beheader, the kidnapper of our mother and the evil one who fathered Ra-Tanox as the successor to the high crown of the Castle Krog, Ra-Tanox, it had been whispered, was of such evil as to cower even the all-powerful underdemons."

As the daylight became brighter, casting its morning glow

through the window of Faro's hovel, the translucent black image of Faro's wife above the fireplace faded to gray. Zennan realized that daylight was beginning to burn its imprint across this land and that he must continue his journey. He rose from Faro's food table, and as he did so, Raffo handed Zennan his cape.

A crash on the outside of Faro's door stood each of them motionless. Another crash accompanied by an anguished cry, which Faro recognized immediately, moved Cerro, the eldest of the sons, to swing the hovel door open. Before them knelt Peldo, sobbing and still pounding upon the air that the now open hovel door had previously filled.

"They stole her," Peldo sobbed. "They stole Meeshannette."

Faro's face turned pale and his knees weakened. He slowly dropped to the floor. "No, no," he cried in anguish. Cerro moved to comfort his father. The two remaining brothers lowered their heads in saddened silence.

"Who stole her!" Zennan demanded. He grabbed the sobbing Peldo and stood the small and impish man up. "Tell me now, who has taken Meeshannette, and what have they done with her?"

The sobbing, frightened creature before him could not look Zennan in the eye. "I don't know. Perhaps it was the evil of the Principles that took her," he said, staring his eyes downward at the hovel's floor.

"The Principles? Zennan queried. "Of such I have only heard through whispered warnings."

Peldo's words came with great difficulty. "Of the Principles we know little, only that they guide the ways of the sorcerer and his soldiers. And I saw the evil one, the Grand Black Sorcerer, dressed in black, sitting upon a great white horse, more powerful than I have ever before seen," Peldo explained slowly.

Faro covered his face with his folded arms. "Why," he asked. "Why now my daughter? Was not my wife enough?"

"Why did you not fight this sorcerer?" Zennan demanded of Peldo.

Peldo slowly raised his head to see this stranger before him for the first time. "Fight? We are not believers in physical struggles. Our greatest efforts are no more than a feeble defense against such powers of evil," he said in his own defense.

Zennan looked, first at Faro, then in turn at his sons. Faro and his two older sons nodded agreement with Peldo's repulsion for fighting.

"You do not defend even your daughter from such demonist behavior?" Zennan asked, already knowing what answer would be forthcoming from a race that refused to consume as food the strength and wisdom of their land's fiercest creatures.

Raffo stepped forward. "I wish to accompany you on your journey," he offered. "I must learn of my sister's fate and free her if that is to be her destiny."

"You have not yet come of age for such a journey," Zennan quietly assured Raffo.

Raffo looked to his father, but the old man sadly nodded agreement with Zennan. Disappointment stole the look of anger from across Raffo's face.

"I will seek the daughter of your stolen wife, the sister of your sons, as I journey toward this Castle Krog," Zennan promised Faro. He looked down upon the much shorter Raffo and placed his large hand on the boy's downcast head. "I will discover the fate of your sister, Meeshannette, and if her destiny is to be such that she should return to you, so it shall be. This I promise to you," Zennan assured him, finally releasing the grip that his other hand still held on the front clothes of Peldo. The quivering, sobbing creature lapsed back to the floor next to Faro.

In a quickly following flurry of activity, the youngest of Faro's sons filled Zennan's satchel with hard bread and a leather flask with the brown grog they had enjoyed. Zennan bid them farewell, but as he walked from the hovel and greeted the light of the morning sun, he was met by a small crowd of villagers gathered outside Faro's hovel, all standing silently still. Faro pulled himself back to his feet and walked out with Zennan.

"What brings my villagefellows before my hovel," he asked.

One of the fellows stepped forward. "Again your home brings the return of the sorcerer and the army of Ra-Tanox," Faro's oldest friend, the father of the wifeless Peldo, said softly.

"They come because you welcome strangers into your hovel," another villagefellow chortled.

"But they have departed without harm to you," Faro offered,

pointing to the dust cloud already a distance or more to the west.

"No harm?" the father of Peldo asked. "They have taken the future bride of my eldest son," he stated in his business-like manner. "My son's children need a mother, and now they will remain without."

"And I have lost my only daughter, in the same vile manner in which I long ago lost my wife, good friend," Faro responded.

Another village fellow stepped out from the small crowd. "They searched for the one known as wishtongue," he said. "And they have taken your daughter instead."

"How could they possibly know of the wishtongue's presence?" Faro countered. "The wishtongue was here and gone in no time. From such great distance, even the Grand Black Sorcerer is incapable of sensing his visit."

"The sorcerer was looking for more, yet he did not sense or discover the object of his search, a search obscured by the power of the wishtongue," the villagefellow said.

Zennan heaved an exasperated gasp of frustration, immediately drawing the small group's attention. "You talk of things that you do not understand, and you show no concern for Faro's great loss," Zennan said. "You should return to your brewpots and attend to the tips of your noses, that business which obviously you know best."

The group eyed the tall and powerful being with suspicion. Slowly they began to shuffle back toward their personal hovels and own businesses.

"You seek what should not be sought," another villagefellow said in retreat. "You will bring grief and blackness to our world. It is written upon the wisps of wind that move through our village. Do not return here if you care at all for Faro and the remainder of his family," he said, as he disappeared inside a neighboring hovel.

Zennan looked apologetically at Faro. "If I do indeed bring such danger to your family, I shall be forever saddened. Your hospitality has been welcome, your friendship esteemed. I will free your daughter, if she is to be free," Zennan said, grasping Faro's forearm in the ancient greeting of trusted comradeship. Faro nodded and smiled as he watched Zennan depart, having chosen to remain on foot rather than accept the horse that Faro offered.

Just outside the village hovels, Wun and Wunto had perched themselves precariously on the ledge of a large rock that towered over the meandering trail heading west. When Zennan passed from the village he saw the two creatures busily chattering between themselves.

"Alas, my two traveling companions have decided to rejoin me, I see," Zennan said, as he passed beneath them.

The two creatures stopped their chatter and clambered down from the rock and took up step behind Zennan.

"You have learned much?" Wun asked.

"Not the least of which is that I can't trust the both of you to stay beside me when your guidance may be of most use," Zennan answered, not slowing his pace.

"Ah, secrets," Wunto said.

"Yes, secrets," Wun acknowledged.

Zennan appeared to ignore his companions, but he was none-the-less listening to them.

"Should we keep secrets?" Wunto asked.

"Best that we do for now," Wun assured.

"We head to the west," Zennan advised.

"Ah, face, once again," Wunto said.

"Yes, I fear you are right," Wun agreed.

"Yet, to save a young maiden from Ra-Tanox's Castle Krog is perhaps worth the effort, more so than other less noble journeys might be," Wunto offered.

Zennan looked over his shoulder as he continued down the path. He was not surprised by his companions' knowledge of his destination and his goals, nor was he remorseful of his promise to Faro. Little could surprise him now. Zennan merely smiled to himself and wondered what the Castle Krog might be like. He increased his gait as the two creatures scampered effortlessly to keep up.

CHAPTER SIX

Meeshannette smiled weakly as her fitful sleep was again interrupted, but this time with a soothing faint blue glow that emerged from the dank air that suddenly swirled around her. This strange but peaceful spirit had come to her before, and, as in the past, she once again welcomed this savior of her mindful being. Slowly she rose from her sleep, not fully conscious, yet feeling alive for the first time since her fateful encounter with the Grand Black Sorcerer. The blue glow calmed her now, although she knew not why, yet she understood. The ambient coldness of the black stone walls of her imprisoning sleeping chamber was pushed aside as the blue glow metamorphosed into a pulsating image of a being, his long and flowing midnight blue robe billowing gently outward, revealing the claws of his feet. Meeshannette's hazy vision was filled with wispy, moving clouds of silver sparkling dust that slowly settled, yet she knew not where.

Moving slowly to the edge of an oversized and beautiful bed made from finely carved woods, Meeshannette pushed the long and silky black braids that framed her face back over her shoulders and stared upward at the pulsating vision before her mind. "From where do you come, old one," she asked calmly.

"I come from nowhere, yet I am everywhere," the wizard responded solemnly, his voice soothing to the youthful woman before him.

"And shall you leave me soon?" she asked.

"While your vision will dim, I shall remain forever in your mind."

Meeshannette, still feeling a dizziness she could not explain, slid down from her bedding that was softer than anything she could ever have imagined. Her bare feet stepped upon the cold stone floor and she respectfully moved toward the wizard. She could not get closer for as she moved, his image moved with her, maintaining the sameness of distance. She stopped and held out her hands.

"Are you able to assist me in returning to my family?" she asked.

"Your fate lies intertwined with the fate of others."

"Indeed that may be so, but shall I know with whom I am to be so closely allied, or is the blackness of Ra-Tanox and the evil of his Grand Black Sorcerer to be my fate?" she asked, her voice true, masked by neither sorrow nor fear.

A crash on the huge stonewood entry doors to her chamber whisked away her dream wizard and with it the comfort that she had felt in his presence. Meeshannette awakened, slightly startled to find herself standing in the center of a grand chamber clad only in a nightsleep gown's flowing folds of softness. She quickly returned to the edge of her bed as the door finished its swing inward. Two corsair guards entered her chamber.

"Why have you come and disturbed my sleep?" she asked.

"You will remain without questions or comments, imprisoned one," the nearest corsair said as he took her arm and pulled at her.

"Ra-Tanox orders your presence at his morning feast," the second corsair said. "And you would be wise to mind yourself in the ways of higher breeding if you seek not to offend the Great One," her rough-handling corsair added.

"Must I appear before your leader in these nightsleep clothes?" she asked. "Or shall you allow me time to present myself in the way of your higher breeding, if this life that you have allowed the evil one to create for you is one that you consider to be of higher breeding?" she said, contemptuously.

"Your continued effrontery will not be tolerated by either us and certainly not by his Greatness," the second corsair said, brusquely.

"You will leave my chambers and return for me only when I am properly adorned for your master."

"Ra-Tanox is also your master, pale one," the first corsair said, as he released her arm. "And it is best you remember that or your life may be quickly shortened." He stepped away from Meeshannette and nodded a slight bow with his head. "We will await your call, but be quick and appropriate in your coming readiness," he added. The two corsairs backed through the opened chamber doors, closing them as they exited, leaving Meeshannette once again to herself and her dreams.

Within moments of the great stonewood doors being closed, inside her chambers there was again a swirl of coldness intermixed with the strangely familiar blue glow. Meeshannette watched intently, her night dreams softly and slowly returning to her mind. An image began to form before her, but was quickly swept away by a momentary frigid wind that emerged from the cold, black stone walls. Meeshannette shivered away the coldness and, as her mind once again cleared of the night's visions, she began to ready herself in the richness of the garments that Ra-Tanox had provided for this newest of his captured prospective courtesans. Here, Meeshannette was presented with her choices from among the collection of exquisite silks and wools, each finer than she had ever imagined possible. Yet the fine clothes that filled the racks behind the mirrored partition were not of colors bright as a spring day, but dark and dreaded as the blackest winter storm. She quickly chose a long and flowing gown of the blackest silken cloth, then carefully adorned the many tight braids of her hair with thin strips of noire silk.

As though they had been watching and knew when Meeshannette had properly readied herself, the two corsairs reentered her chambers. "You will now accompany us to the master's feast of morning and remain quietly in your proper place," said the first and tallest corsair, who earlier had grabbed Meeshannette by her arm. He again reached for her silk-covered arm sleeve, but she pulled away from him.

"It would be in your best interest to leave your hands far from my body. Or are you willing to compete with your master's desires for my personal attentions?" she asked, defiantly. At her words, both corsairs froze their desires, belligerence giving way to submissive acquiescence.

Standing away, the first corsair bowed his head slightly in mocking acknowledgment. "You shall follow between us, and we will deliver you to your destination," he said, with evilness lacing his words.

"After which you will be wishing instead for our attentions," the second corsair chided. He laughed a chilling laugh. "Obviously you insignificant creatures from the outway regions of the empire do not know the stories about such sweetly inconsequential creatures as yourself laid bare before the Great Ra-Tanox."

"I have no fear of your pitiful leader, just as I fear not your amateurish attempts at forced seduction. Lead on, heathen creatures, and I shall follow, stepping not upon your repulsive footmarks."

Meeshannette spaced herself between and to the side of her two tormentors as they passed through great black crystalline archways. The castle was indeed expansive, Meeshannette thought to herself, her eyes prying into its deepest recesses, probing for a possible escape opening from this horror. From her earliest year, with no mother to protect her, she had become expert at avoiding her older brothers in their rough play, often escaping between their slow moving bodies, secreting her tiny frame in the smallest of hiding places. She often ducked into the trunks of lightning-hollowed trees or climbed high among their limbs or squeezed into the slimmest of rocky crevices where they would not think to search. But, before she could discern a route for escape, the corsairs presented her before the banquet table of Ra-Tanox. They cast their eyes downward with their heads bowed low as they backed their way from his presence. Meeshannette stood facing her seated captor.

"You have taken me . . ." Her words were cut short when Ra-Tanox slammed down a silver bowl hard upon the table before him.

"You do not speak without my permission," Ra-Tanox commanded. "Stand in silence until I am ready for you." He continued drinking from his ebony goblet filled with the elixir of Nador.

Calmly, Meeshannette obeyed, but her mind and eyes continued their exploration of the castle.

Ra-Tanox set the empty goblet on the table before him. "You will forgive my rudeness," he said, his voice oozing sarcasm. "Perhaps my beautiful guest would care for food and drink?"

Immediately, from behind a nearly invisible partition, a hunched-back servant appeared and refilled the empty goblet with elixir. The servant's downcast eyes never lifted their view from the ground before him as he set forth another goblet of crystalline blackness filled with elixir. Ra-Tanox motioned for Meeshannette to step forward and take the goblet.

"I do not welcome your hospitality," she said.

At Meeshannette's words, the servant, slowly backing away from the presence of his master, raised his eyes slightly from the floor toward her, then quickly disappeared before Ra-Tanox could notice his purposeful indiscretion.

"I do not offer, but command. You will drink with me and you will remain pleasant, or I assure you that the short remainder of your life will be significantly less pleasant than it is presently."

Meeshannette smiled. "Your offer I accept," she said, briskly stepping up and taking the goblet from the long table of Ra-Tanox. She swirled the fragrant liquid about its black crystal bowl, inhaling its sweet, intoxicating aroma, an aroma that suddenly seemed strangely familiar.

"Your familiarity with the magical potion my sorcerer brews for me should not come as a surprise. Following your arrival at the Castle Krog last night, you were given a sampling of its power, a power used to secure complete cooperation from those who partake," Ra-Tanox said. He sipped again from his goblet.

A surge of terror suddenly spread its fire through Meeshannette's belly, as incomplete flashes of a horrible image passed worm-like through her mind.

Ra-Tanox smiled a dangerous, calculating smile. "Yes, my dear, you have joined those so honored to have served my, how shall we say, higher spiritual needs." He laughed heartily, knowing this young woman, like those who preceded her, would be at first repulsed, but would ultimately feel privileged to have served the greater needs of the empire. "You will learn to accept me, or you will regret having ever entered my castle."

Once again revulsion shivered through Meeshannette's body. She knew that maintaining control of her mind was essential to her survival, yet her mouth was not so easily slowed. "Already I regret having been abducted from my home by creatures so vile that even my pigs failed to acknowledge their existence."

"Perhaps you are a witch in the pig hovels of your worthless family, and it was your presence that frightened their silence," Ra-Tanox countered.

"Or perhaps I have merely grown fond of the vile smells of our pig pen slop pond, which is the reason I do not relinquish my last meal upon your table," Meeshannette said.

"You mock me in ways that others have never dared," Ra-Tanox wailed, slamming his own crystalline goblet of elixir down upon the table. He stood to his full height, towering over his newest acquisition.

Meeshannette, too, slammed her goblet onto the table, spraying the black liquid across the food spread before her.

Anger flashed across the face of Ra-Tanox, but it quickly softened, if only slightly, as his attention was drawn to the expansive entrance to his dining area. Meeshannette, too, found her attention drawn suddenly away from her tormentor.

The Grand Black Sorcerer, his strides long and powerful, appeared at the entryway. He motioned for his accompanying sirocco officers to remain, as he continued forward to the table of his master.

"I trust your next journey, my most evil and trusted sorcerer, will prove more successful than your most recent, which provided only this single and most disrespectful female for my entertainment," Ra-Tanox said.

The sorcerer cast his eyes down upon the female standing beside him. "Perhaps our discussion should not include your . . ." His words quickly faltered, his mind being suddenly invaded by foreign feelings. An evil shiver coursed his body, a shiver that he could not immediately shake away. Finally, he slowly continued speaking to Ra-Tanox. "This feeble creature you have before your greatness possesses more than that which appears before your immortal eye. Her beauty is deceiving. She must be removed from this room immediately and sequestered where light and wind may never again discover her presence."

A moment of fear crossed Meeshannette's mind, but did not linger. Instead, strength came to her at a time when most others would certainly have trembled, and this new-found strength showed in her face.

"Why does this smallest of creatures disturb you so?" Ra-Tanox asked his sorcerer.

The sorcerer remained silent, crossing his arms and closing his eyes. Ra-Tanox knew well the stubbornness of his powerful sorcerer and rather than command him to speak, thought it best to remove the obstacle of his abstinence. Ra-Tanox motioned toward the entry, and the same pair of corsairs who delivered Meeshannette immediately returned. Ra-Tanox nodded toward Meeshannette, and the two corsairs each grabbed one of her arms. She struggled to pull away, but only momentarily as the corsairs intensified the strength of their control, forcing her into submission.

"Place her in the deepest of the dungeon cells, and treat her as she deserves," Ra-Tanox commanded, then added, "but let no harm come to her that you do not wish upon yourselves and your kin one hundred times over."

Meeshannette struggled once more, turning her head back toward Ra-Tanox as she was led away. "Your powers will not protect you forever," she said. "You will fall, destroyed by your own evil."

"Remove her from my vision before I have her tongue removed to silence her insolence," Ra-Tanox screamed. He turned to his wizard as the two corsairs quickly removed Meeshannette from his sight. "You, my evil Sorcerer! What have you to say now about your fear of this village female? What is it that she could possibly disrupt?"

The Grand Black Sorcerer slowly opened his eyes, transferring the consciousness from his trance to the beckoning of his master. "This female that my soldiers have delivered to you is much more than she appears," he mouthed slowly.

Ra-Tanox leaped up onto the table and stepped over the food that separated himself from his sorcerer, moving his own face close to that of his most evil servant. He said nothing immediately, letting his thoughts move from his own mind into that of his Grand Black Sorcerer.

"What you are thinking is of no consequence," the sorcerer proclaimed.

"Then perhaps I should simply have this omen that you insist is my demise burned at the stake, while I sit and enjoy the taste of her boiled blood."

The Grand Black Sorcerer turned away from Ra-Tanox and squeezed his hands hard to the sides of his head, feeling pain like he had never before experienced. The pain quickly subsided, but not without leaving an indelible mark upon the sorcerer. "This woman, the one called Meeshannette, she holds within herself the answers to questions not yet being asked," he said.

"And, my most favored and trusted Grand Sorcerer of knowledge, to what questions does she hold these most mysterious of answers?" Ra-Tanox demanded.

"Power, my great master. The power that moves the universe. It is a force so potent that it remains separated until once in each eternity it joins together with the possessor of its counterpart. Paired, it creates an omnipotence which not even the most powerful of masters is capable of conquering." His eyes lowered as he turned once again to face Ra-Tanox.

Ra-Tanox laughed. "The female appears not to be a witch, and certainly she possesses no special powers, not even powers capable of removing herself from the chains of my dungeon." He sat in silence for a moment, finally turning to his sorcerer. "And where, tell me, may her counterpart hide, this half possessor of a power so potent that I should be concerned?"

Now the sorcerer focused his vision tightly upon the eyes of Ra-Tanox. "Mysteries exist that evade even my most powerful of incantations, master. A wind, cold and bleak, present yet unattainable, has visited your empire. It flies free among the hovel villages along the farthest fringes of your empire. And, there are signs present that an elder wishtongue has once again come among your multitudes."

Ra-Tanox, his eyes suddenly fired with hatred-driven anger, lashed out at his sorcerer. "You dare to spout such blasphemy from your tongue? I commanded that the name 'wishtongue' never again be uttered during my lifetime nor following my departure to my next empire." Ra-Tanox drew his dagger, its oversized onyx-encrusted handle gleaming in all its evil blackness.

Quickly the Grand Black Sorcerer lowered his eyes to the floor before his master, yet made no effort to escape the pending death blow coiled but an arm's-length to his front. The sorcerer knew that his life would not end today. He remained the most powerful sorcerer within the bowels of the Ra-Tanox empire. And with the reemergence of the wishtongue, and the potential threat of an unknown power more powerful than himself, Ra-Tanox would not bring harm to his Grand Black Sorcerer.

Both beings simultaneously twisted their thoughts to the cold chill that once again and without warning spread throughout the room. "Stop this infiltrator," Ra-Tanox shrieked. The ribbon of cold shifted slightly away from his voice, then returned, swirling its wind around Ra-Tanox. Again he shrieked, "Be gone, wind of death, be gone from before the sight of my eyes and the touch of my hand." He snapped his head toward the staring sorcerer. "Cast this dispersion against my power from this room. Cast it out immediately, Sorcerer," Ra-Tanox commanded.

The Grand Black Sorcerer stepped back from Ra-Tanox, momentarily escaping the wind that swirled also about him. A second wave of cold streamed into the chambers creating its own ribbon of swirling wind about the Grand Black Sorcerer. Fear crossed the sorcerer's dark and wrinkled face, deepening the lines that already creviced his life form. The two wind ribbons now grew bright, emitting a translucence that glowed yellow then green as they left their two crazed captives and swirled momentarily into one entity, colder than the coldest of winters. As suddenly as they had appeared, the two ribbons separated and streaked from the room, leaving Ra-Tanox and his sorcerer gasping for breath.

Finally, desperately, Ra-Tanox gathered himself to the point of speech. "What evil is this that invades my domain, now with ten times the bitter cold as before," he uttered, trying to scream terror into his wizard, but gurgling only short, raspy breaths of words.

Studying his choices, contemplating carefully the words he would use to describe the vision he had just witnessed, the Grand Black Sorcerer finally coerced an opinion from his own lips. "The two powers of which I had earlier warned have now united the winds of their singular essences before us."

"And what harbingers of menace shall result from this chance mating, Grand Black Sorcerer?"

"I cannot say with the certainty of time, only the certainty of actions, Master. The two beings of whom I spoke are now aware of each other's presence, yet the duration of their communion before us indicates that they have not yet come to understand the powers that await them if they ultimately unite as one."

"And you say this pitifully weak hovel-female now in my prison is the supposed partner in this conspiracy against me?"

"Believe not that a conspiracy exists, great Master. What befalls our future is fate, fate as yet unknown to us." The sorcerer raised his caped arm across his forehead, allowing the soft black fabric to cascade before his face. He closed his eyes, but only momentarily, the vision striking hard into his mind, stronger than he had ever before experienced. "The woman, Meeshannette is her name. Her heart must be taken from her body upon the full moon of this night. Eating of its raw flesh while it still pumps hot through her body the blood of her innermost being will transfer the power she possesses to he who consumes its crimson juices. Then, and only then, Great Master, will we be able to plan for the annihilation of he who seeks to join the forces of the universe against the great Ra-Tanox."

All fear had now left the mind of Ra-Tanox as he paced slowly across the great floor, his mind seeking thoughts that he knew would come to him. The destruction of the two halves of such a dichotomous power, and his assumption of its control, would certainly elevate his own powers. Such successful action surely would ensure dominion over all lands of light that extended beyond the borders of the great darkness his family Tanox had thus far created. He ceased his pacing and turned to his awaiting sorcerer and screamed his orders.

"Corsairs, present yourselves before me, I command you now!"

Immediately the two corsairs who had earlier removed Meeshannette returned again to face Ra-Tanox their master. With their heads bowed low, neither spoke, waiting in silence for his command.

"Return to the woman prisoner and bring her immediately to the Chamber of Voices," Ra-Tanox ordered. "Do not make me wait. Now, be gone from my sight." He turned to the sorcerer. "Bring with you your greatest of powers my wicked sorcerer," Ra-Tanox bellowed, as he quickly headed for the doorway. "We will steal away from this female those powers you say she possesses, but does not yet comprehend."

The Grand Black Sorcerer followed closely behind his master Ra-Tanox as the great one charged off for the Chamber of Voices, deep in the bowels beneath his castle.

CHAPTER SEVEN

A partial moon shone dimly, its warm, golden glow that Zennan had known in his homeland transformed to a strange orange fusion in this strange land. His night fire burned warm, though its few flames flickered low. Once again, Wun and Wunto appeared to have abandoned him, though their absence concerned him little now. Zennan was certain they would return with the morning light. And if they didn't, he would continue his trek toward the west assured that the castle walls of evil that he sought would soon find their way before his path.

Zennan's light slumber was suddenly stolen from him as a wind as wicked and cold as he had ever felt shivered coldness through to his spine. It was a cold so deep and controlling that even his warming fire visibly diminished its soft, flickering light and was extinguished. Two winds, the one from his west being met by a second that seemed to arise from his own being, spun wildly about him, swirling outward, then inward, becoming one. The circling winds again moved outward from his body, coursing as one, separating, then merging once more. As the winds united, at his feet the warming fire suddenly burst forth from the small remnants of charred-woodfuel, raging into a blue-white flame brighter than he had ever before seen.

Zennan, rightly assuming that a sign was being visited upon him, stood to his full height, allowing his cape to drop to the ground about his feet. Suddenly the newly raging flames of his warming fire leaped upward and joined the winds that now swirled above him. Higher they ascended into the sky, then returned to the ground, scorching the duff surrounding his feet.

As quickly as the fire and wind had burst upon him, they were gone, replaced by the bright shine of a golden moon. As he watched, the moon's face darkened back to its diffused orange glow, softening the black shadows that his small warming fire again danced around him. Zennan reached down and picked up his cape, pulling it back over his shoulders. He hoped that the wishtongue might return and interpret what he was feeling and what he had encountered. But neither the wishtongue nor the wizard of blue light would return to him this night. He settled back to the ground, pulling his cape snug around his shoulders to ward away the returning coldness that was natural and expected as the first days of the new season of growth were not yet upon the land about him.

Wun and Wuntu sat on rocks looking down upon the light of the campfire's last flickerings, mindless of Zennan's awakening to the new day, discussing the avenues that he might choose on his continued trek toward the Castle Krog.

"He again sleeps soundly," Wuntu jabbered to his companion.

"For once, but his eyes will open wide in moments that are as fleet as the flicker of his most bushy lashes," offered Wun.

Their chattering voices greeted Zennan's mind as it quickly shed the shroud of night that slowed his thoughts. They both watched Zennan intently as he sat up, the cape slipping from his shoulders to his lap. Zennan shook his head, and both creatures turned back toward one another and chattered quick spurts of incomprehensible babble. Wun stopped and looked at Zennan.

"Nourish yourself quickly, for the winds of change dictate that we must move from this land to the sanctuary that awaits us," Wun explained, expecting that Zennan would remain confused, but caring only that the message was properly delivered.

Zennan felt Wun's words, not in the identical manner as before with contempt cast his way, but deep from within himself. He was beginning to understand and comprehend what his two companions were telling him, although confusion still reigned.

"You are right," Zennan said, looking about him and for the first time beginning to see what this land beyond the end of the beginning of light held for him. He stood up and stretched, then quickly gathered his meager belongings. "We must make careful haste onward. Today's sun already burns too quickly toward the end of its wick, although now the days will continue to grow longer before us."

Wunto and Wun looked at each other and smiled.

"He is learning," Wunto said.

"Yes, he has quickly assimilated much, but much remains before him," Wun answered.

"Much," Wuntu agreed.

They hopped down from their rocky perch above Zennan and scampered along the meandering trail. Zennan quickly followed behind. When they reached a path fork, not easily discernible to the unaided and untrained eye, Wun and Wuntu chose the trail that headed still west, but now slightly south. Zennan hesitated for a moment at the fork, but only because he could not easily distinguish either trail, which obviously were little used by the few inhabitants of this barren and desolate land. He chose the path followed by his two companions.

When the sun passed its zenith and tumbled downward toward the far horizon before them, their path again began to ascend a steepening hillside. And as they climbed higher, the scrag brush that had tangled periodically at Zennan's feet grew sparse, slowly replaced by patches of soft grass, then by taller plants of a kind he had never before seen. Finally, his two friends stopped at a place where the smallest of waterstreams tumbled down from the hills above and disappeared into a mass of strange vegetation that towered high above Zennan's head.

"Tis time that we break for nourishment," Wun said as he plopped himself down on a small round boulder that was perched next to a group of greenish-blue plants. Wunto sat next to him on another equally stream-rounded boulder.

Both immediately broke off one of the long canes of the greenish-blue plant and appeared to bite into it. Zennan watched for a moment, amused at this sight of these two strange creatures sucking nourishment from a plant. He then maneuvered himself through the tumble of boulders that surrounded the tall cane plants where the small stream of water entered the patch of blue-green. He dropped to his belly and just as he started to drink from the stream of clear, cold water, the ever-present voice of one of his companions spoke to him.

"You assume that in this strange land what appears familiar to you is indeed the same as that which you knew in your old life,"

Wun said, now suddenly and quietly perched atop a large stone near where Zennan lay.

Zennan hesitated for a moment, then began to move his face toward the cold water, but again hesitated. Finally he pulled back from the stream and sat up.

Wuntu plucked a small leaf from the end of one of the tall canes and scrambled over the rocks to where Wun and Zennan sat. He carefully set the leaf upon the slowly trickling water and immediately the floating leaf began to smoke. In a short moment it turned into an ugly and crinkled black mass as flames burst forth leaving only remnant ashes that were quickly swallowed by the waters that carried the smoldering mass to the base of the cane grove where it disappeared.

In silence Wun handed Zennan an arm-length piece of the cane. "The waters before you that you believed to be cleansing and life-giving, because such is so in your homeland beyond the end of the beginning of light, here carry poisons that eat life from nearly all that it touches," Wun said.

Wuntu stepped up beside Wun. "The poison is filtered by the base of the watercane, which, since the time of the last coming of ice, has built immunity to the consuming fire that destroys all else that is living. Slowly, the cane filters clean liquid through its brackish bottoms to the green life stems above." Wuntu bit another piece and sucked into his body the cool liquid the watercane poured forth.

Zennan quickly bit into the cane he held and savored its cool, sweet liquid as it tumbled freely into his mouth. When he had drunk his fill he dropped the last piece of cane and looked around. His two traveling companions were once again not within his sight. He walked around the small watercane grove, being careful to leap well across the path of the firewater. Still they were not there, so he headed forward along the trail that still angled upward into the western hills. He knew he couldn't wait for his friends to decide to return before he continued his journey, not if he hoped to find Meeshannette, the stolen daughter of Faro. And for a reason unbeknownst to him, other than his first attraction to her, his inner feeling was growing from the kindly promise to a sad old man, to a life-compulsion to find this young woman, a woman who remained a stranger, yet who was inexplicably known deep within him.

The nearly indiscernible pathway wound higher, periodically tracing its way near the course of the poison stream. Twice Zennan's passage crossed the stream's liquid fire, but his path was made easy over large stones evenly spaced in the spoor. As he continued onward, the sparse vegetation turned to a multitude of twisted pygmy trees with their small, gray-green leathery leaves that turned their edges to the sun as it tracked its heat across the sky. He climbed still higher to where the scrag pygmy trees were in-turn evicted from their living space by larger trees that reached to touch the sky, while lush green ferns bordered what had become a much more obvious trail.

The farther the trail meandered, the steeper its downside ran until the trail had become but a narrow ledge clinging to the cliff face of reddish-orange stone worn smooth by forces ancient and persistent. The shade from the tall trees Zennan had enjoyed now disappeared, their bodies too massive to cling to such sheer cliffs. He continued onward, watching carefully his footing on the narrow trail, wishing not to tumble to lifelessness in the abyss below him. As he rounded a blind corner a small child ran into his legs and yelled out in surprise. The youngster looked up at the giant towering above him and backed away slowly, silently. Zennan again walked forward and the boy turned, and as sure-footed as the mountain goats that ran wild in these mountains, he scampered away, quickly disappearing around another cliff corner from the direction he had first come. Zennan continued onward, more slowly, cautiously, now being uncertain what warning the boy might sound and how the elders of his village might respond to an uninvited stranger in their midst.

* * *

Within the darkened halls in the deepest chambers of the Castle Krog, tongues of fire from the Inferno of Tanox transformed the nearby tiny stone cell where Meeshannette sat into a wet, dripping heat sump. Intolerable as her situation appeared, she knew that her life would not end in this chamber of horror. Escape was possible, only the opportunity had yet to present itself to her. Time would change that, as it always had when she was forced to escape the teasing harassment of her elder brothers when they too had become intolerable, even for her. She pulled her long, raven hair up on her head and bound it in a tight knot, allowing what little free air existed in the cell to move across her neck, providing a fleeting sensation of cooling.

In the far distance Meeshannette heard the slam of one of the dozen black iron doors that the corsair guards had passed through when they imprisoned her here. A moment passed and another door, this one closer, squealed open on its rusty hinges, then slammed closed. Voices began to emerge from the thick silence that surrounded her. Meeshannette quickly sat as far back on the plank bed as possible and pulled her legs up to her chest, burying her face between her knees, yet allowing space enough so she could see who it was that might open the door to her cell. Two voices became distinct before growing silent outside her door. Keys clanked and the door opened allowing a weak ray of light from an outside torch to spill across the corner bed where Meeshannette sat.

"Look, pity our poor guest who sobs as though still in her mother's arms," the tallest of the corsairs remarked with a chuckle.

From between her knees, she watched both corsairs approach. Meeshannette pulled back from them, pressing herself against the hot, wet wall. The smaller corsair was the first to reach for her. He grabbed her arm and attempted to pull it away from its locked position wrapped around her legs. She resisted and he pulled harder. The taller corsair laughed at his smaller companion's trouble. He stepped to the edge of the bed and grabbed her other arm. Meeshannette resisted at first, then as both corsairs together pulled hard, she suddenly sprang away from the wall and over her two keepers. Off-balance, the two corsairs tumbled backward to the hot stone floor, confused and astonished at what had just occurred. Before either could regain control of himself or the situation, the raven-haired girl snatched the round iron key ring from the smaller corsair's black leather belt and slammed the chamber's iron door closed behind her. She quickly twisted the correct key in the lock, turning her captors into captives. The two corsairs chose not to yell for help because they knew that in these lower cavern levels there existed no one but themselves who might assist them. Now it was the two corsairs who curled into fetal positions on the wood plank bed awaiting their fate when the wrath of Ra-Tanox discovered and reacted in his manner to their incompetence.

Outside the locked chamber now, Meeshannette followed the route through the dark, sweat-dripping cavern tunnels that she had memorized during her first and hopefully last journey into the deepest depths below the Castle Krog. But the tunnels appeared different now that she was moving through them in the opposite direction. As she climbed the carved stone stairways, at each new level she was confronted with several tunnel options. At first she had no problem finding her way, because only one of the tunnels at each level was controlled by a locked iron door, with the others being open. Since her forced journey downward required the corsairs to open a locked door on each of the last five levels, she merely chose the door-guarded tunnel and used the stolen keys to open her path to the next higher level. But from the sixth level upward she was confronted with six tunnel options at the top of each stairway, all of which were controlled by iron-barred gates. Meeshannette chose as best she could, but she knew that guesses alone would not get her back to the castle's main level. Still she continued, hoping there was more than one possible avenue through to the final level.

Passing as rapidly as she could through the darkness of her sixth level guess, Meeshannette encountered a cavernous room where locked iron-barred cells held unknown dozens of pathetic creatures who both stood and sat huddled together in large masses. She realized that her sixth level tunnel guess was an error as she had never before encountered these cells nor had she ever seen another living creature in the tunnels. She continued onward, past the imprisoned creatures.

A shrill scream shot through the tunnel and echoed into the hall that Meeshannette had entered. It made the blood in her veins run cold. She stopped her escape, standing motionless in the darkness just paces beyond where the cells were filled with the unknown creatures. The scream echoed once again through the tunnel and was answered by an even more tortured scream that emerged from the captive creatures. Their discordant wails increased and became such that Meeshannette's ears shrieked for relief from the pain. She held her hands across her ears attempting to reduce the level of noise, but to no avail. Following untold moments of torturous waiting, the wails subsided, allowing her mind to once again work as it had when her brothers, screaming and yelling their playful threats, chased her across rocky fords and through thick woodlands. She quickly backstepped to the cavern's cells where the howling creatures were imprisoned, chose the correct key from the stolen ring and opened the locked doors that held them captive.

* * *

A heavy fog saturated the Chamber of Voices, and the thick air swirled as Ra-Tanox shrieked his anger. "Where are my corsairs, Sorcerer? Why have they not yet returned with this feeble female?" he screamed.

The Grand Black Sorcerer remained near the entry allowing his master to work through his seething anger. When Ra-Tanox again chose to face his evil sorcerer, the wily one bowed his head in anticipation of what he already knew would be his master's command.

"End my wait and bring her to me yourself, now!" Ra-Tanox commanded.

The sorcerer responded as expected to his master's demand. He nodded and bowed as he backed from the Chamber of Voices. As he reached the doorway, the long since departed human spirits who had died in the horrors conceived by Ra-Tanox and his ancestors began their full-moon howling serenade. The Grand Black Sorcerer glanced upward at the swirling vapors that had evolved into faint vestiges of their original selves. Several dived downward at the sorcerer, who merely pointed the power of his hand, reeling them backward into a disheveled gaseous eddy that remained suspended a dozen body lengths above his head. Ra-Tanox again wailed at his sorcerer, but the sorcerer quickly slipped from the cavernous chamber.

As the sorcerer passed down the first stairway, a cold and powerful wind pressed him hard against the cragged stone wall. The wind passed him swiftly on its way up the stairway, and the sorcerer rebounded as quickly, hurrying his pace downward into the bowels of the deepest chamber. At the bottom of the first set of stairs he chose the center of the five tunnels that lay before him and moved as if riding upon his own wind down to the next set of stairs. Just as he reached the first of its steps he slowed for a moment as the howl from the Chamber of Voices increased its intensity in response to the cold wind that had passed him and had continued on to where Ra-Tanox awaited. Before the Grand Black Sorcerer made the next lower level, he heard the howl of Ra-Tanox vainly attempting to command away the invading winds of fate that swirled about him whipping the Chamber's voices. The grand sorcerer hurried his pace, descending to the next chamber level and chose its second tunnel from the left. Finally, the ranting voice of Ra-Tanox faded completely from his ears. But with the welcome silence came also the invading image of the fate wind that had passed him at the first cavern level and now surrounded Ra-Tanox. The image was of confusion, not yet a person, although the Grand Black Sorcerer knew it must be the girl, Meeshannette. He further quickened his pace onward through the tunnel and then downward to the next lower level.

  Another mind image surged upward toward the sorcerer, but in his present, scattered state of mind any reasonable interpretation from its confused meanings was impossible for even a great sorcerer, at least without benefit of slow and deliberate focus. He had no time for such things, not if his intuition served him as well now as it had always served him in the past. A screeching howl joined in the image surge, and when the discordant noise reached an ear-shattering crescendo, a stream of four-winged bats screamed through the tunnel from his front. As he stopped and braced himself upon a small ledge that had been hewn into the rock wall next to the stairway, the bats and their screams passed by. A low reverberation followed the bat screams, and it rumbled continually, although more slowly. The sorcerer, still pressing his body into the shallow wall depression, took the few seconds spaced between the attackers to focus his mind more sharply upon the vague and fleeting image of Meeshannette. Rather than the girl, what entered his mind was an image of two corsairs quivering before him in a combined fear that overwhelmed all else.

"Burn, my failed corsairs. Burn like the straw that you perch your two worthless bodies upon," the Grand Black Sorcerer wish-commanded.

Down in the lowest chamber two corsairs leaped in agony as at first their clothing, then their flesh, burst into flames. But sounds of their tortured screams and the remnants of their flailing bodies failed to pass through the locked iron doors that separated the end of the soldier-jailers from their successful escape to the upper cavern tunnels.

As the sorcerer howled his pleasure at his incompetent solders' demise, he allowed the surging image of confusion to reenter his mind. Just as the swirl of madness was beginning to slow and meld into an image of sense, the low rumble that had been slowly approaching was upon him. The confused vision that slowly had been merging into a comprehensible mind-image suddenly coalesced into hundreds of creatures with stinking, rotting bodies and deep resonant and pleading cries of guidance for their sightless eyes. Even the evilness of the Grand Black Sorcerer quivered in disgust as the mass of creatures continued their surge past him. The mass quickly ascended the stairway, leaving the sorcerer alone. He turned his mind back toward the caverns below, searching and probing their many hollows and crevices for a sign, a feeling, a sense for where the girl Meeshannette lay in hiding, trying to escape her deadly fate within the waiting Chamber of Voices. She was nowhere.

The Grand Black Sorcerer, his wickedness useless to him this moment, wailed his hatred at the winds of fate that were aborting his mightiest attempts for control of a mere mortal, a lowly hovel girl. Like a great weight striking his entire body, his mind focused upon an image of Meeshannette, but it was an image free of the chains of the Castle Krog.

"Impossible!" he bellowed in arrogance. "Impossible!" He knew that immediate action was required. He began the long climb back to the top chamber where his sirocco troops awaited his commands.

* * *

Meeshannette held her breath as long as she could, but finally, as she run-squatted among the surging mass on their upward coursing migration, she was forced to suck her lungs full of the putrid air that oozed from the jailed creatures she had unleashed. She had immediately detected their blindness and was uncertain how they could find-follow one another in such a close-packed bunch, let alone find their way out of the chamber tunnels. But she knew the confusion they would create was her only hope for avoiding detection by the guards that must be present at the final chamber levels.

Meeshannette caught a glimpse of the Grand Black Sorcerer clinging against the tunnel wall as her mass of long, scraggly-haired creatures surged her toward the final level of caverns. She knew that her choice had been a good one, although the smell she was forced to behold was much more stomach wrenching than the foulest of her family's slop-rolling hogpigs. When they burst through the final arched doorway into the daylight, she quickly separated herself from the mass of creatures, taking refuge among carved stone barrels stacked high against one of the coal-black castle walls.

Almost as quickly as Meeshannette dropped in among the carved stone barrels, a massive, black iron gate opened before her, revealing a courtyard where she found herself watching helplessly as a small troop of mounted sirocco troops descended upon the creatures who unknowingly had aided her escape. Unmercifully, they charged their great gray steeds into the mass of creatures, creatures that she witnessed in the light of the early evening were quite pitiful beings. They appeared to her to be the creatures possessing strange powers and special mind-knowledge in tales she heard told by her great grandfather when she was first old enough to sit upon his knee. Unlike in her great grandfather's stories, far too many of these creatures today died, pierced by lances and trampled in brutal charges as the troops pushed the living, throbbing mass back toward the cavern entrance from where they had emerged.

Meeshannette dropped back behind the barrels, and when finally sounds of the murderous assault had diminished, she cautiously peered between two of the stacked stone barrels. She ducked down slightly again when the Grand Black Sorcerer entered the courtyard through the still-open iron gate. As the night when he kidnapped her, the evil one sat atop a white steed, a riding beast larger than any she had ever before seen. The sorcerer ignored the chaos around his horse's mighty limbs, seeming to sense an invading power that he could neither identify nor locate. Meeshannette imagined that he was sniffing out her presence and slid her body again out of sight behind the barrels. She looked around, seeking an escape route that would take her from this madness.

As Meeshannette's eyes calmly and methodically searched, she again felt a strange and unwelcome burning inside. She wished away the uncomfortableness and then began to move away from the courtyard, scraping her hands and knees across the rough-hewn cobblestone, keeping a large stack of stone barrels and wood crates as a wall between herself and the sorcerer. In moments she reached the south castle wall and quickly sought the smallest crevices for handholds and searched for cracks that might create footholds. She found none. The sheer black stone of the monolith she faced was far too smooth and polished for climbing.

Already the commotion in the courtyard had ended, leaving a sad and quiet pallor suspended low over the castle grounds. Meeshannette remained furtive in her movements along the length of the great wall even though she neither heard nor saw another being sulking about. Pressed close to the wall, she passed near several stone structures, each empty and without benefit of either windows or doors. Cautiously Meeshannette entered the third structure's open doorway seeking a hiding place where she could spend moments concentrating on a plan for escape, rather than having to constantly remain alert for soldiers wishing to return her to the evil that Ra-Tanox commanded. She found a corner room, the only one with windows and doors that offered several escape alternatives and slid herself down onto the floor, using the wall as a backrest.

As her mind drifted through escape scenarios, all of which appeared impossible, her quiet was shattered by the sharp clash of a horse's metal-clad hooves upon the cobblestones just outside the window above her head. Meeshannette scooted quickly across the floor to the opposite side where an open doorway awaited to aid her escape. Just as she reached the door and peered around its edge, she was confronted by two of the sorcerer's soldiers trotting on foot directly toward her. They hadn't yet seen her, so Meeshannette moved quickly to another of the escape routes. Two more corsairs approached and she saw that the leading soldier caught a glimpse of her. Without hesitation, she stood and sprinted toward the one open window and dove head first through it, rolling as she hit the outside cobblestones. Her flying body frightened the great white steed into rearing, nearly throwing the sorcerer to the ground. The sorcerer managed to hang onto the reins, but by the time he had repositioned himself in his saddle and settled his horse, Meeshannette was back on her feet and running away from where the soldiers were converging on the structure she had just vacated.

"Here, you imbecilic creatures of arms, the girl escapes from this side," the sorcerer screamed. He reined his horse around and spurred the white steed into pursuit. "Move toward the south gate and prevent her passage," he commanded as his great animal rapidly closed the distance to the frantically running girl. "Do not allow her to escape a second time."

Even without looking, the pounding doom of the sorcerer's horse told Meeshannette that she must do something now or forever remain the mad ruler's chattel. A final burst of foot speed brought her to the edge of another building just steps before the sorcerer's horse. She made a quick right turn around the building, hooking the wall's edge with her hand to quicken her change of direction without losing momentum. The sorcerer flew by, his horse skidding across the cobblestone surface. Before Meeshannette lay another open courtyard with only a small, stone-walled well within its center. She continued her sprint to the well and stopped at its edge. Already soldiers were closing in on her from the front and two other sides, and now the sorcerer was riding deliberately toward her, sensing he had won the race. Meeshannette, without even looking down inside, leaped over the stone wall and into the well, grabbing the bucket-end of the rope to slow her fall downward. When the rope caught at its knotted end, she was thrown hard against the rough-hewn inside wall. She looked down and could see nothing but black, with only the musty odor from below drifting up through her nostrils. Although stuck, a length of the rope still dangled below her, and she began letting herself down. Above, a laugh as black as the stormiest night she had ever trembled through as a small and motherless child, boomed out above her. She looked up and saw the weaseled face of the sorcerer.

His soldiers began to crank the handle to bring her upward. As she clung to the rope, not wishing to let go and die alone in the blackness below, she spun slowly in a circle just as her mind raced in circles seeking an escape. As she rose slowly upward, before her she noticed where the glint of light that reflected off the black walls of the well suddenly disappeared. She took a chance and swung herself to where she could kick her body away from the nearest wall and then released her white-knuckled-grip on the rope. As she fell outward and down toward the black, shineless spot on the wall, Meeshannette held her breath still expecting to smash into the stonework and tumble downward to her death. Instead, her intuition won and her body fell through the non-existent wall. She landed hard on her feet inside a small side tunnel. She immediately collapsed in the darkness, exhausted, from both the physical strain and from the mental effort that went into convincing herself so quickly that releasing her hold on the rope might be her only savior.

Echoing down from above, an angry and anguished scream reverberated off the walls, penetrating her refuge tunnel. She could hear the sorcerer screaming at his soldiers for having lost his prey, allowing an insignificant female hovel dweller to escape. Meeshannette wasn't sure she had escaped. Surrounded in cool, damp blackness, the light from above barely penetrated the main well shaft to the depth she had fallen. It penetrated not at all inside the tunnel where she rested.

"Ahhh," screamed a soldier, on his way past her, falling to his death in the abyss below. There was no sorrow in her feelings, only thoughts about how she would escape from her new prison cell. Slowly, carefully, so as not to reveal to any soldier who might be carefully listening from above that life still breathed from within her, she pivoted her body inside the narrow tunnel. Even more slowly Meeshannette took her first step back into the depths of the savior tunnel. Another step. Nothing. Still no ending wall confronted her passage. She continued on into the blackness, forced by fate into allowing the stone-lined cave to take her wherever it might lead.

To Meeshannette, time had ceased to exist. Cutoff from all sight sensory judgment, neither day nor night existed in her own little world. Only an occasional rat squeal caused by a misplaced blind step broke the silence. Still, she pressed onward until she finally hit a wall blocking her path. Feeling to her left, another wall met her groping hands. Then into the right side. Blackness and nothing. She turned right and continued forward, but now her blind path was also taking her downward, not quickly, but steadily. Her only choice was to continue onward, and as she did, the air became warmer, wetter, less breathable. She began to chant softly to herself, the only song she remembered from the short time she had with her mother.

"High atop the greenspar tree
the minstrel bird sits alone and free
Climb the trunk the cat does try
only to see the orange bird fly
Gliding high on soft white clouds
high above life's great black shrouds
Fly as free as the fastest breeze
and back you'll be atop the greenspar tree"

From deep within the black silence the drip of a water droplet echoed through the tunnel. Meeshannette softened the already nearly silent chant of her mother's song, repeating the simple verses. Her head scraped the rocky ceiling, so she lowered herself carefully to her hands and knees and continued forward. The stone floor quickly shred the fancy dress she still wore following her last encounter with Ra-Tanox and now scraped roughly her bare skin. She stopped singing and crawling when her hands touched a pool of liquid blocking her path. Meeshannette dipped her finger into the unseen water and touched it on her nose, sniffing for some recognizable odor. The smell did not seem harmful, so she tasted a bit of the liquid, her subconscious thirst suddenly surfacing. It was sweet and refreshing, so Meeshannette dipped her cupped hands into the pool and drank her fill.

She listened for the sound of water dripping. What had been a single drop now echoed from the tunnel's stone walls as a steady, tumbling cascade, although small it remained. Meeshannette moved ahead, carefully, sloshing silently through the collected pool. Her hands again struck a solid wall before her. She felt both left and right. The tunnel split here, so a decision was needed. To the left, Meeshannette imagined seeing the smallest speck of light far in the distance. She closed her eyes and the light speck remained. It was only her eyes playing tricks in the blackest darkness she had ever encountered. Or was it? Meeshannette slowly turned to the left, and as she moved forward the sound of water dripping was magnified, but its noise no longer echoed from the walls. So too, did her wishfully imagined point of light become larger. She felt upward and found nothing. Slowly she raised herself up from her crawling position and onto her feet and reached high, still feeling nothing above her head. Meeshannette, able to stand once again, hurried her pace forward down the tunnel, now feeling a much welcomed breeze that touched her face and cooled her sweat-wetted body. As the light grew brighter, so too did the air become cooler that blew across her skin.

The blackness that was slowly being transformed to ever lightening shades of gray across the smooth stone walls created its own deceptions. The light speck was not as quickly reached as Meeshannette had anticipated, now appearing to actually grow more distant with each additional step forward. She stopped her advance and rubbed her eyes free of the salted perspiration that had failed to evaporate. Now, the hole of light was pulsating before her, sending shafts of its warm yellow light ricocheting off the wet floor beneath her feet. Confused, she stepped forward, slowly at first, then at a normal walk, softly whispering more of her mother's song.

> "Little minstrel bird fly away
> amongst the clouds where you play
> Safe here you are sure to be
> back so high in your greenspar tree
> Little bird your heart beats wild
> Cry your tears and be gone my child
> The winds will take you safely free
> Be true oh darling,
> you're a part of me"

Finally, the light speck again sped toward her with each of her quickening steps, and when Meeshannette reached the edge of the lighted portal she ended her song once again. She moved with stealth, staying low as she peered through the round hole's opening, hoping that escape and safety awaited her eyes. Panic is not what came to mind, but frustration and sorrow invaded Meeshannette's heart. Before her lay the cells she had emptied of their prisoners not too long before. They were bare and silent. If she had known that her release of those pitiful creatures would bring a brutal death to so many, she would never have allowed them to leave. Yet, their lives, deep in the dungeon of Ra-Tanox would cause her to remove life from her own veins should she be so imprisoned in such a squalid and hopeless confinement. The thoughts were hurtful, yet fleeting, as she moved past the rusted iron bars.

Only moments passed when Meeshannette reached the top of the stairway where she had originally chosen the cellway as her escape route. Now she chose an alternative entryway, but before she could move into it, the sound of footsteps, hard in their slaps upon the cobbled floor, grew from silent patterings to echoes that penetrated to her soul. She backed from her chosen hall and into the stairway landing, listening carefully to the approaching steps. They were coming from the hall she had chosen, so she quickly slid back into the empty cell hallway and scrunched her tiny body deep into the darkest corner just past the entry. Meeshannette's heart pounded away the seconds until finally a horrid stench preceded a dozen of the surviving creatures that stumbled out past her hiding place and into the center of the hallway between the rows of prison cells. Two soldier guards chased after the creatures and cracked their great whips at the pitiful beings now huddled into one ball in the middle of the hallway floor.

Meeshannette hunched lower into the shadows watching intently for an opportunity to escape back into the stairway landing. The guards' whips cracked in unison across the quivering ball of life, squirting one of the creatures away from the group. It scampered down the hall, and both guards, laughing at the pitiful attempt to escape, pursued the being, again cracking their whips. The creature jerked to its left and tumbled into one of the empty and open cells. Both guards chased into the cell and laughed as they whipped it unmercifully. Meeshannette took the chance, but rather than returning to the landing, she instead crept toward the ball of creatures. She saw eyes, several of them, deep green and shining, staring at her. She ignored the stares and crawled to the cell and quietly closed the great iron door. The soldiers were so intent on beating their one small prisoner that they didn't hear the cell door closing. The iron lock clanked secure, safely separating the two guards from Meeshannette and the remaining creatures.

Immediately the bundle of pulsating fur separated into the remaining eleven individual beings. Without hesitation they surrounded Meeshannette. She stood silently and watched them, each and all amazed yet unafraid. The green-eyed creature nearest her reached its slender arm up holding the stolen cell door keys that she had dropped during the first escape. She made no attempt to take them.

"You, female villagefellow," the closest of the guards yelled at Meeshannette as he charged toward the closed cell door. "You have played your last trick upon the soldiers of Ra-Tanox." He pulled his own set of keys from his belt and reached through the iron bars with the keys in his hand to unlock himself and his partner.

The creature that held Meeshannette's keys used them to lash out hard at the soldier's outstretched hand. The guard screamed painfully and dropped the ring of keys as he jerked his arm back into the cell's safety. Suddenly, his partner screamed a surprised and anguished cry and dropped to his knees. The creature that had felt the guards' slashing whips cut across its back had clamped its long, daggeresque teeth into the guard's lower leg. As the guard struggled to beat the attacking creature away, his partner rushed to his rescue. Too close to use his whip on the thrashing beast, he attempted to grab his hands full of the scraggly fur and rip the attacker away.

Outside Meeshannette watched, frozen in her steps at the sudden turn-around. The creature carrying her keys quickly opened the cell gate, and his remaining friends rushed in, wrapping themselves in a savage, writhing ball around the two guards. The struggle lasted only moments, and when the beasts moved away they left two stone-quiet guards lying on the filthy cell floor. As the group of creatures moved back outside the cell and circled around Meeshannette. She watched, fascinated with these strange creatures that could, during one minute be able only to submit to the slashing cracks of two guards' whips, and moments later, with such incredibly swift savagery, turn their attackers to withered corpses.

Meeshannette raised her hands. "I wish you no harm," she said, not knowing whether they could understand her, but for this moment unaware of any alternative action.

In unison the creatures backed several steps away from the stranger before them, all that is but the largest and most scraggly of the beasts, the one who held Meeshannette's stolen keys. He stepped up to her, his deep-set green eyes blazing. She stared into his eyes, her mind working quickly.

"You are a strange one to be here among us," the creature said.

Meeshannette smiled. She knew if these creatures would take time to speak to her it wasn't likely they would harm her. But then she thought about all those who had died up on the courtyard because she had freed them. "I am truly sorry for the tragic fate of all your friends," she said, softly.

The creature answered without hesitation. "It is of no consequence that many of our ones were destroyed by the soldiers above. Any sense of loss we have encountered today is easily exceeded by the excitement that overwhelmed our senses at having been released following so many lifetimes of confinement," he said. "We have been here since before any time which we can remember."

"How is that you do not remember your lives before this prison?"

"Our ancestors were brought here by the father of the father of Ra-Tanox, long before we lived," the creature explained.

"Oh," was all the Meeshannette could say.

The knee-tall creatures standing about her again moved in, each in turn touching her smooth skin. The leader slapped their probing hands away.

"You must forgive my brothers and sisters. They have never before seen one such as you."

"It's quite all right," she said, trueness of heart filling her words. "Do you know a way out of the many caverns and tunnels that infiltrate this beastly bastion?" Meeshannette asked.

"We have never before been as far as we have gone today," he offered. "Perhaps together we shall be destined to find our escape." The creature hesitated for a moment. "Although I am not certain what we shall do in the outside. The descendants of our ancestors, in their time, told us many stories about the world of light, stories which our wise ones memorized and passed to us, and we to our young."

"Ah," Meeshannette sighed. "But I'm afraid we must first escape much darkness before we can hope for you to see the beauty of light and allow the scent of clean, fresh air on a cool spring morning to pass through your lungs. Come, we must leave before more guards descend upon this place."

CHAPTER EIGHT

The child that Zennan had encountered much earlier had disappeared and neither his elders nor his village had yet appeared before his path. The narrow trail still hugged the cliff face, but now twisted ever slowly to the right. Zennan continued, caution preceding each of his steps, his vision being able to capture only a short distance of the curving pathway before him. As the sun was beginning to set behind the distant hills across the broad valley west of the mountain, he climbed still higher. The trail turned even more sharply to his right and grew too narrow for him to pass. Zennan shuffled up to the ledge and peered cautiously around the corner of red rock. The narrowed trail continued only another two body distances, then ended. Zennan moved back to a wider spot in the trail and sat to rest, wondering where the child and his trail had gone.

"Oh, he is there," Wun said, walking in front of his companion around the corner from where Zennan had just looked and seen nothing but the trail's end.

"Yes, yes, confused he does appear," Wuntu replied.

Zennan looked down at his two occasional companions. "From where do you two come?" he demanded. "There is no trail beyond that corner."

"We tell him that he must not view this world as he does his own," Wun said.

"And still he does," Wunto added.

The two sat beside Zennan, dangling their short legs over the edge of the cliff.

"Tis a long way down," Wun said, stating the obvious as he peered over the ledge.

"Tis the reason to look up when down is not the way to go,"

Wuntu said, scratching his scraggly head beard.

Zennan, knowing that he should not be annoyed with his two friends, could not remove such feelings from his mind. He closed his eyes for a moment thinking about the constant babbling of his tagalong creatures, at least when they decided to honor him with their presence. Finally, his eyes opened as he looked up to the cliff that towered upward behind him. Clinging from well-formed hand and footholds, Wun and Wuntu were looking down at him.

"You two proceed, and I will follow," Zennan said, knowing that these two creatures that he had earlier mocked and thought of as not even worthy of his killing, had once again shown him the path that he had lost. He motioned them ahead, but already they had climbed well beyond his reach. Zennan pushed his carryall bag from his side around to his backside and began the arduous climb. No match for the creatures' agility, Wun and Wuntu were quickly gone from his sight. Zennan's focus was not on his two companions, only on the tiny hand and footholds, struggling for adequate grip on miniature appendages better suited for less significant creatures.

Sweeping up from far below, Zennan felt the first swirl of cold air strike his face. He expected it to cease as cliff-side breezes often did. Away from the cliff face a black raven effortlessly rode the rising air current, quickly becoming but an insignificant sky speck. The raven was gone, but the wind persisted, soon turning cold and blowing harshly upon him. As the trail continued its twisting climb, the wind that swirled produced a harsh, shrill whistle as it flowed unevenly around the rocky overhang that had appeared above Zennan's head. The sunlight was shadowed, darkening Zennan's sight as he carefully picked his way around the side of the overhang, finally pulling his body to a resting place on a ledge that lay below yet another overhang. Here, the shadows were blasted away by the setting sun's last brilliant luminance, its harsh golden glow lighting a slender, yet passable trail.

Still, Zennan was forced to hug the path's cliff face, bent at the waist so as to clear the ledge that trailed above his head. He fought for a foothold along the path that again was eroding from what already was nothing but a narrow mountain goat trail. Zennan thought fleetingly about his earlier encounter with the wizard and later with the wishtongue, only to busy his mind once again with more important matters as he felt for solid footing with each of his steps. Again, Zennan's steps ceased at the sudden end to the trail. He looked above his head to where the ledge now gave way to a series of rising and more obviously formed footholds. As he reached upward and grasped the first rocky handhold, the ledge beneath his lower foot gave way, the crumbling stone cascading into the abyss below, well beyond his sight. He held on and once again began his climb upward, moving away from the cold wind and golden light as darkness descended.

Before the night's blackness forced closure to his exhaustive day's travel, the small handholds had become steps. They in turn became a narrow trail that once again allowed Zennan to speed his pace. Still, the path was narrow and the cliff drop precipitous and long. He reached the top of his climb, entering a village of stacked-stone huts perched near the cliff-edge, while a meadow, its yellow flowers glowing golden in the rising half moon, spread out wide before him. As Zennan had become accustomed, Wun and Wunto were nowhere in sight, but, many dozens of villagers wandered about, all but one ignoring his presence. Standing beside this single attentive villager, who stood tall and stared Zennan's way, was the small boy of his earlier encounter. A villager, likely a parent, took the boy's extended hand, then moved toward Zennan, but stopped a comfortable distance from him.

"Who dares trespass upon my mountain and do damage to my great highway?" the villager's deep and powerful voice boomed.

Zennan froze his movements, only his breathing continued, slow and steady. "Who speaks to me with such power that cracks the mighty rock of this mountain claimed by you?" Zennan asked, his voice, without melody, booming forth to match the power of this villager.

"Who is this bold and lost trespasser who dares demand my name?" the villager answered, the power of his voice echoing through the distant canyon.

Zennan thought for a moment, seeing that the villager was smaller and less powerful than himself and without weapons of any discernible size. The villagefellow wore a tunic of roughly woven fabric, perhaps from the hair of sheep, and his face was free of hair, though a ring of fine brown hair surrounded the top of this villager's head. Finally he answered. "I am called Zennan by the people of my land, a land distant from all that you know."

The villager stood motionless for several moments as he evaluated this stranger, then smiled broadly. "Your journey has been long. Come, you will join with us in our evening meal, my friend," the villager offered. He walked up to face Zennan and extended his open hand.

Zennan recoiled at the unknown gesture. "Stop, stranger. Your life is of value to me and I wish you no harm," he said.

The villager obeyed Zennan's request, stopping his hand movement toward this tall and strange visitor to his village, yet not dropping his extended hand to his side. "I offer my hand, empty of weapons and void of threats to your hand of the same circumstance," he said, his voice sounding strong and confident to Zennan's ears.

Zennan's mind traced back to his childhood and one of the forbidden stories told him by an ancient talltalist. This extending of a weaponless hand was a gesture even his talltalists had laughed about, knowing that warriors of ancient time were equally skilled with either of their hands at disposing of their enemies. Zennan made his choice.

"I do not bring harm with my presence, only my wish that you allow me sleep and nourishment before my departure to the Castle Krog," Zennan said.

Now it was the village greeter's turn to step back, his initial cautious-yet-confident manner transformed to one of fear and anger. "Be gone, you portender of all that is evil," the greeter demanded with as much voice command as he could build.

"I do not forebode evil nor bring nefarious actions against your village," Zennan said.

Squeezing harder the hand of the youngster, the villager scrunched up his face in cautious belief of this stranger's words. "Only evil would seek the evil of the Castle Krog," he offered, knowing that such explanation might enrage this beast before him should it be that secrecy was required of his journey to the place of the ancient Principles.

"I have come seeking to end this evil darkness that pervades the lives of my people and of all those whom I have encountered," Zennan said.

"A dream, a dream this must surely be," the villager offered solemnly. "Your sumptuous thoughts are better held captive in the sleeping mind and not allowed loose in the conscious ways of the living. And certainly not here in this land whose occupants cowardly kneel to the powers of the family Tanox," he finished, awaiting the reaction of this stranger. He reached down and plucked his young son into his arms.

"Your son is a fine representative of your blood," Zennan offered, his words true to his thoughts. "It is for our children that I seek knowledge of the evil one who shrouds this land in terror and keeps my own people captive, sequestered in darkness in a foreign land where we were shunted a millennium ago, a land that lies well beyond the beginning of the end of light."

"Your words mean much to us who live on the edge, though I fear that success is not the destiny of your long and arduous journey. But, I must not cast doubt upon your noble quest. Please, join my family for this night, and I will provide nourishment for both your belly and your mind," the villager offered.

"Your offer of nourishment is accepted no matter its form or its intended destination," Zennan said. "What may I call you, so we may seal our friendship?"

"My name is Morro and this is my son, Morro," the villager said.

"Both father and son of the same name?" Zennan queried. "Does that not create confusion?"

"Ah, to a stranger our tongue-names sound as one, yet we ourselves hear the subtle vocal inflection that distinguishes our people by similar names. And, also, seldom does the call of one's name go unaccompanied by a message that easily reveals for whom the discourse is meant," Morro explained. "Thus the family Morro is preserved and our lineage most easily followed when necessary." He motioned for Zennan to follow, as the night was becoming dark and a return to his home was required.

Zennan followed behind, but his curiosity overcame him. "But with such naming practices is it not impossible to relate tales of honor for those who distinguish themselves in battle or to dishonor those and their families if such a need should unhappily arise?" Zennan asked, his voice returning naturally to its sing-song melody.

Morro turned and looked strangely at Zennan, having never heard such melodious speech ways before. "It is the village immortal who bears such burden, be it good or bad," Morro said. "The individual is the responsibility of our village-whole. Our oldest and wisest of ancestors discovered that the simple act of assigning responsibility to the individual would not absolve the village-whole of the consequences of actions destructive to our people." Morro paused, allowing Zennan to think upon this statement about a practice obviously foreign to him. When Zennan's thoughts had coalesced and returned to Morro's presence, the villager continued. "Thus we have also assigned the goodness that our people as individuals bestow as that bestowed by the village-whole."

"Tis a strange way you have, Morro. Yet I can see the wisdom in your ways, though your customs are not for a warrior civilization such as mine," Zennan explained to the uncomprehending villager. "We have need to assume individual responsibility for both good and bad." Zennan remained aware of Morro's continued quizzical looks.

"Come, we must continue on." Morro turned toward his home, his son twisting around in his father's arms to better view the stranger who again took up pace behind them. Morro wished to help this stranger understand his village ways, so he continued his explanation as he walked. "Suppose that one of your kind is cruelly beaten by his father, tortured by his mother and laughed at by his brother," Morro said. "If this child then strikes out in anger at another, perhaps even killing this other person, is it the child who is responsible for behaving in the only way that he has come to understand? Or is it the parents for treating him suchly, or is it the village-whole for allowing the parents to treat the child suchly?"

"The questions you ask are without answers," Zennan responded after thinking hard upon this query.

"Ah, but the answers are there, if we are not too frightened to seek them, nor too weak to hear them, nor too stubborn to accept them."

"Perhaps," mused Zennan. "Perhaps seeking the truth is not always so easy, nor is the truth always easy to accept."

"You will find that the same truth is different for different people in different times, I am afraid," Morro sighed.

They walked past numerous small abodes, each slightly different, yet each much the same with their mud and stone walls topped with a tile-like roof. There was very little green vegetation and only a few small garden patches spread among the homes.

"Ah, we have reached my family's home. Join us inside." Morro lifted the outside latch swinging the heavy wooden door open. He stepped back and allowed Zennan to enter first. The young Morro quickly twisted around and out of his father's arms, dropping cat-like to the floor where he scampered alongside Zennan.

Inside Morro's stone-walled home, on a sleeping cot that filled one corner of the room, two more small children sat playing with a young, flaxen-haired woman. They paid little notice to the stranger who had entered their home.

"We have a guest for this night's meal, and he is in need of a place to allow him time to rest his eyes," Morro announced. "Zennan, this is my wife, Mirro, and our two daughters, Mirro and Mirro," he said, gesturing toward the cot. Mirro smiled and got up from the bed, leaving the two small Mirros to bid for each other's attention.

"It is my pleasure to make your stay worth the time it took you to travel such a long distance," Mirro said.

Zennan bowed low. "Your welcome is most appreciated," he replied. "I have had few opportunities during my journey to spend time among such a fine brood."

Mirro frowned, her eyes squinting obvious displeasure with Zennan's choice of words, yet curiosity poked her thoughts, for she too, had never before heard such a melodic voice-talk as Zennan's.

"You appear confused," Zennan offered, himself not understanding the look that Mirro quickly and consciously lifted from her face, wishing not to offend one who unintentionally offended her.

"We do not speak of our families as broods," she said, motioning with her head toward the farthest and darkest corner of the room. "The newly born dog-pups that suckle their mother we call broods, not the children of our females," she said.

Zennan bowed low. "Please forgive me, dear Mirro. I did not wish to purposely offend those who so graciously offer me a meal and the comfort of their home," he said. "I have encountered others who practice ways that I do not understand."

"Because our ways appear strange to one who has never before been among us does not make them strange to those of us who live among those ways," Morro said. "Please, sit, my new friend. I will answer the questions that curiosity creates in your mind, and perhaps you can answer mine as you seem quite unaware of the powers that you seek to battle."

"Mirro," Morro said, "please bring this weary traveler a mug of our best brew juice so we may sit and discuss all that needs to be discussed."

Mirro smiled at the prospect of providing her husband's guest with another surprise, because she thought that he certainly could never before have sampled their village's prideful product. She disappeared for a moment down a set of steps, which Zennan had failed to notice, and returned with three mugs filled to overflowing with a frothing amber liquid. She sat on the stone bench beside Morro and across from Zennan. As the children played upon the corner bed, the two family elders and their guest sipped from the mugs.

"Tis a mighty fine brew you have created," Zennan complimented honestly, already feeling the results of its mind magic.

"I thank you for your good words, but you should be asking about the castle and the evil that lives there," Mirro offered, gulping down the last half of her brew. Zennan saw what she had done and quickly did the same. Mirro took his mug and stood. "I will get us more." She looked at her husband. "He seldom drinks, so he sips slowly, not wishing to feel too strongly and too quickly the mind effects," she said. Mirro disappeared down the steps and returned with both mugs filled, giving Zennan his, and as before, taking a seat next to Morro.

Morro's sipping momentarily turned to a loud slurp, then, harder than needed, he crashed his mug down upon the table. "I will tell you a story, much of which has been passed down from the very beginnings of time," he announced loudly.

Mirro interrupted her husband to explain to Zennan, "He becomes the great story maestro when he has drunk too much, which seldom takes him much drinking time."

Morro ignored his wife, taking another quick drink to wet his throat before starting his words. "In the blackness of time that stood eons before the time when my many-great-great grandfather's great-great grandfather first worked upon these lands, fierce battles were fought across our world. Fires spread everywhere, and everywhere desolation and destruction were at hand. For our ancestors who followed in the footsteps of our defeated warriors, pain and death were all they knew and, indeed, all they expected of life. Powerful armies destroyed our desires and then laughed hungrily at our weakness and our pitiful abilities to sustain our lives, our people, our culture. For us, there was no fighting back, no sense of future.

"It was said that there emerged from among an ancient and magic-caste tribe to the east, a leader. He was a stranger among us, his ways as strange as his speech. He promised that his family Tanox, of which he was the first, could restore life to our living, restore honor to our domain. He took the name Aa of the family Tanox, and became known as that. It was such that his promises rang true. He lifted the veil of the blackest of darknesses that had enslaved our peoples." Morro took a long slow drink from his mug, savoring the liquid's tangy fullness.

Zennan finished his second fill and Mirro again took his mug and her own empty mug to the cellar and returned moments later to the table with them refilled. Zennan rolled his eyes at the prospect of having to drink another, because already his head was spinning, and he did not favor ever being out of control for fear of the consequences. Zennan thanked Mirro, but decided that he would slow his drinking by making appearances to more fully savor the strange and intriguing flavor of this unknown amber.

"So, if this family Tanox freed you and your kind from the dark powers that controlled your lives, why do you so hate and despise them now?" Zennan asked. "Your story has ended, yet without an ending."

"Ah," Morro answered. "My story does not end here, for the family Tanox continued to reign. At first the leaders treated most with fairness or so it appeared, their taxes minimal, their requirements of us nonexistent. But as the centuries passed and the generations of Tanox leaders changed, so too changed the temperament of their rule. At first my ancestors accepted their increased demands for taxes and the requirement that each of our young males spend time during their coming-of-age years in the deep mines of Tanox, a dangerous undertaking for anyone. The Tanox leaders, after the passage of more centuries further increased the greatness and power of their armies. They began taking our older sons also, molding their minds with tales of greatness if only they would serve the needs of the master Tanox. When we fought such demands, we were simply too weak to win against the power of Tanox, a power that created a magic as powerful as the underworld gods. Thus through the following centuries of sitting idly, we allowed our guardian father to become our sinister uncle. We called upon the power of our own ancient ways, seeking help from our wizards and wishtongues, but alas, even they, scattered wide and far, could not for long fight the all-powerful Family Tanox.

"In the beginning, in single and carefully chosen small battles, our people could drive away the soldiers of Tanox, but no more." Again, Morro paused in his story to sip from his mug and wet his dry throat. He continued: "Deep from within the bowels of the Castle Krog, an evil fire is said to burn, and he who harnesses this fire so powerful, as a farmer harnesses his oxen, will control all in his domain, a domain extending to wherever he wishes to plow. Such evil it is said, has never before been controlled, yet those same unknowns who speak these words insist that such undergod power now lies near the grasping hands of Ra-Tanox, the most recent to ascend to rulership of the Family Tanox. His power already is more than all his predecessors combined, and his use of evil magic is said to extend beyond the powers of even the most powerful of wizards and wishtongues. His army grows larger and stronger with each passing solstice, as he continues to seek the most powerful of powers and to capture all the lands of our known world."

Morro again sipped brew from his mug, closing his eyes for a moment of appreciation of its fine flavor. Zennan awaited more words from Morro, but Morro's eyes grew heavy, and quickly he sank into a deep sleep. Mirro carefully got up from her chair and motioned to Zennan to do the same.

"Morro loves our special brew juice, especially the amber," she said. "But, he would do well to not over indulge himself. He will remember nothing of this upon the sunrise."

Slowly, with dizziness attacking his senses, Zennan rose from his chair and moved away from the table. He noticed that the three youngsters had also fallen into a deep, yet restless sleep, lying curled upon the corner bed in a single, tangled ball of arms and legs.

"When sleep finally comes to you, you will close your eyes in the safety of our cellar," Mirro said.

"Is there need to be wary?" he asked.

"Always diligence is necessary in this land so near to the Castle Krog."

"Am I that near to the castle?"

"A walk of three days for us," Mirro replied. She looked deep into Zennan's eyes. "But perhaps only two days for you," she added. Again she looked into his eyes. "And what are your plans once you reach the great castle?" she asked.

"It is difficult to know," he answered as honestly as he could. "I shall wait and see upon which side of the tree the wind blows, then move to follow the guiding wind with the silence of a stealth master.

Mirro finished the last of her brew and set the mug upon the wooden table, then wiped her hand across her mouth. She looked up at Zennan. "Is it not silence amidst chaos, or the animal that is not where it should be that stands out in the hunter's eye?" she asked.

Zennan mused carefully Mirro's words, then spoke slowly. "Possessing a hunter's eye has never been my aim, yet the understanding of such skill is present in my desires. I remember a story from one of our oldest and wisest of talltalists, the story of a great hunter who had lost his sight," Zennan said, allowing Mirro time to focus upon his words. He continued: "His brother, Weogot, advised this once great warrior and hunter, whose ancient name was Geofgot, that because he was blind, he could no longer provide for his wife and children, and that he, Weogot, as his youngest brother, would meet all the needs of Geofgot's family, including those of his wife. The great warrior, Geofgot, was not to be spurned and humiliated by a sibling whose only intention was stealing all that was due Geofgot, the family's eldest male child-descendent. So, Geofgot trained his mind's ear to learn when an animal was near by detecting the most faint of sounds, sometimes by the absence of sounds where sounds should be; his nose became keen, knowing the scent of danger when danger was near. He became a proud and able-hunter providing for his family, and ultimately, the protector who killed his seeing-brother when his brother attempted to steal his wife away from him."

Mirro removed the three empty mugs from the table as her husband snored in deep thought. "Your story is of interest, Zennan, but of little use against the Castle Krog," Mirro said.

Zennan smiled his knowing smile. "My story is one of great assurance, my newest friend. It shows that one can quickly improve upon personal skills, transforming himself from the hunted to the hunter, if incentive enough presents itself."

"Stories are easy to tell," Mirro offered, as she again went to the cellar and quickly returned to the table with two mugs refilled. "Living the truths of such stories is more difficult."

"Agreed," Morro snorted as his mind moved from sleep to semi-consciousness. He slowly raised his head and groggily grabbed for Mirro's mug of brew. She pulled it away before he could reach it.

"Enough brew for you tonight, I do think, dear husband," Mirro said. She quickly returned her attention to Zennan. "But for most, especially those who are nonbelievers during these times, anything too difficult is indeed avoided."

"You are certainly correct, Mirro, that which is difficult is often and too easily avoided by too many, perhaps a reason that today we all share so much misery and fear," Zennan said. He thought for a moment as he sipped his brew, then continued. "But when one truly believes that he will accomplish what must be accomplished, he certainly is other than a nonbeliever. And I believe that I truly have the will to defeat the evil that inhabits the Castle Krog."

"Perhaps," Morro mumbled, knowing better. With his mind groggy with the desire for sleep, he again reached for Mirro's mug. She allowed him to grasp it and sip a small amount. He smiled as he savored the tasty liquid. "Yet, with my help, perhaps you can better blend with the people of this land."

Mirro looked at her mate, surprised. "You are offering to accompany this stranger to the black castle?" she asked. "I believe that you are intoxicated with drink and have much need for sleep."

"I think that I may be of some assistance to this one named

Zennan," he said.

"I do not seek your personal help, especially if you or your family will be endangered," Zennan replied.

Morro looked startled and suddenly very awake. "I did not offer my assistance for your benefit," he said. "What I am offering is for you to accompany me on my own personal journey to the Castle Krog."

"I see," Zennan answered, not really understanding what point Morro was attempting to make.

"Should you awaken tomorrow with these same thoughts, dear Morro, you two should leave as the sun rises above the mountains to the east and before the children rise," Mirro said, smiling.

"You wish your husband to accompany me on a trek from which his safe return is considerably less than assured?" Zennan was startled at Mirro's quick agreement, without benefit of even the most limited discussion between them. He wasn't sure that Morro would be as quick to join him once morning arrived and the brew's affects had worn away.

* * *

They entered a chamber whose air was blacker than the blackest she had ever before felt. Meeshannette stepped cautiously down upon the mush ground that oozed a thick, sticking syrup between her bare toes and over her feet. The creatures whose scents she followed as they led her onward through the abyss below the Castle Krog, moved nimbly, their eyes made dark-sensitive by virtue of generations of their dungeon-evolved ancestors. Often the creatures' powerful odor drifted lightly away and mixed with the rising gases formed from the rotting masses of dead organic matter that lay just inches below the syrupy liquid walking surface.

Far ahead, a squeal rippled its curdling effect backward to Meeshannette who trailed nearly a full distance behind the lead creature. Another scream answered the first, and yet another scream followed the second. Feeling her way through a bend in the tunnel's route, her eyes met the first speck of light to pierce the blackness in the passing of many time periods by her estimate.

As they continued forward and toward the light opening ahead, Meeshannette heard each of the creatures' tortured squeals of pain, watching, with her own sense of heartfelt compassion, as each turned backward to face the darkness, their eyes unaccustomed to such painful brilliant light.

Meeshannette's pace hastened as the footpath became more visible and certain the closer she drew to the opening. Now, she could see outside, a view of trees and flowers, living things not found inside the walls of the Castle Krog. She stopped just short of the tunnel's opening where the oldest of the creatures had stopped, his back still facing toward the outside light, his eyes squinted nearly closed, a smile across his face.

"We must leave this tunnel of evil and find a place where safety is assured, my friend," Meeshannette said. She knelt beside her creature friend and took his hand.

"That which blinded our brothers and sisters at the apex of our first escape and led to their slaughter, again stands in the way of our escape from our ages of imprisonment, I am afraid," the creature explained. "We are destined to live here on the edge of light, waiting for a time when darkness must no longer fill our eyes and light is once again a welcome visitor." The other creatures gathered around Meeshannette and their leader, their eyes, too, turned away from the sun's direct light.

"I am sorry that you may not attend me on my journey, my friends. You have my life, should you ever desire it for what you have done for me." Meeshannette promised.

"It is I and we who owe you much, my friend," the leader offered.

Meeshannette stood and walked to the opening, then turned back to look at her friends. Already they had begun to move back into the darkness. She hoped they would do well with their newly won freedom, limited as it was. She offered one last wave of her hand, though she knew they would not see the biding gesture of her departure. The syrupy ooze that creeped from the tunnel's floor and spread out into the light that lay before Meeshannette trailed into only the faintest animal path that wound down through the scrag trees and creviced boulders that littered the desolate landscape.

Meeshannette spent much time and effort trying to follow a

trail that she thought to herself fought tenaciously against being followed by a creature of her size. From a few hardrock scrag trees and sporadic brushweeds, the rocky ground turned to ochre soil that fed larger trees and bushes whose long, tendril limbs reached downward, catching her skin with rows of spindle thorns. She fought through them, finally emerging into a small yellow-grass meadow. Cautiously, Meeshannette eyed the edges of the empty meadow, searching for anything that could either help or hurt her. She saw nothing of significant consequence, so she ventured into the opening.

From the center of the meadow, through a narrow break between trees, she spied a steep-sided mountain in the distance, barren of green and surrounded by a misty cloud layer. As Meeshannette sat and rested, she watched the mountain's surrounding clouds slowly dissipate into nothingness, all the time thinking whether from atop such a height she might discover a landmark that could lead her quickly from this ancient land of sad creatures and evil madness. Her gaze refocused back from her mind thoughts to the yellow-grass meadow that surrounded her. Nearby, several tiny, six-legged fur creatures emerged from smallish ground tunnels and began to nibble the edges of an orange-striped fungus cap. Although Meeshannette had never before seen such plants, her stomach forced her hands into plucking one of the caps from the ground. For only a moment, the fur creatures scampered into their hideholes before quickly returning to their cap eating, ignoring this newcomer sharing their meadow.

Meeshannette nibbled into the succulent cap and involuntarily soured her face to the taste that greeted her. Although strong, the sensation was not altogether unpleasant once past the initial sharp slap upon her tongue. She took a second bite, this one deeper into the fleshy cap. Immediately, the sharp taste she expected was replaced with a bitter burning as, in her hand, the remaining fungus cap poured out its slickery orange liquid. Meeshannette instantly flung the cap well beyond where she stood and spit repeatedly, attempting to remove the spongy flesh from her mouth. Finally, with the flesh gone, the bitterness that first invaded her taste sense turned sweet, sending unknown, yet pleasant sensations through her body and mind before slowly and finally dissipating to nothingness.

Once again, Meeshannette focused upon the distant mountain. From its western-most slope a strange blue light glistened upon the white snowfield that covered the highest, rocky precipice. All around her, the fur creatures squealed. She turned her eyes toward them, and watched as they dropped their tooth-riddled fungus caps and looked toward the distant mountain. Their fur prickled outward from their slim bodies, showing an obvious sense of alarm. A moment later they squealed again and disappeared back into their tiny hideholes. They did not return to the surface.

Meeshannette looked again at the mountain. The blue light blinked off, then on again, repeating several times before it was gone. She breathed deeply, then began her journey to the blue sparkle mountain.

* * *

Zennan's eyes opened much later in the morning than he had planned, and what greeted his vision was Morro's grinning face just inches from his own. Startled, he sat up quicker than he should have, gaining the most unpleasant feeling left over from his previous evening's encounter with several too many mugs of Mirro's special amber brew. Zennan had expected that morning would come with Morro holding his throbbing head accompanied with a desire to not move from his bed, rather than partnering with a mere stranger on such an unplanned and treacherous quest. Instead, within a short time, Morro simply kissed his wife Mirro and his three children, then slung the burlap sack of food to his back in readiness to depart.

Now, as the sun still lay low in the morning's red and clouded sky, Zennan trailed a few paces behind Morro, impatient at the slow pace he was forced to maintain. Yet he dared not lead, for Morro appeared very familiar with the path, even when it split into several arms or disappeared into none. A small branch snapped behind Zennan, unnoticed by Morro. Zennan turned to look backward, but saw nothing. Looking forward once more for several paces, a branch again snapped, followed by a muffled sneeze.

"Wun, I suspect?" he queried out loud, without another glance behind.

"It surprises me not that you cannot yet tell that I am Wuntu, but Wun is nearby," Wuntu replied.

Zennan stopped and turned to see his two periodic traveling companions.

"EEeeee," cried Morro, startling Zennan.

Zennan turned forward to again face Morro. "What is this alarm that you cry?" he snapped.

"EEeeee," Morro again howled. "Such madness has mushened your mind."

Wuntu hopped toward Zennan, causing Morro to leap away, keeping a safe distance between himself and these creatures. Now it was Wun who stepped forward. Morro's face visibly paled. He spun around in panic and flew into a scramble-run down the trail that quickly turned into a narrow passage between the gray scrag trees that festooned the pock-marked landscape they had entered. There was a loud and sharp crumpling crash, then silence.

"It seems that the power of your presence is mightier than I had first suspected," Zennan said to Wun. "Perhaps the two of you should stay here while I go and see if my friend Morro has suffered too greatly from the surprise you have unsuspectingly visited upon him."

Wun sidled up to Wunto who stood in the middle of the trail rubbing his fingers through his head hair. "Perhaps your friend should be blindfolded so that he is not permitted to view that which he doesn't understand," Wunto said. "Too often, it is the fear of the unknown seen by the eyes of the unknowledgeable, rather than the sound sense of a good and rational mind, that dictates re-actions and thoughts about new and untested matters and masters, if masters we were to be."

Zennan became thoughtful. "Why would you conclude that you are masters of this one named Morro?"

"We assume nothing," Wun answered.

"We are but responding to a behavior that would dictate that we should not be seen by this one named Morro," Wuntu added.

"At least not until such time as he knows us by more than what his blind eyes so selectively allow him to visualize," Wun concluded.

A long moan emerged from the distant brush. Slowly, amidst

crackling branches and the rush of an escaping covey of semi-flightless feather creatures, Morro crawled back out to the main path. He looked toward Zennan, fear still strong upon his face. Quickly the fear eased as his eyes did not meet with the sight of the two small creatures of a darkness perceived but not known.

"Morro, my friend, you need not fear my friends," Zennan assured him. "Allow me to introduce Wun and Wunto." Zennan turned, and with the sweep of his arm he meant to show that his two small and amicable friends were not to be feared. But as too often occurred, they had made themselves invisible.

"I shall not fear your friends, if indeed they be friends and not creatures of deceit," Morro responded, stooping and brushing away the dust and brush that adhered to his rough cloth clothing.

"I assure you, these two, wherever they have again chosen to hide, know enough about me and my quest to have sabotaged my way on many occasions if that was to be their choice." Zennan walked forward to where Morro now stood continuing to brush himself off.

"Then I will allow them to know me as the one called Morro, if you will call them from their hiding place."

"I fear that I have not the power to call them from anywhere at any time of my choosing. They come as they please and have proven to be masters at disappearing when I think that their assistance could be most welcome," Zennan said. "Come, we must continue, and when the two known as Wun and Wunto again make themselves visible, I shall prove that they mean no harm to either of us."

Morro thought to himself for a moment. "It is good that we depart. The day shadows will soon begin to grow long and we have much distance yet to travel," he said.

CHAPTER NINE

Black as black might ever be, the smoke of Tanox oozed slowly from the smoldering fire that burned below. Twisting ribbons of the blackness swirled upward then parted as the rambling words of the Grand Black Sorcerer mixed with the dank air deep within the walls of the Castle Krog's Chamber of Voices.

"Peer through time
where smoke masks pain,
with eyes of blackness
their blood will rain.
Part the darkness
shadowed by light,
my power rightly
will blind their sight."

His words faded, while just beyond his feet the smoke vanished as the smoldering flames surged upward through crevices of volcanic stone that lined the lip edge of the abyss. The sorcerer looked around through the musty ancient air that surrounded him in this primordial chamber of horrors. He was not alone, but while he could feel the presence of another, he did not know where the trespassing power rested nor why it had not yet become visible before him. He waited patiently in darkened silence as he closed his eyes, wishcommanding the intruder to come forward. The flames subsided and the black smoke returned, but not to their usual ordered ribbons of flight, but to wispy flittering flights of uncontrolled chaos.

The sorcerer could remain silent no longer. "Come forth with your presence and let yourself be seen by my mind and felt by my senses," he demanded, while stretching his arms upward and spreading his fingers to their farthest reach.

"You are much as I anticipated, yet more than I thought," a soft voice oozed, near but unseen.

"Ah, so my night dream antagonist has returned," the sorcerer replied, recognizing the ancient voice. "It has been many lifetimes since we last met," the sorcerer offered, knowing now who was so near, yet beyond his mind's control. "You are not the one who has invaded the places of sanctuary of my master Ra-Tanox."

"I am many, in both form and sense," the wavering voice offered. "You have done well to bide your life through such a long and dark existence."

"You have not yet answered me. From where do you speak and from whence do you come, blue lighted one?" the sorcerer asked. He stepped around the smoking abyss, only to be no closer to the place where he felt the voice might be stronger.

"You have doubted my perseverance, Sorcerer, which has often been the downfall of those wishing for power. It would appear that you are capable only of sniffing the edges of the endowed strength of others, lapping up leftover crumbs of nothingness," the blue voice said.

"My time shall come, perhaps sooner than you might imagine."

"Time is not measured by my imagination, sorcerer. But time will indeed play a role in what is to come of this world," the stranger's voice oozed.

The faint blue light glow that had grown inside the cavernous Chamber of Voices, now slowly subsided, as it and the wavering voice merged with the ancient stone, becoming hard edged and silent.

The sorcerer motioned the disappearing image away with a wave of his black gown-covered arm. "You shall not hinder me in this age of change. Too many ancients cowered at your presence and bowed to your commands," the sorcerer said, his voice tense and strong. "I am not the same soft-crust bread of the old ones whom you so easily mushed and molded," he mouthed silently. "That, you shall come to know, personally," The sorcerer ran from the chamber, climbing quickly the stone stairways and charging through ancient passageways, finally emerging into the morning's light.

Moments later the Grand Black Sorcerer joined his awaiting troops and all were quickly outside the castle walls. A great red cloud of dust was flung skyward by the iron-clad hooves of his sirocco soldiers' gray mounts, causing the sun to rise a deep crimson behind them. The Grand Black Sorcerer, mounted upon his great white steed, set a pace that forced the breaths of his soldier's horses to gasp hard for the thin air that was being sucked away by the cool dawn winds from the east. The sorcerer's chosen trail ran toward the tallest eastern mountain in the distant range that rose high as one of three land boundary markers of the Ra-Tanox empire. To the far west, a fourth boundary, a great and wild turquoise sea, served the needs of border guards, allowing no trespassers to step into this land that few cared to live upon. The sorcerer's soldiers dropped into a shallow, rock-strewn valley, a land absent of all but the most stubbornly tough vegetation.

* * *

Morro was the first to sense the coming danger. He hurried his pace to catch Zennan who had decided to lead his band of sometimes four, because now the trail to the west was quite easily discerned.

"Good sir," Morro hush-yelled. "Good sir, we must take cover quickly, for I feel the coming of an evil whose forces are not to be toyed with." Morro had stumbled quickly around the trail and was now walking backward in front of Zennan.

"I have no time to allow fear to direct my travels, my friend," Zennan answered as he maintained his pace causing Morro to stumble backward even faster.

"EEeeee," Morro cried as he stumbled nearly into Wun who stood directly in his path. Wun stepped quickly aside, letting the falling Morro land upon a rounded rock that caused little pain and no injury.

Zennan stopped and breathed a sigh of feigned concern. "Wun, what have you done to my new friend Morro?" he asked.

Wun glanced at Morro who was quickly trying to scramble

back upon his feet. "It would seem that I have done very little. Why must you insist upon this unneeded one accompanying us on our journey?" Wun asked.

"Yes, why do you not listen to us?" Wuntu asked, as he popped his head out from behind a larger rock, startling Morro who was now standing against a massive and oblong obelisk in the center of this vast desolation.

Morro purposely restrained his startled reaction to the second creature, although sweat broke out across his brow and trickled down the side of his stub-pug nose. He tried to ignore the two strange creatures. "Please, Zennan, we must take hiding cover. The time too quickly grows short," he pleaded.

Wuntu hopped around from behind the rock, as Morro carefully eased himself a safe distance away from the unwelcomed travel companion. "You would be wise if you chose to hear the words of this near-sighted creature who calls himself Morro," Wuntu suggested. "Often boldness and ignorance create the same result." Wuntu stepped back behind the large rock, quickly followed by Wun. Morro looked at Zennan, then he too disappeared behind the rock.

Zennan shrugged away his disappearing friends and started once again westward. Only a few steps had separated him and his three friends when Zennan felt thunder vibrations through the graveled ground beneath his feet. He looked ahead and in the second that it took for him to focus on the cloud of dust rising quickly and coming in his direction, Zennan jumped behind the rock joining Morro in the hollowed cavern in the backside of the great stone. He pressed himself against the opposite side of the small hollow, facing Morro.

Morro cringed as he awaited the appearance of Wun and Wuntu, knowing he would be forced closer to these creatures than he had ever before been forced in his entire relatively uneventful life, closer than he had thought possible even in his worst night dreams. But as the seconds passed and the thunderous vibrations of the approaching horsemen grew dangerously close, Wun and Wuntu failed to make Morro's worst fear see truth.

"Where are they?" Morro whisper spoke.

"Who?" Zennan answered.

"Those two disgusting creatures, of course."

Zennan looked around and out of the cavern's entrance and didn't see either Wun or Wuntu. "I have come to the true belief that one should never expect either Wun or Wuntu to be where you would either expect or never expect them to be," he said. He ducked deeper into the hollowed rock cavern as the thunder of iron-clad hooves crashed all around them, echoing off the rock surfaces inside their small rock cave. Red ground dust suddenly swirled thickly inside the small cavern around Zennan and Morro. The shrill sound of horses, fighting the commands of their soldier mounts to stop instantly, suddenly surrounded the rock. Outside the small cavern, now obscured from view by the constant cloud of dust being thrown up by the dancing horses, the soldiers waited in silence as a hundred horses stamped nervously.

Around the rock rode the Grand Black Sorcerer, his great white horse a full head taller than the gray steeds of his sirocco troops. He pulled his reins hard as he stopped beside his lieutenant.

"Perhaps what we are searching for is not to be found in the great distance we have thus far traveled. What we search for remains nearer our castle," the sorcerer revealed.

"What might it be that awaits the blades of our swords and the points of our spears, Great One?" the lieutenant asked, masking his irritation that he and his soldiers had been forced to travel so quickly so far from where they needed to be.

"You will know when I wish you to know, but it is near, though faint and scattered, its scent remains before my powers of perception." The sorcerer allowed his horse to circle his lieutenant, as he sniffed the air, his mind attempting to penetrate the latent image of all those who had passed near this place.

From inside the shallow cavern, Zennan and Morro stooped low and remained silent, their view outside remaining as obscured as the sorcerer's view was of them. For a moment, as the sorcerer's horse stopped again on the opposite side of his lieutenant, the dust swirled a small hole through which Zennan gained a view of the sorcerer. At the same immediate time, the sorcerer felt a power penetrate his being, but before he could focus his mind upon the spell that was casting itself upon him, the dust hole swirled closed, ending Zennan's view and the sorcerer's point of convergence on the hiding place.

The sorcerer threw his arm forward, now pointing to a different mountain in the nearest distance. "We will find what we search for near the top of that peak. Ride hard, my faithful soldiers, and you will end your day basking in the glory of a successful hunt."

The lieutenant rode forward, leading the soldiers toward their goal. For a moment, the sorcerer remained behind, turning his white steed in a tight circle, knowing that another power was nearby, yet outside his reach. Finally, he spurred his horse forward, away from the rock. After the noise of the horses' hooves subsided Zennan and Morro carefully peered outside, watching the sorcerer's back become smaller as he rode away toward the red dust cloud that rose, its distance quickly growing longer.

"They ride the same direction that we must travel," Morro said, wiping the sweat dust from his brow.

"Yes, they do. Perhaps they will lead us to what we seek," Zennan mused.

"Or to our deaths," Morro complained.

"Death is never far from the boundary of life," Wuntu squealed from high atop the obelisk.

"Nor is life far from death," Wun added as he popped out from behind his partner.

"What quiz is this that you two creatures spew from your fuzz-covered brains?" Morro demanded.

Wun and Wuntu disappeared behind the obelisk and two eye blinks later reappeared behind and much nearer to Morro.

"The question might easily be answered if it were a quiz we entertained," Wun said.

"Yet we speak, not in questions that should confuse, but only in statements that must be true," Wuntu answered.

Zennan pulled the strap of his carrybag over his shoulder. "Enough of your constant biddle. We must move ahead quickly, lest the dust trail we are to follow disappears," he said. He breathed deeply only twice, then paced forward through the faint trace of dust that still clung to the air about him. Wun, Wuntu and Morro followed in step, toward the ominous mountain that stood before them.

* * *

In her shallow dugout at the base of the blue sparkle mountain, Meeshannette had spent a long night shivering away the cold that constantly stabbed her body. As dawn broke, slowly spreading its red glowing warmth down upon her, Meeshannette once again set out, climbing the steep goat trails that meandered up the mountainside and through narrow passages between red boulders and black walls of ancient lava flows. Several times her way was blocked at the end of her chosen path, forcing her to backtrack to the last split in the trail and then try an alternate pathway.

Finally, as the sun reached its noon zenith and began descending westward, she had come within view of the top of her blue mountain, but the red soil and rocks issued no sign of the blue glow that had sent Meeshannette on her long and arduous journey to the high point view she had imagined would be here. At last, standing atop its highest pinnacle, she shaded her eyes from the sun and viewed the rock-strewn lands that lay as far as her sight could take her mind.

It was Meeshannette's vision that first imagined the tiniest swirl of a moving red dust cloud, but quickly her mind confirmed what her eyes had told her was growing larger and closer to her mountain. As she watched through the shimmering heat waves that emerged from the mountainside and across the distant redlands, the column of horse soldiers, led by the sorcerer sitting atop his large, white steed, approached the blue mountain. Even here, at a distance so far, Meeshannette could feel the eyes of the Grand Black Sorcerer piercing the air, penetrating her mind. She shook away the evil feeling, knowing she could not allow herself to be drawn into the powers controlled by one of such utter darkness.

Even from atop her blue mountain Meeshannette tried but could not see anything that appeared familiar to where she either had been or cared to go. And with the evil one continually drawing his army of horse soldiers closer, she dared not linger away any more of her precious time. Yet she was unsure of where she should turn. As she gathered her meager belongings, a rough and thin sheep hair shawl, which had inadequately shed the night cold from her body, Meeshannette decided that she would not go either directly toward nor directly away from the approaching riders. She scrambled down from the mountain, crossing back over the goat trails, this time making no misturns. As she neared the bottom, the mountain's steepness flared outward, broken now only by the red boulders that were scattered everywhere before her.

Safely behind her, a small cloud of dust puffed outward from the most distant ridge of the mountain that she could see. Knowing that the riders would certainly continue onward to the top of the mountain from whence she had come, Meeshannette now turned and trotted back to the border of jumbled red rock columns she had sighted from above and knew must be very near where the riders' earlier trail had already crossed her own. Finding the trail did not take long, as the rutted path beaten deep into the red soil over the years by the hooves of galloping horses was easily discerned. She knew they had come from the Castle Krog and did not wish to return to that prison of the mind, body and soul. As the strange red rock dust columns once again appeared to be moving closer, she slipped into a concealing hollow between two of the largest boulders near the trail. There she sat and rested.

Hunger invaded Meeshannette's mind. Her empty stomach gurgled and cramped as she finally relaxed, her advancing thoughts hoping the soldiers would soon pass by on their return way to the castle. Then and only then could she continue on her return journey home in relative safety. Meeshannette pulled her legs into her chest and rested her chin upon her scraped and swollen knees, closing her eyes. It was at that moment when she felt their presence. Yet, she remained calm, knowing she could outrun anyone who might attempt to capture her, especially here among so many dodging and hiding places. She closed her eyes once again as she focused her thoughts and energy.

"I see that we are not alone among these reddened boulders of this ancient and forgotten land," the voice chanted softly.

Meeshannette, startled by the unannounced voice, remained still.

"Oh, but this one is so very pretty," a second voice chimed.

Immediately, Meeshannette knew these kindly voices meant her no harm. A smile came across her face as she opened her eyes and lifted her head from her short moment of thought. She stepped from her hiding place.

"No," she screamed, fear and loathing instantly crossing her face and filling her mind. "You cannot be here."

The guttural laugh that emerged from deep inside the sorcerer knew no bounds or limits. He stopped only long enough to repeat in his disguised and pleasant voice the message that had captured Meeshannette's trust. "Oh, but this one is so very pretty." The sorcerer then repeated his sickening laugh.

Meeshannette darted quickly to her left, but was grabbed by two of the sorcerer's sirocco soldiers, their grip remaining strong and unrelenting, even when she relaxed her own struggle for the immediate time. Her eyes screamed her hatred as they pierced the heartless soul of the sorcerer. His laugh died quickly in reaction to his prisoner's focus on him.

"You have done well to evade me and my powers for even such a short time," the sorcerer said, meaning his words.

Meeshannette did not answer.

"I have a master who demands your return to his side."

"And I have a father who awaits the return of his only daughter."

The Grand Black Sorcerer reared his huge stallion and the great white beast danced around in a complete circle, its front hooves finally crashing down into the red dirt only a hand-length's distance from Meeshannette and her two guards. The guards involuntarily jerked back from the flash of hooves that passed their faces and the red dust cloud that spewed upward. Just as they did, Meeshannette ripped her arms from their grasp and dodged quickly beneath the sorcerer's horse causing the animal to rear in panic, nearly throwing its rider to the ground. As the sorcerer fought to regain control of his mount, and while his soldiers pulled back trying to avoid the beast's pounding hooves, Meeshannette darted out from beneath its danger and ducked her body under two more horses causing them also to rear in startled reaction. In the sudden chaos she dodged around another mounted soldier and into the jumble of red rock columns that lay just steps beyond the small cave where she first rested.

"After her you fools, after her," the grand sorcerer raged, finally bringing his mount back under his reined control. "Bring me her head securely attached to her shoulders or I shall have each of your heads upon my dinner platter."

A half dozen soldiers dismounted and chased the fleeting shadow, while others, still mounted, attempted to pick their way through the tightly wound maze of red rock columns. Meeshannette glanced back over her shoulder just in time to see one of the mounted soldier's horses about to trample down upon her. She dove for a small, natural arch formed from the wind-blown sand and water-scoured columns and disappeared from sight just as the sirocco soldier crashed his mount into the barrier column. The horse stumbled to its knees, stunned but unhurt, as the soldier passed over its head, smashing himself unconscious into the column before dropping hard to the ground. His body slumped over the hole that Meeshannette had crawled into, blocking its view from the soldiers who arrived but a moment's tick after him.

Out the other side Meeshannette emerged from the stone tunnel on her knees and quickly was up and running around and behind several more columns. She turned sharply to her left and began a long circular trail back toward where she had first escaped, knowing that her captors would not expect such an action. She stopped and scooted down on her belly and crawled up to the head-width crevice that separated two rock columns. From her vantage point, Meeshannette could see the sorcerer whipping his horse into short frenzied runs, first to the left, then to the right, and then back again in confused frustration. When several soldiers returned from where she had first escaped and said something to the evil one, the sorcerer flailed his arms in the air. Meeshannette dropped her head behind the stone as the sorcerer's vision momentarily passed in her direction.

Before Meeshannette could again raise herself to witness what she hoped would be the quick departure of the evil soldiers and their leader, she felt the cold grip of a large and strong hand around the back of her neck. Even before she could think to react, another hand, equally as large and strong, wrapped itself around her mouth, closing off her breath.

Behind Meeshannette, a voice of calm and pleasant sound addressed her. "You have come a great distance and unaccountably survived what obviously has been a significant trial."

Meeshannette pulled back from the voice, imagining it to sound just as the impersonated voice the evil sorcerer had sounded before she was momentarily captured among the red columns. While the hand over Meeshannette's mouth remained tightly grasping, the second hand that wrapped around her neck released its pressure, then pulled her to her feet.

"You have been born with the luck of a princess, dear lady," a second voice said softly to her.

The holding hands slowly released and spun her around to face her captor. "You have done well, Meeshannette, to get this far on your own."

Meeshannette's fear and loathing melted, and a smile spread across her face. She leaped up and wrapped her arms around Zennan's massive neck and hugged him long and hard. Looking over his shoulder she saw two strange creatures and the one called Morro.

"It would appear that we have created much happiness," Wun said.

"I believe that happiness existed without our help," Wuntu answered.

Meeshannette's happiness was cut short by the shrill cry of the sorcerer who caught a glimpse of this gaggle of outsiders in the land of Ra-Tanox.

"Ahheee," cried Morro, when he saw a dozen sirocco soldiers charging around the columns and up the slight rise to where the Grand Black Sorcerer pointed and they stood.

"Quick, we must leave this place as rapidly as my two friends have again retreated," Zennan said.

Meeshannette looked around her. The two small creatures who stood near her only moments before were nowhere to be seen. Only Morro remained. "Where have those two adorable little creatures gone?" she asked as Zennan grabbed her hand and led her to a small cave entrance.

"I no longer try to keep my eyes on those two or it would be all that I ever did, and I would not be successful in any manner. But we must now disappear or we will become nothing more than pigpen fodder for the soldiers charging down upon us," Zennan said.

He pushed Meeshannette in front of him, followed by Morro, and the three instantly disappeared as the pounding of horses' hooves crashed through the dirt where they had just been. The soldiers passed on to wherever it was they were aimed, while inside one of the small caves carved into hundreds of the red rock columns, Meeshannette crawled through the blackness followed by

Morro and encouraged by Zennan. As her hands became raw from the rough stone floor she traversed, a bright circle of light suddenly appeared ahead of her. The hole become brighter and larger as she and her two followers came closer to its end. Once there, Meeshannette cautiously peered outside, and her eyes were met by those of Wun and Wuntu.

"We are safe now," Wuntu said to her.

"Yes, safe we are now," Wun agreed, standing upon a rock, peering outward across the open land of rock spires and columns. He placed his hand across his forehead, saluting away the sun's glare.

Meeshannette crawled out of the cave and stood before Wuntu. "How could you two get here before us?" she asked.

"Only moments before, if not less," Wuntu answered.

"Oh, much less, I should think," Wun assured.

Morro, followed quickly by Zennan, crawled out of the narrow cave. Zennan stood a breath behind Meeshannette. He touched her shoulder, and while his touch upon her sent a wave of unknown warmth coursing through his arm and into the deep recesses of his mind, Meeshannette did not apparently display the same reaction. "It serves little purpose, I have discovered, to attempt interrogation of either of these two strange creatures, as their answers, if any, are generally obscured in purposeful confusion," Zennan said.

Wuntu scampered down from his rocky outpost and he and Wun stood before Zennan and Meeshannette. "Shall we continue forward?" Wuntu asked.

"I see no reason not to, unless of course we choose to continue backward." Wun answered. He scratched his head, then lifted his foot up to his waist and with his short, stubby fingers scratched between his furry-covered toes.

"Scritch scratch?" Wuntu queried.

"Again it is so," Wun responded.

Zennan stepped around his short friends. "It's unlikely these two will be particularly helpful, so perhaps we should continue on by ourselves," he said. "I believe that our good guide, Morro, a man of great courage, will serve us well."

"Do you know the direction we must travel?" Meeshannette asked of Morro.

Before he could answer, Zennan responded to her query. "I

have traveled far on my journey, yet now it appears I must first return you to the safety of your father's home before I may continue."

Meeshannette reached out, and with both her hands, tightly squeezed Zennan's arm. "Your strength is great and your quest of greater importance. I have decided to accompany you on your road wherever it may take you," she said without hesitation.

Zennan placed his powerful hand over Meeshannette's slender fingers. "The dangers that both you and I have encountered have so far been little compared with what I am certain to face in the future. In the land that lies beyond the beginning of the end of light the strength of my enemies is significant and the dangers unknown, though we know them to be great," Zennan said.

"They are our enemies together, my friend, and those dangers I am willing to accept, just as you are." She released her hands from his and stood tall, her eyes now filled with respect and determination. Meeshannette closed her eyes for a moment and her body shuddered in remembrance before she continued. "Already I have been held by and escaped the chains of both the Castle Krog and the evil master Ra-Tanox. I have met others who have been held captive and now have escaped those chains. None of you know the castle or its many corridors of terror."

Zennan looked deep into her eyes and knew. "Shall we continue? Much remains before us." He turned to Morro. "I will be grateful if you would continue to direct our course, but I will understand should you choose instead to return to fill the needs of your fine family."

Morro scratched his chin hairs, which were untrimmed and growing longer each day, staying only momentary with his thought. "My family is of much concern, but the world of all our children is of greater concern. There remains much time and distance that must pass beneath our feet. For this reason, I choose to continue on our road, if there remains assistance I may offer," he announced.

"Very well, my friend," Zennan said. "I believe that we should first find nourishment and drink to build our strength before we continue on our journey."

"An idea worthy of a great leader," Meeshannette said.

Morro nodded his agreement.

CHAPTER TEN

A cold, dark wind drove through the canyons and valleys that furrowed down from the great mountains guarding the Castle Krog from the sea to the west. A coterie of soldiers redirected the few cityfellows who wandered the night streets of the castle grounds away from the darkness where Ra-Tanox, caped and hooded, strolled beneath the new moon. Above him beams of black lights beaconed their ominous warnings across the lands of the family Tanox. Ra-Tanox stopped, heeding the crash of horses' hooves that rapidly approached from the far darkness beyond the courtyard. His soldiers moved quickly and without needed orders to the shadowed edges of the stone walls and awaited the arrival of the gray-steeded siroccos and their sorcerer. Ra-Tanox pushed the hood of his cape from his head.

Illuminated by a striking beam of black light, the white horse of the Grand Black Sorcerer flashed a blue and purple sheen as its metal-shod hooves scraped across the stone-paved court. The sorcerer pranced his horse for a moment in front of Ra-Tanox before dismounting and allowing one of his soldiers to manage its reins.

"I see that you have again returned to face me without the villagefellow girl. Perhaps I should find another sorcerer, one more capable of capturing a helpless female," Ra-Tanox threatened, as he angrily jerked his capehood back over his head.

The sorcerer stood tall, now less willing to be intimidated by the potentate that loomed before him. "Your power would be diminished without me to guide you through the intricacies of your reign. There are threats that you do not understand, dangers that loom not far from these ebony stone walls of false impregnability."

"Your tongue may not long be coupled with your head, Sorcerer,"

Ra-Tanox said, his voice made purposely absent of the anger that he felt invading his being.

High above Ra-Tanox and the sorcerer, the castle's beacons of black light were suddenly swirled crooked and forced downward by a cold twisting wind, a wind that also intercepted and pushed aside the usual cold night bluster that washed down from the mountains. Immediately, Ra-Tanox recognized that the new wind was the same as that which had earlier invaded the innermost sanctums of his castle.

"Wishtongue!" the sorcerer screamed, his obvious panic cowering the coterie soldiers who quickly sank deeper into the shadows.

Ra-Tanox pointed at his sorcerer whose initial defiance had vanished with the sweep of the invasive winds. "You have failed to return the girl, yet it appears you have successfully allowed the winds of the wishtongue to again follow your trail to my domain, Sorcerer."

"The wishtongue found the Castle Krog and the sanctum of Ra-Tanox long before I tracked after the girl your lumbering castle guards allowed to escape." The sorcerer softened his defiance with a bow of contemptible respect.

Ra-Tanox strode around and behind the sorcerer who stood motionless, awaiting his master's next commands.

"Your powers seem to have lost their spark of magnificence, my Grand Black Sorcerer. Perhaps there is someone better suited to meet my needs than you have become," Ra-Tanox half mumbled, knowing that such was not so, but feeling frustrated because all was not as it should be. "If what you have foretold, that this fleeting spore of a female holds part of the key to the future empire of Tanox, then perhaps you should continue your efforts to locate and capture this foe who at present appears mightier than your magic."

The sorcerer turned to face Ra-Tanox. "It is not the powers of my magic that have weakened, only that I momentarily misjudged the devious and slipperiness of one so futilely weak, yet desperate." He quickly spun around and remounted his great white steed, then looked down upon Ra-Tanox and trumpeted his anger and frustration:

"As the winds that darken
this world to black,
let them spin and return
my great powers back.

*Upon this titmouse
creature so weak,
I will crush her life
before again we speak."*

The sorcerer's great steed reared high, yet as its powerful hooves clashed down upon the ebony stones of the courtyard grounds, the wind of the wishtongue spun harder as if to answer the challenge of the evil one. The sorcerer shrieked his cry skyward, but again the wind answered, muting his words while whisking his great black robe up high and over his head, then quickly abated to still nothingness. The white steed reared once more before the sorcerer spurred him around and galloped hard back across the courtyard pavings and out beyond the Castle Krog, followed by his mounted, exhausted and confused sirocco troops.

A hushed quiet fell across the courtyard. A shuffle of leather-clad feet drew Ra-Tanox's attention to a cityfellow who was using his one good leg to drag his second withered and useless limb behind him across the black stones. A coterie soldier moved out from the shadows and grabbed the useless and pitiful being.

"Bring that sullen and broken creature before me, soldier," Ra-Tanox commanded, angry still with the arrogant and disrespectful departure of his sorcerer.

Immediately and without struggle the soldier brought the man to face his monarch. The intruder, hooded in a ragged, gray woolen mantle, did not look into the eyes of Ra-Tanox, but instead stared downward at the feet of the great master.

"You dared to hear the words spoken between me and my sorcerer?" Ra-Tanox raved.

The man did not answer, but stood hunched, his weight bearing heavily upon his one good leg. The soldier cracked an amber cane across the back shoulders of this pitiful witness to the sorcerer's insolence.

"Speak to me, you fitless little fool, or your tortured screams will be added to the growing chorus in my Chamber of Voices," Ra-Tanox commanded.

Without raising his head, a voice emerged from beneath the hood of the cityfellow. "Trust is what one must have, yet he who holds power seldom trusts even the most trustworthy."

The soldier again crashed his cane across the stranger's back. "You will not speak with such words and in such a manner to the Great One, sniveling creature," he ordered.

"If truth is to be feared, then you should fear your grand Black Sorcerer most of all. It sounds such that his loyalties are only to himself," the stranger answered. The faintest snicker slipped from the lips of the shadowed cityfellow, unheard by the soldier, but sensed by Ra-Tanox.

"Take this miserable insolent to the Chamber of Voices where I shall enjoy forcing the song I wish to hear from his vile lips and worthless body," Ra-Tanox ordered.

Instantly the wind of the wishtongue flew with a fury never before felt within the castle walls. Even as Ra-Tanox spoke his deadly threat, the face of the suspect, already obscured by the darkness that surrounded him, sank still deeper into the hood of his cape with only the pale momentary flash of yellow escaping. Again, the soldier crashed his amber cane across the cityfellow's back. As he grabbed the cityfellow's arm sleeve, the cape's woolen cloth collapsed into an empty rag pile at the soldier's feet.

Ra-Tanox shrieked his terror: "Yeeaah, a wishtongue trick." He stumbled backward, away from the heaped cape. "You, soldier, burn that cloth, burn it," he yelled. "Then drown its ashes in the acid of Kryt." He backed still farther away, fear shivering through him. "Burn it, now!" he screamed.

Before the soldier could bend down and pick up the fallen cloth, the wind swirled harder and harder, its force growing in strength, enough now to pick up the cape and send it spiraling upward. The soldier grabbed for the cloth as it passed in front of his face, but with another shriek of terror from Ra-Tanox, he instead quickly cowered as the cape dropped down slightly just before speeding upward through the broken beacons of black lights high above the castle walls. As the cape disappeared from sight, a blinding yellow flash scattered the black light beams across the sky. Instantly, Ra-Tanox retreated back into the false sanctuary of his chambers. In the far distance, Ra-Tanox imagined that he heard the laugh of the Grand Black Sorcerer echoing and amplifying itself off the ebony walls from outside the Castle Krog.

* * *

"The most thoughtful and carefully laid plans are by necessity never allowed to reach complete and unmitigated fruition," Wun squeaked. He scrambled around and past the long strides of Zennan, then joined Wuntu who already scampered easily backward, facing Zennan as they traveled toward the far mountain forest.

"Nor does entering the savage world of the unknown without a plan serve the best interests of those who seek the power of knowledge," Wuntu offered.

Zennan ignored them. His mind wandered in circles around Meeshannette who walked next to him, easily matching his gait.

Wun and Wuntu both felt the breath of the cold wind before it also struck Zennan and Meeshannette. "The air is stirred by a power," Wun offered.

"Tis the truth. Power greater than ours is stirring in a way that has not occurred since before the age of our most distant remembered ancestors," Wuntu said, as both he and Wun turned in their strides to face the bluster.

"Is there a reason for your concerns?" Meeshannette asked, smiling now at the curiosities who trotted before her.

"Pay them no attention that you do not wish to have wasted," Zennan said.

"They offer little of use and seldom make sense," Morro added in disgust.

"Ah, perhaps a demonstration would do you well," Wun said.

"Oooh, is that so wise? They may not be ready for such exhibitions so early in their adventure," Wuntu replied, concern lacing his voice.

"Little can be accomplished by waiting still longer, I am afraid."

Wuntu scratched. "Perhaps you are right. I will prepare myself," he said.

Immediately Wuntu scampered ahead and quickly disappeared behind a jagged stone plant. At that same moment the wind increased its attack upon the faces of the remaining travelers. Meeshannette drew herself closer to Zennan's side, while Morro used his hand to shield his face from the stinging grains of wind-tossed sand. From behind the stone plant yellow lights flashed alternately from spiny wings that shot outward from its scrag twisted trunk. The wind, still buffeting tiny, sharp-edged ground pebbles off their faces, suddenly subsided and the yellow lights stopped. From behind the stone plant a caped and hooded stranger emerged, his eyes hidden in darkness, his arms folded across his chest. Zennan stopped and Meeshannette huddled close to his side, while Wun scampered off to sit atop a nearby large, rounded stone.

"It has been some time since you and I have shared company," Zennan said, lowering his head momentarily in acknowledged respect.

"I see that Meeshannette's adventure has turned out well," the wishtongue said, returning a respectful nod. As he raised his head, a slight flash of yellow escaped from the eyes buried beneath his cape's cover. "Farro would thank you heartily for the safe return of his only daughter."

"Would thank me?" Zennan asked, not certain he understood the words and tone of the wishtongue's voice. "You seem uncertain that I am able to return her safely to her family and home," Zennan challenged.

"Already, you have decided to continue upon your quest, and the much-spirited Meeshannette has demanded that she accompany you," the wishtongue countered.

"This decision is by her choice and against my best judgment," Zennan answered in his own defense. "Her will is as strong as a northern gale and changing its set direction equally impossible. Yet, while I have failed so far to reach the closed gates of the Castle Krog, already she has successfully escaped the innermost chambers of this evil monastery. I continue only to hear murmured and fearful whispers about the far-reaching powers and darkness of the Principles from the mostly pitiful creatures who inhabit this land near the end of the beginning of light."

"Fear such powers, rightfully so," Wun chimed from atop his stone perch.

"Respect the fear that naturally accompanies the unknown," Wuntu added, his sudden appearance unwitnessed as he emerged from behind the stone plant nearest the wishtongue. He quickly hopped over and sat atop another rounded stone at Zennan's side.

Wuntu's voice startled Meeshannette for a moment, but she quickly regained herself, already becoming accustomed to the unannounced appearances and disappearances of these two bespectacled creatures. She focused her eyes on the darkness within the wishtongue's hood as he quietly and momentarily returned to the innermost thoughts he held.

Following several moments of silence, "You have become special in these dangerous and changing times, Meeshannette," the wishtongue responded in a slow, deliberate cadence.

"I am but a small creature in the great and evil lands of the Family Tanox," she said softly. "The dust my feet moves will do nothing to bring down the mountain of what will be."

"The dust your feet raises has already partially obscured and bent the sight of Ra-Tanox. He knew nothing of the latent powers that you possess deep within you. Yet the evil sorcerer, black in his thoughts and dark in his actions, knows that the seed you carry is one that threatens his own visions of greatness."

Zennan put his arm around Meeshannette's shoulders and pulled her toward him. "You speak of things about which we know nothing," Zennan declared. "Seed? What seed is this that you speak of?"

Tears welled in Meeshannette's eyes. Her voice was no longer strong. "That is the ill feeling that I have within me," she cried. "It cannot be so. Such evil should not be possible."

"Much that should not be possible becomes truth within the walls of the Castle Krog," the wishtongue explained.

"But, I did nothing for which I must be ashamed. I escaped from my dungeon with help from some most pitiful, yet brave creatures, many of whom were killed. How can such an ugly truth be told?" Meeshannette sank to her knees.

"Indeed, you did nothing that could tarnish your heart or blacken your soul, yet an action was taken upon you without your knowledge or acceptance," the wishtongue said, softness covering his words. He turned to face Zennan. "There is much you must learn, Zennan, if you are to free yourself and your people from the chains that strangle life from even the light that fills the skies," the wishtongue offered. "There are times when the life of one should be sacrificed for the good of the many, even if the one is an infant child."

Meeshannette, her hands rubbing her thin and as yet unchanged belly, looked up at the wishtongue. Grief filled her heart and confusion gripped her mind. "Child?" she said. "A child is a sacred thing, a life which may not be extinguished simply because it is not wanted," she stated as a fact for which there could be no misunderstanding. "A child is not inherently evil or good, but is only what its parents teach it to become. It must be given the opportunity to find and follow the light of goodness." Tears filled her eyes and her body quivered in confusion.

"Agreed," the wishtongue replied. "But a child should only be brought into this world of darkness if it possesses at least the smallest chance for light to enter its mind and heart. Any other action places a cruel and unjust demand upon the child. And, such is not possible with the most evilist of seeds planted in such a treacherous manner by Ra-Tanox. This is a child who is destined to bring down upon this world only darker shades of the blackest of evils. This is a child who invariable and uncontrollably will inflict death and suffering on others, many times over." The wishtongue turned and walked away, back toward the stone plant from where he had first emerged.

Zennan knelt beside Meeshannette and pulled her tight to his body. At first she pushed away, repulsed by the thought of what grew between them, but quickly allowed and welcomed the warm comfort Zennan willingly offered.

"Wishtongue, you need . . ." Zennan stopped because when he looked up from Meeshannette, the yellow-eyed stranger had disappeared. So, too, had Wun and Wuntu. He turned his attention back to Meeshannette and held her tighter. Her tears flowed freely down her cheeks and wetted his chest garment. Morro stood beside them, a sudden sadness also casting its grief upon his heart and mind.

* * *

Whimpered fear and loathing, soft and muffled, echoed in near silence down the long stone corridor. Those few trusted coterie soldiers who imagined the sound, quickly sent such thoughts from their minds, fearing for their own lives should Ra-Tanox discover their knowledge of his weakness. Inside his Black Crystal Cavern, Ra-Tanox lay face down on his great bed of thorns, his robe crumpled atop his prone and quivering body. Finally, succumbing to his need to confront the power of fear that invaded deep inside him, he screamed a silent scream and leapt from the bed. His robe floated to the floor next to him, and he stood naked, except for a black satin loincloth and the black and orange swirling tattoos of flame that covered his back and chest.

"It must die," Ra-Tanox wailed. "My power will not be shared with anyone, especially my own corrupted prodigy." He grabbed his robe from the floor and draping it around his shoulders, ran to the towering crystalline doors. His sweating hands slipped from the handles on the first try, but he quickly pulled the right side of the massive double doors open and swept his languid body outside and down the shadowed corridor.

"Guards, bring Lakat, my sirocco commander to me. Bring him to the Grand Hall immediately!" Ra-Tanox yelled, as now he sauntered the length of the corridor. Slowly, he gathered within himself the facade of his earlier command composure, as his coterie soldiers scrambled to find the leader of the sirocco horse troops.

When Ra-Tanox reached the Grand Hall, his loyal commander already awaited, standing ready with an extended and offered black crystal goblet filled with the elixir of Nador. Ra-Tanox slipped into an awaiting robe, and then submerged his anger as he accepted and drank quickly the much welcomed black liquid offering.

"I have ignored you and your loyalty to the family Tanox for much too long, Commander Lakat," Ra-Tanox said.

"I await your royal orders, my most powerful and generous master," Lakat answered, bowing low and holding the position until he was offered another nodded acknowledgment from Ra-Tanox.

Now back under control, Ra-Tanox sipped slowly from the crystal goblet, then spoke again, motioning for his old and loyal soldier who stood before him to rise. "You were a friend to my father and served him well, if I am to remember the stories that were told to me."

Lakat bowed low once again as he spoke. "Yes, Master of the Family Tanox, your father was a great leader, a greater warrior, a master of the battle. My memories of him live on deep and indelibly within my soul."

"And you learned all that my father could teach you about battle, Commander Lakat?"

Lakat thought carefully and quickly about his answer, not wanting to offend Ra-Tanox, yet also not wishing to offer more than he was able to give. "I learned all of which your great father was kind enough to allow me, yet for one of my sort to be allowed to know all that Qa-Tanox possessed would be foolishness, sir."

"Good," Ra-Tanox responded. "As you did for my father, you will become for me. With the absence of my sorcerer, you will again do the leader of my armies."

"I would be honored, Great One," Lakat said proudly, with only the slightest hesitation in his voice, which Ra-Tanox noticed.

Ra-Tanox, raising his goblet in a partial toast, moved around behind Lakat, who dared not turn to face the great leader of the Empire of Tanox. "Your hesitancy, is it something with which I should be concerned?" Ra-Tanox tested.

"My concern, great one, is about where my rightful place might be. Shall I continue to answer the call of the Grand Black Sorcerer? Or will the words I give to my soldiers come directly from you, Great One?" Commander Lakat turned slowly, his eyes cast only partially downward as he faced his master.

Ra-Tanox lowered his drink and held it out toward Lakat who stared at the black elixir, unsure of what was expected of him. The slightest hint of a smile came to the right side of Ra-Tanox's nearly lipless mouth, although to Lakat's anxious concern it remained imperceptible. Slowly, hesitantly, Lakat reached for the black goblet, and to his surprise and concern, Ra-Tanox released the power of the chalice to him.

"Drink from my crystal the noir elixir of my power," Ra-Tanox issued slowly, giving no reason for Lakat to expect that his master's words were anything less than a command.

"You honor me with such a memorable request, my master." Lakat drank slowly from the goblet, savoring the warm liquid as it tumbled down his throat, quickly filling the deepest reaches of his body. Finally, he tipped the emptied chalice level and held it back toward the outstretched hand of Ra-Tanox. Just as Ra-Tanox accepted the return of his goblet, a cold wind swirled through the room, cascading shivers down Lakat's spine, which quickly pushed the last warming breath of the noir elixir from his body.

To Lakat's surprise, Ra-Tanox let the crystal goblet slip through his fingers, and it smashed on the floor, spreading its black shards across the smooth, stone surface.

"He's back," Ra-Tanox screamed. "He's back. Get him out of here. You're my commandant, get him out of here!"

Lakat, confused and battling an inherent and rightful fear that invaded his mind for not knowing why such a strange cold should panic Ra-Tanox, drew back from his master and withdrew his battle adz, swinging it into the ready position. Yet, who or what was it that he, Commandant Lakat, was to confront with his great battle skills? Certainly not the wind, for the wind could never be defeated.

"Destroy it! I command you to destroy it," Ra-Tanox screamed again. He stumbled backward trying to escape the stream of cold, but it circled after him, swirling his robes and scattering the long braids of his gray-streaked black hair that trailed down his back. Ra-Tanox fired a look of both anger and helplessness to his commandant.

"I saw this only once before, when I still remained an aspirant, much too young to join the great army of Qa-Tanox, your father king," Lakat retorted, keeping smoothness and calm in his voice. "And," he continued, "my own father told me of such things, and that, while rare and evil, indeed, battling such a force as the wind of ancient and withered wishtongues was as pointless as slashing the air with even the greatest of battle axes or scimitars."

"Do not bore me with your ancient and useless excuses," Ra-Tanox bellowed. "Instead, tell me how you will destroy this vile intrusion upon my world." The wishwind lifted itself upward, into the inky heights of the black crystalline wall spires where it swirled faster and faster its ominous, yet voiceless threat.

"I know the secret of how to kill this wind, but I must travel with my army to the great Plain of Wishtongue where I can destroy the wind at its source," Lakat offered, lowering his great adze.

"Then do it now!" Ra-Tanox screamed. "Do it now!" His face screwed from tortured pain to an evil smile as his black eyes focused upon the gray eyes of Lakat. "And should you happen across the path of my Grand Black Sorcerer . . . ," he hesitated a moment, "introduce the edge of your weapon to his throat. Succeed and all the powers of my once trustworthy sorcerer will transfer to you."

The order to kill the Grand Black Sorcerer at first startled Lakat, but the thought of possessing such all-powerful control of the empire would lend itself to his becoming the most potent of commandants in his family's lineage.

"Your wish shall be my most fervent command, Master Ra-Tanox."

"It is not merely my wish, Commandant Lakat. Fail and you will live eternity in the deepest bowels of the Inferno of Tanox, while your screams will forever join those already in my Chamber of Voices, voices from the dead and those wishing they were dead."

"I understand," Lakat said, bowing low as he backed out through the great double doors. "I shall not fail you, Great Master."

CHAPTER ELEVEN

Wun and Wuntu squatted themselves atop two low stone promontories and watched quietly as Zennan and Meeshannette sat before the blazing flames of a midnight fire. The fire was not for comfort, as the night had remained warm with the rocky earth slowly releasing upward its collected warmth stored from the day's early summer sun. High above in the night sky, an occasional streaking skystar momentarily marked its passage with its glowing line of light that slashed its way across the blackened covering. Zennan placed his powerful arm across the shoulders of Meeshannette. She looked at him, her mind filled with both hope and despair.

"Will it be long before the blue wizard about whom you have spoken appears before us with his guiding wisdom?" she asked Zennan.

Zennan gave a gentle squeeze to her shoulder. "There is little that I have been able to predict with respect to these creatures of the night. The wizard of blue light has visited me but a few times, and always at times of his own choosing."

"Must we wait here, or can we continue alone and still hope for success?" Meeshannette asked, already knowing the answer.

A light breeze stirred the fire's coals, lifting both the flame and a scurry of embers skyward. Zennan watched with hope that it was a sign, but their glow dimmed and their movement ceased as quickly and unannounced as they had begun. Again, he turned his attention to Meeshannette.

"With the departure of Morro to his homeland during the last full moon, we are two standing alone who must act as one if we are to defeat the evil that must be defeated," Zennan said. His eyes scoured the darkness beyond the light cast by their fire, hoping for something that would provide him with hope.

"I wish that Morro could have stayed with us," Meeshannette said as sadness escaped her eyes. "Although his thoughts were sometimes strange, he did provide us ideas with viewpoints of value," she added.

"Morro truly was a friend, and a friend he will continue to be, but his family had more need and more right to his presence than we. We were right in offering him our best wishes for happiness," Zennan said.

Meeshannette smiled her understanding as she slowly and gently rubbed her ever-so-slightly protruding belly. "What am I to do, Zennan?" she asked. "What am I to do with this child?"

Zennan did not have an answer. He squeezed her ever so kindly and closer to himself. A moment later he cast a glance up at the stones where Wun and Wuntu had sat, but where they no longer were perched. He looked around quickly and did not see them, although his vision could not pierce the surrounding darkness at much distance beyond the dancing orange light cast by the slowly dying flames of their fire.

"It appears that once again our two friends have left us," Zennan whispered, for no reason other than not wishing to interrupt the nighttime quiet.

"They really are quite likeable creatures, those two you call Wun and Wuntu," Meeshannette said softly. "Perhaps they have left for a reason, but likely they will return by morning's light."

"Or perhaps they are merely sleeping in the rocks that lie just beyond our vision." Zennan released Meeshannette. "Come, our fire dies and wood fuel is scarce. As it is late, we should attempt sleep because the sun will soon enough wash away the darkness. I fear that tomorrow's only reward will be a long and difficult journey deeper into the unknown."

Zennan kicked the ground smooth of its larger stones and spread his cape upon the reddish dirt. "Sleep, dear one. Sleep so you may be rested and strong," he said.

Meeshannette did as Zennan requested and was quickly drawing toward a sound, yet periodically restless sleep. As her soft panted breaths became deep and restful, the coals of the dying fire once again stirred to life. Zennan became aware of the change about him. From within the coals, a swirling wind circled and tumbled upward, taking with it orange ember sparks, which slowly transformed their color into a blue as crisp as the coldest winter's ancient ice glacier.

"Where is it you hide, Wizard?" Zennan asked, his voice calm and melodic, his mind at restful ease. "Why do you wait until my companion has drifted into night dreams before you show yourself and your powers before my dying fire?"

The ground fire flared its flames, blue and hot, as a voice as cold as Zennan had ever before heard pierced his back. He turned slowly to face the wizard cloaked in an azure robe of shiny flaxen cloth. The wizard and Zennan stared at one another in silence that screamed an unknown conflict.

Finally, Zennan spoke. "Have you come to aid my journey into light, or have you instead come to cast me into a darkness deeper than tonight's starless and moonless sky above?"

The wizard stood silent for an eternity of moments before responding. "I have come," he finally said, then let silence grow again before he once more spoke. "I have come as an emissary of grief that you must bestow upon the one lying before us, peacefully asleep in her unresolved conflict."

"I do not wish to understand your riddles, wizard, and even less so if what you are offering are words harmful to one so beautiful and innocent." Zennan stood firm behind his words.

The wizard did not play his word games with Zennan this time, but instead spoke directly, simply, strongly. "The one before us carries a seed which holds the essence of one so evil that even Ra-Tanox and his sorcerer fade to but a shade of the lightest gray in comparison." Zennan began to speak, but the wizard raised his hand, stopping Zennan's thoughts before they could become words spoken in anger. "The one she carries is destined to become the 19th in the Tanox lineage. His name shall be Sa-Tanox, and his evil shall be darker than any of the Tanox masters before him and it shall be cast upon the earth for a thousand of the longest lifetimes."

"This is truth that you speak?" Zennan asked, knowing deep from within that it was so.

"A truth so hard that the mightiest blades of Urbon could not penetrate its shell and spill its blood." Finally the wizard moved slowly to stand over the prostrate and sleeping body of Meeshannette. She stirred slightly as he looked down upon her. "It is neither my temperament nor my liking that one of such peacefulness and beauty should come to bear an evil so powerful that the world already unknowingly trembles in anticipated horror."

Zennan also moved closer and knelt beside the sleeping, but innocent harbinger of evil. Gently, so as not to wake her, Zennan smoothed his hand over Meeshannette's head, following her long and trailing raven hair over her shoulder. He looked up at the wizard.

"What must I do, wizard? What must I do to ensure the safety of my people, and to save all good creatures from this evil that so cowardly hides within such pureness?"

The wizard flared his robe slightly, its soft, billowing lines flashing its azure sparkle in a halo around his body. He spoke quietly, so quietly that Zennan had to strain so as to hear his words and understand their meaning.

"There exists but only the smallest of chances that Meeshannette's body will expel the evil seed before it reaches its maturity, but if a child is born, it must be set upon a raft of tules to be swept over the great Falls of Kelto. In only this way, will the life of the child be extinguished, and its evil forever cleansed from the earth."

The shape of Meeshannette stirred in its sleep, as though hearing the wizard's instructions. Zennan knelt beside her and again caressed her shoulder and head. Her stirrings eased and she was quickly back at peace.

"I understand, Wizard, yet Meeshannette's feelings and thoughts do not mirror ours," Zennan offered, standing once again to his full height and shaking his head in knowing concern. "Already the wishtongue has spoken similar words to us, and their meaning was deflected by Meeshannette from the reality that accompanied them."

A near smile, imperceptible, yet there, moved to the blue wizard's crooked mouth. "It is in you, Zennan, to change such feelings. Yes, it all lies deep within you, but you must work hard to find it if our destiny as presently foretold is to be altered." With these last words, the image of the wizard quickly faded, just as the morning light slowly brightened the edge of night.

At his feet, Meeshannette stirred from her slumber, slowly opening her eyes to the misty remains of the blue wizard. She blinked away the sleep from her eyes and the image was gone. She looked up, and Zennan filled her view.

"You are awake early, Zennan," Meeshannette said softly. She tried to blink away the fuzziness that filled her mind, but was not successful. "I had a dream as strange as any I've ever before experienced," she said.

"Dreams can tell us much," Zennan answered, "if only we can learn to listen to their voices, understand their songs, and believe in the truths they reveal." His voice had momentarily resumed its melodic resonance of old. "What is it that you have dreamed, dear Meeshannette? What is it you remember that you may share with me, so that I may, if required, assist you in understanding that which is not fully understood?"

"I am to be a mother, that I feel, that I know," she said, her words voiced slow and strong. "But there is danger, and yet I know not what it may be. My dream ended before I could hear all its words and understand its message." She sat up, and Zennan helped her up to her feet. She kissed his cheek gently. "Perhaps what I remember are the blue wizard's words that I am still hearing, words that came to me in my night dreams."

Zennan smiled, knowing that Meeshannette had not dreamed the blue wizard's words, but heard them true as they intertwined with her mind's night thoughts. "I am not worthy of someone so beautiful and intelligent," Zennan said, his finger touching his cheek where Meeshannette's lips had just kissed.

"No, it is I who is not worthy of one so strong, of one so capable of leading us from the darkness that has engulfed our lives for generations."

"Then," Zennan said, "let us who are unworthy of one another become one in our battle against the Principles of darkness that pervade our land and smother our people. Come, we must trek to the lands at the base of the great mountain barrier and await this child's birth in a safe refuge. Only when the newborn child is safe can move against the evil leader of darkness who hides in his Castle Krog."

They soon gathered their meager belongings and headed away from the red earthen-towers and scrag brush, walking toward the lush forest lands where the great River Kelto tumbled from the high cliffs. Wun and Wuntu were not to be seen.

* * *

The Grand Black Sorcerer had remained near the Castle Krog, though not inside its walls. He entered now, secretly moving briskly down the ancient passageways. He returned here as needed to slowly, secretly and more fully absorb the great and little-understood powers of darkness, tho powers that fired upward from the Inferno of Tanox. Since the beginning of the most ancient times, those same fires had been fueled by a powerful evil lodged deep within the darkest passages of the earth's center mass. From there they were melded with the first members of the emerging family Tanox through sorcerers.

The Grand Black Sorcerer could sense that inside the Castle Krog, Ra-Tanox was thrashing about spewing his confused and maniacal rantings, knowing his fear would not allow the powers of evil to replenish themselves within him. While Ra-Tanox grew weaker, the strength held by the Grand Black Sorcerer increased with the passage of each full moon that crossed the night sky, a strength that was not being shared as required by the Principles. The evil and its power that was to pass from the sorcerer to Ra-Tanox instead twisted in its passages and flared outward from its intended target, fading into useless fog when sharp focus was required. In his own methodical and magical way the sorcerer continued practicing with his newly discovered and stolen powers. He was determined to control the tools that would allow him to reign over all who breathed the air upon these lands.

The Grand Black Sorcerer knew of the coming child; he was also aware that with the power of Ra-Tanox slowly fading, it was the child, and the child alone, who challenged his future command of these lands that stretched as far as the eye could see and the mind could envision. His ongoing inability to capture and destroy a woman so small and insignificant was like having the great death raven hover perpetually above one's head. He had sent his couriers and spies as far and wide as the known lands of darkness stretched, but one by one they returned, each with empty hands and unwelcomed answers. The only ones who remained afield were the soldiers of Commander Lakat. From Lakat he had heard nothing, not even rumors of success or failure.

At last, the time had come for the Grand Black Sorcerer to lead his remaining loyal sirocco horse soldiers across the empire's vast and empty lands and begin the destruction of each village until the secret of Meeshannette's hiding place was revealed to him and to the onyx blade of his waiting sword. When finally his soldiers mounted their gray steeds in anxious anticipation of the destruction that lay ahead, the sorcerer advised them that they would be either successful in their assigned endeavors or sentenced to live in their burning coffins forever. Galloping across the great red plains to the edge of the mountains where the farthest villages subsisted on the very edge of the end of the beginning of light, they struck ruthlessly. Entire villages were removed from existence, their inhabitants slashed, burned, enslaved or sent scampering into fearful and certain death upon a land that the sorcerer had made inhospitable to the very breath of life.

It was an escaping villagefellow who stumbled half dead into the river's shallows at the edge of a small and what appeared to be abandoned village, delirious in fear and absent of the nourishment required to survive for even another hour. Meeshannette, her belly now plumply filled with its new life, a life which only slightly slowed her movements, managed to pull the tall, thin fellow from the water's eddy and onto the sandy shore. In the warm sun the stranger, his clothes ragged and tattered, his face and limbs equally bruised and abraded, slowly returned from his unplanned but seemingly destined mission to the land of the dead. Meeshannette gave him milk from her goat bag, which he slurped down weakly and hungrily. The bedraggled stranger-in-need looked up from the goat bag, his eyes slowly focusing on the beauty that blocked his vision of the blue sky above. "Are you an illusion in my death dream here to make my passing more pleasant?" he asked weakly.

Meeshannette smiled. "As your body regains its lost strength and your mind regains its focus, you will see that I am but a villagefellow just as you." She pulled the goat's milk bag from the stranger. "You should not take so much of this rich nourishment so quickly," Meeshannette advised. "You are a strange one to me, your clothes and your speech. From where have you traveled, or should I better ask, from where have you escaped?"

The stranger reached for the milk, and Meeshannette allowed him another small drink before she again pulled it away upon his choking. He looked again at this beautiful lady before him. "First,

I should introduce myself," he said weakly. "My name is PEarlOch, eldest father of the family EarlO." He attempted to straighten his long and ratted, curly brown hair, but with no success. "My village was attacked a fortnight ago by a black and evil wind. A black-caped monster who sat upon another monster, so large and white, a fire-breathing beast as I could never before have imagined."

Fear crossed the eyes of Meeshannette. "The Grand Black Sorcerer from the Castle Krog, I am afraid," she mumbled.

At her words, immediate fear stung the eyes of PEarlOch as he lay on the ground before Meeshannette. "You speak of this monster as one you know. But how could you know of such evil and still be here to speak of it, unless you are a part of . . ."

Meeshannette placed her fingers upon PEarlOch's lips, quieting his words. "Do not fear, my new friend. The evil black sorcerer is neither a friend nor an ally. I was merely lucky to escape my encounter with him from inside the black-walled castle."

"From in . . . inside the castle?" PEarlOch stuttered in amazement. "We too, have had young and eligible ladies taken from us by the soldiers of the Great Ra-Tanox, yet none has ever returned to us. You are indeed as lucky as you are beautiful."

"You must be quiet now. Let's get you to my shelter where you may rest and nourish yourself." Meeshannette helped the tall, frail fellow to his wobbly feet. "You may tell us in more detail how you came to be here and about the fate of your village and its fellows."

"Us?" he inquired, remnants of his recent fear rising to the surface of his mind.

"Yes," answered Meeshannette, reassuringly. "You have nothing to fear. I and my companion Zennan will protect you, should that become necessary. But such action is unlikely to become reality as our temporary home is difficult and dangerous to find for the unwary and unknowing, and has little to offer the outside world should such discovery be made." She steadied PEarlOch and together they walked slowly along the narrow and winding pathway that passed through the weeping trees that thickly bordered the river.

They broke into a small natural opening in the weeping trees where the river split, sending a small and narrow channel to the opposite side of the clearing. At the head of the water's split, a small conical refuge made from stripped bark and thatched river tules sat nestled neatly into its surrounding world. Zennan came around from behind the living refuge carrying a large fish with its silver and gold scales shimmering in the warm red rays of the late afternoon sunlight.

"Who have you discovered?" Zennan asked. He dropped his great fish to the ground upon seeing a stranger who was weak and quickly failing what little strength remained in his body. He grabbed the slim fellow's body and supported and guided PEarlOch to the inside of their living refuge where he helped him to lie atop one of the grass beds. "You have endured much trouble, that is easy to see," Zennan said.

The little fellow heaved a sigh of relief as he allowed himself to rest upon the soft grass blades beneath him. "And you must be my savior's husband," PEarlOch announced, assuming it must be so.

Zennan laughed, while Meeshannette turned away, blushing. "I might someday wish that such could be true," Zennan said. "But I am only a friend who promised another friend that I would help bring his youngest child, his daughter Meeshannette, back to his side after she was stolen from her village."

Meeshannette poured a hot cup of willow tea and offered it to the grateful PEarlOch.

"Then where is it this young girl's husband hides? Does he not care for his wife and child enough to aid in her return?" PEarlOch asked, unable to ignore Meeshannette's belly swollen large by the child she held within.

"I am not a wife, only a mother-to-be, but not of a man I would ever choose to have as my husband," Meeshannette said, being quite honest and forthright.

"Oh, I do not understand," PEarlOch responded. "Why would you wish to choose a husband by yourself, when your elders would have the knowledge and wisdom to choose the man who would be best for you and their future generations? Truly, my injuries are not so serious or such as to cast my memories and life's understanding into meaningless chaos, thus making good and proper sense escape my grasp." He rubbed his bruised forehead as he resumed his stare at Meeshannette's child-filled belly.

Meeshannette began to speak in the first wisps of anger that infused her thoughts, but her father's words that, "Only the fool speaks in anger to another fool," made her remain silent for the moment. Zennan did not remain so.

"You come from a land where wishes and actions can always be true to one another?" he asked PEarlOch. As he spoke, Meeshannette quietly went outside and quickly returned with the great fish that Zennan had earlier caught.

"There is no one who can guarantee that actions will work in perfect concert with one's wishes," PEarlOch answered. "But certain things," he nodded toward Meeshannette, "certain harmonies are within the actions and thoughts of all of us, including the young and impish."

Zennan looked toward Meeshannette, then back at PEarlOch. "Meeshannette's powers of harmony are greater than either you or I will probably ever understand," Zennan explained, more for his own self-understanding. "She has a magical power that captivates, yet frees the will and strengthens the heart. What she has within her at this moment is not of her will and certainly not of her wishes." Zennan drank from the stewing tea that Meeshannette offered him. PEarlOch did the same from that which Meeshannette's soft hands had earlier placed before him.

Zennan looked again at Meeshannette as the last rays of sun spilled through the small window opening and created a glowing halo through the fringes of her raven hair. He turned his view again upon PEarlOch who also stared at the beauty of Meeshannette.

PEarlOch thought back to Meeshannette's few words to him as he lay in his mindless stupor upon her discovery of his dying body. He vaguely remembered that she was stolen by the soldiers of the Castle Krog. Indeed, he had heard the whispered stories of kidnapped women, even those from his own village, being forced to bear and rear children for the masses of evil who inhabited that foul and bitter place. Perhaps, he mused, those stories were true. He thought better of Meeshannette. PEarlOch now understood that perhaps wishes and destiny were seldom close friends, but they sometimes became passing strangers who occasionally traveled together. He silently sipped his tea, a concoction sweet to his tongue that pleased him greatly, but also one that released, along with its flavor, a feeling with which he was not familiar.

As night fell and tumbling light from the full moon shone down through the river tules and upon the thatched refuge of Zennan and Meeshannette, the time had come that Zennan had anticipated, yet loathed. Pain stabbed at the young Meeshannette's body and her muffled cries filled the air, intertwining with the soothing sounds of the river's water cascading over the rounded boulders of its gravel bed. As the sun rose into the sky from the east, the sharp screams of a newborn infant filled the crisp morning air, competing with the cries of squawking birds and the squeals from small and chattering fur creatures that bounded about in play and feeding.

As Meeshannette lay quietly, her child wrapped in a blanket of dried and woven softgrass leaves, PEarlOch sat back in contentment and confusion. In his village, which he was sure no longer existed, such a thing as a fatherless child could never have happened. Such was not their way. He would offer this young mother his advice, but he did not know what advice he could give under such strange and unpleasant circumstances. The more he thought about it, the more uncomfortable he became. Finally, he approached Zennan. "Sir, it is not my intention to offend one who has certainly and without concern for herself or himself saved what remains of my pitiful life, but I feel that I must leave your home as I am unable to remain in a place where a fatherless child lives, if this is indeed the life that has become the fate of this infant."

Zennan nodded his acceptance of the beliefs of the stranger called PEarlOch, although he himself could not understand why such was so. As Meeshannette slept peacefully with the sleeping child upon her breast, PEarlOch bid his host farewell and respectfully asked that his most gracious and thankful tidings be offered to Meeshannette upon her awakening. Zennan agreed, and PEarlOch, with strips of dried fish carefully wrapped and placed in his bulky pocket, started off down the river's edge on a trip he hoped would lead him back to his village and put him once again with those whose ways he better understood and could accept—if any still lived.

It had been quiet since PEarlOch departed, with the exception of the new child's occasional cries. Zennan prepared all that was needed to make the journey to Morro's village where Meeshannette had finally agreed to return and leave the child, at least until she could return to her own home. Zennan battled mindthoughts that pushed him to act upon the words offered by the blue wizard. If the child was truly the bearer of evil as foretold through the wizard's voice, then it must be destroyed in the manner as described. Yet, Zennan could not tell Meeshannette of this need because he sensed that each day her maternal hold upon the child that had grown inside her was becoming stronger. Doing so would surely break her heart and her spirit. Still, the child must be cast into the river and allowed to drift over the falls to its certain death if the evil the infant indeed possesses was to be erased forever from the face of the land.

Meeshannette had strolled to the river's edge to bathe away the remnants of displeasure left by the birth of her child. She carried the boy child close to the warmth of her breast and the beat of her heart, yet still she was repelled by the thought of the child's origin. But, she reasoned that it was not the child's fault nor burden concerning who his father might be. She also knew that she could not care for this new child, if she was to accompany Zennan on his quest. Though she had thought that it would be useless for her to have expected Zennan to take leave of his focus and assist her while she awaited the birth, Meeshannette was both surprised and comforted when Zennan insisted that such be the way of his actions. He made her torturous wait much more bearable and her inner feelings less guilty for having allowed this to happen to her.

As Meeshannette placed the wrapped child upon the earthen bank, a sudden flurry of wind and wings exploded from the river reeds and adjacent willows as the water boiled with the thrashing tails and fins of fish. She stood looking over the reeds and down the river but saw nothing unusual. Silence now greeted her ears. The birds were gone and the fish once again swam silently below the water's surface. Then it came, gently at first, barely perceptible and certainly not identifiable. But the quivering vibrations that spread across the ground beneath her feet grew stronger and faster. For several moments, her mind failed to comprehend the identity of these strange and strengthening temblors.

"Meeshannette!" came the loud cry of Zennan from their near distant lodging. "Meeshannette!" thundered again from Zennan's lungs.

From nowhere apparent, Wun and Wuntu suddenly appeared

before Meeshannette. It was at this moment that Meeshannette instantly understood what she was feeling, even without Wun's urgent request.

"You must hide the child, for if the sorcerer captures its heart, he also controls its mind and the power it holds," Wun said.

Meeshannette did not fully understand the significance and exact meaning of Wun's words, but she did know that her child was in danger. She looked around, and seeing the large dead and rotting willow trunk near where she stood, Meeshannette used her crude cutting tool to remove a portion and widen the opening that entered into a pecking bird's nest. Inside this soft, punkwood she softly pushed her infant child, carefully filling the chamber's entrance with grasses that would allow breathing air to enter, but muffle and soften the cries that were sure to squirt from the infant's lungs as he began to feel the unwelcomed coolness of the water through this wooden vessel.

Meeshannette waded into the icy water pushing the log, with its natural-appearing long and broken limbs, along the shallow, quiet surface, leaving it hidden among the tall watercourse reeds. She turned around to see that Wun and Wuntu had again disappeared after having offered their initial warning. She raced back to the lodge clearly expecting to see and meet Zennan, but what confronted her was not the vision expected. Instead she was greeted by the pounding hooves of two of the sorcerer's mounted sirocco soldiers, their long, black leather capes spread behind them in the wind created by their charging mounts. From her side, another mounted solder suddenly burst from the low hanging willows, but just as he reached for the unsuspecting Meeshannette, Zennan leaped from the branch crotch of a taller willow and smashed his extended feet into the chest of the soldier.

A great gush of air blasted from the soldier's lungs as his body greeted the ground with a thunderous crash of leather and iron. Meeshannette looked up to see Zennan now mounted upon the great steed. He jammed his heels into the beast's flanks and as it reared and then charged forward past her, Zennan reached down and with all the strength massed in his great arm, swept Meeshannette from her feet and swung her around behind him and onto the horse's hindquarters. The horses of the remaining two soldiers flared in surprise as they stumbled over the fallen soldier, their riders barely able to hang on and avoid being cast to the ground as was the first soldier.

As Zennan spurred his stolen horse, crashing through the riverside tules and willows, Meeshannette screamed into his ear her need to return to the river where she had placed the child. Her yell caused Zennan to rein his horse to a stop as Meeshannette again pleaded to regain her child. Zennan's mind was met with the fleeting thought that this was an opportunity to allow the child to be destroyed as had been decreed by one much older and wiser than he. Yet, with more soldiers likely nearby, he knew that it was equally likely that the child would be captured and taken to the feet of Ra-Tanox, forever bidding an unwelcomed end to all those who had successfully remained beyond the Principles and the beginning of the end of light.

"Where is it you have left the child?" Zennan yelled, as his horse circled in its excited state of ready.

"I placed my child, whom I was going to name in your great honor, in a log upon the shallow waters hidden among the thick tules along the main river's edge," she said, quickly and now more calmly. "He should be safe from the grasping hands of the Ra-Tanox soldiers," she added.

"Perhaps, but he will not be safe from the probing mind powers of the Grand Black Sorcerer, should his evil self be near the patrolling soldiers."

"Truth fills your words, Zennan. We must get to the child, if we are to ensure his long and safe life."

Meeshannette held tightly around Zennan's waist as he spurred his horse toward the river. Yells and chants emerged through the thick willows from that same direction. It was the sorcerer himself who had crashed in upon their temporary shelter and was now leading his soldiers toward the child's hiding place. Zennan charged his horse forward in the direction of Meeshannette's extended arm as she pointed toward the river's shoreline thicket.

"There," Meeshannette screamed into Zennan's ear, "there, floating beyond the reeds is the log hiding place of my dear child," He spurred the horse hard as the force of the beast's powerful strides churned and splashed the cold waters of the river high over their heads. But his direction was momentarily intercepted by one of the soldiers who suddenly crashed through the tules. Zennan swung hard, hitting the soldier's head, causing him to fall from his saddle, his left ankle now broken and his foot caught in the stirrup. Again Zennan galloped his mount toward the small log as the horse-churned water's waves suddenly and quickly pushed the small boat out and into the river's quickening current. Before Zennan could again break free from the surrounding and attacking soldiers, the grass-covered hiding log disappeared into the churning waters beyond the reeds.

Down from the small hill behind the shore, the Grand Black Sorcerer suddenly emerged, sitting high upon his great white horse. "Capture them you fools, capture them now or you each will pay the cost through tortured pain that will be with you for ten lifetimes," the sorcerer commanded, as he pointed the remainder of his accompanying solders to the water's edge.

But Zennan expertly maneuvered his kidnapped mount around the pursuing soldiers, eluding their grasps, frustrating their efforts. Meeshannette clung tightly behind Zennan, her arms wrapped around his chest, her heals dug deeply into the horse's flanks.

"We must save my child," she screamed. "We cannot allow the river nor the evil of this sorcerer to steal my baby."

"If the river has taken the child, it will save him from the tentacles of the sorcerer, this I am sure of," Zennan reassured her. He bashed away the grasping hands of one of the soldiers who reached to pull Meeshannette from their galloping horse. The soldier dropped hard to the muddy ground at the river's edge as Zennan kicked his mount into a sprint away from the remainder of pursuing soldiers.

From atop a nearby sandy knoll, the Grand Black Sorcerer watched from beside a single thorn tree, his frustration and anger growing as he witnessed his soldiers' failure to capture the intended prey. His horse reared, and he raised his black onyx sword skyward. As his great white beast settled back upon all fours, the sorcerer was suddenly surrounded by a wind that swirled its way from the cold river water, sending sand grains and small stones stinging across his leathery cheek. Instantly, the sorcerer knew what he needed and yelled commands that instantly stole the chaos from his soldiers.

"The child we seek has been separated from the womb of its mother and now travels away from us, down the river before you," the Grand Black Sorcerer screamed. "Find that child and bring it to me, either dead or drawing its small and pitiful breaths, it matters not." He charged his white steed off his high shoreline perch and into the shallow waters along the river's edge. As the sun's rays shimmered across the cascading rapids the sorcerer caught an even stronger sense that what he sought was concealed from his sight, yet remained very near. He again spurred his horse forward as his soldiers scattered about searching frantically for a child, but not knowing where it was to be found.

More than two full distances down the river, with the soldiers and sorcerer now ignoring his escape, Zennan, with Meeshannette frantic behind him, guided his horse through the willows, tules and thickening reeds that grew up through the shallow sideline waters. She excitedly pointed toward a piece of broken log that floated out beyond the reeds. It linked momentarily to a thick green reed cluster that tirelessly fought against the bounding waters. As the horse galloped near, Meeshannette's excitement turned to frustration when she realized it was not her hollowed log. She watched as the escaped tree limb suddenly broke loose from its watery mooring and quickly was swept into the thundering rapids that lay just beyond the reed and tule shallows. Zennan spurred his horse around and they continued the search, always moving downriver, leaving farther behind the pursuing soldiers of the sorcerer.

As the sun finally set, bringing the darkness of a moonless night to the river's edgeland, Zennan stopped and slid the exhausted Meeshannette down from the equally exhausted mount. She sank to the ground and quietly wept at her loss as Zennan stood above her, feeling her sorrow, yet silently and secretly hopeful that the child died in the great and powerful falls whose sound thundered from beyond the next bend in the river. But now it was too dark to continue their search. Their eyes would have to wait until tomorrow's sunlight before Meeshannette could hopefully discover the fate of her child, and Zennan could discover the fate of their world.

CHAPTER TWELVE

Fog hung low throughout the maze, clinging to the edges of mineral towers that marked the southern boundary of the Ra-Tanox empire, a wasteland where outland villagefolks lived. It had been a long and hard two full-moon journey for Lakat and his command of soldiers to reach this place, which they had only heard of through story and rumor. Yet, none had complained about their encountered miseries, especially the confusion and backtracking they were forced to endure during their journey as they constantly faced avenues that circled them back to starting points that were days old. The hope that they could successfully serve the needs and desires of the great Ra-Tanox by capturing the infant child more than comforted and consoled their most disheartening and disturbing feelings. The rewards offered them and their success were truly generous.

Lakat slowed the pace of his following column as darkness lowered its curtain before their searching eyes. Yet, Lakat would not allow himself, and thus his soldiers, to cease their efforts. He had determined that upon the death of the Grand Black Sorcerer, that he, who would become known as Lakat the Fearless, could successfully command the powers that would seek escape from their domain of darkness. But it was another matter to predict and especially ensure the destruction of one so strong and whose heart and magic were driven by the deepest depths of the Fires of Tanox.

A slender slash of jagged light shot through the surrounding mineral towers, blasting molten gravel into the lead soldiers, toppling them from their frightened mounts. Lakat had expected such a potent and unannounced encounter with the powers of the Grand Black Sorcerer's strong magic, but he had not realized that now would be his time for confrontation.

"Charge forward against the light, my faithful soldiers," commanded Lakat. "Do not fear for your lives. It is not the winged evil of the sorcerer that can defeat you. It is only fear that can defeat you if you are so weak as to allow it." Lakat took the lead in galloping his mount through the last vestiges of rocky columns as more bolts of lightning slashed their way through the scrambling columns of his faithful soldiers. "Follow my lead and maintain your staunch belief in the power of Ra-Tanox, and we shall triumph in our great mission." Lakat drove his spurs hard into his horse, pushing it to its mightiest effort.

Suddenly, Lakat, followed by the soldiers who were allowed by destiny to escape a gravelly and fog-encrusted burial, emerged from the mineral columns and their lightning bolts and passed directly into the quiet and peaceful midst of a score of villagefellows. These villagefellows, fat in their content living and warmed by their blazing spot fires, busily hovered around ancient tree-stump tables, bartering and trading, bantering and gossiping. Surprise came to both the soldiers and the villagers simultaneously, but the villagers scattered immediately in as many directions as there were fellows. The horse soldiers were startled by the sudden changes around them and reacted by charging in a dozen different directions in chaotic pursuit of their prey. Their great skills as horse soldiers, however, were not an equal match for the long practiced panic sprints, erratic dodgings, and quick hidings of the villagefellows.

Within moments of realizing the wastefulness of his soldiers' valiant but futile efforts, Lakat yelled commands for them to reassemble before him. The chaos and confusion was stronger and louder than Lakat's command voice, so it was some time before order again prevailed. At last all was quiet, and Lakat pranced his horse through the column and to the front of his remaining soldiers' hastily established formation. He stood high upon his saddle stirrups attempting to better view what now appeared a s a long-ago abandoned village. It was remarkable, he thought, that so quickly there was no longer evidence that life existed before him.

"You—you who have hidden yourselves from my view, come forward so that we may talk," Lakat announced to the furtive inhabitants of the abandoned village. There was no response, only the slightest breeze rustling the sand at the horses' hooves. He called louder, "Kind villagefellows, we mean you no harm, but only wish to ask of you several questions about strangers who may have passed this way."

From beneath a sandhill in the distance a muffled, yet shrill voice spoke quickly. "Your actions appear as an attack and your demands as commands that you believe we must obey. You are not of a peaceful sort. Be gone from our midst."

Lakat charged his horse at the speaking sand mound and drove his lance deep into the hill. The blade passed through the sand touching nothing but its dulling grains and rock shards. He turned his horse and charged the mound once more as his soldiers, their own horses prancing nervously, watched and waited for orders to attack these helpless and obviously cowardly village creatures. But Lakat was not destined to silence forever this voice that dared ignore his command, and worse, commanded him to leave the village. Again, Lakat's lance drove into the sand, deeper this time, striking something solid. Yet it was a strange mass that solidly grabbed the shaft of his lance and held it tight in place as his horse thundered by. Lakat screamed as his impaled and now immovable lance propelled him from his horse, smashing him hard upon the shadowed ground.

"Your life ends at the end of my sword," Lakat screamed in anger as he sprang to his feet, unwilling to acknowledge the throbbing pain that he felt in his back. He pulled his great sword from his side scabbard and, remaining on foot, charged back to the mound that still held his lance stiffly in place. He slashed the edge of his sword down hard upon the top of the offending sand hill, cutting deeply into the soft pile. A blast of gray-black ooze blew back up on him, causing Lakat to drop his grip on the sword and grab for his blinded eyes.

"Eeiiiaa, what secret breeders of evil have we come upon," Lakat screamed in terror as he frantically rubbed to clear his eyes.

His lieutenant dropped from his horse and ran to his commander's aid, but once at Lakat's side, he was bewildered as to what could be done.

"Lieutenant Motah, where are you?" Lakat cried.

"I am here, here at your side, Commander," Motah answered. "I do not know what I can do."

"Kill this fiendish attacker," Lakat demanded. His vision was slowly returning, but only to his left eye. He pointed at the pile of sand. "End whatever life it is that lies within that sand heap. Do it now, Motah."

Motah looked at his Commander Lakat and hesitated. He motioned for two of his soldiers to dismount.

"Destroy the one that lies hidden in this sand heap," Motah ordered. "Destroy this one before it again can harm our commander and further hinder us in our mission for the great Ra-Tanox."

Instantly, the two soldiers pounced upon the sandhill with their drawn dirks, slashing and stabbing through the sand. But when they had dug deeply enough into the hill to reveal the head of Lakat's captured lance, there was nothing remaining but more sand. The standing lance tumbled to the ground and shattered into tiny shards of black glass, which were quickly lost among the sand pebbles.

"Ignore the signs that fall before you, if you are truly loyal soldiers," Motah ordered.

Lakat's eyes were now partially clear of the temporary poison that had immobilized him. "Dig until you strike the Fires of Ra-Tanox if you must, but discover what has attacked my sight," Lakat uttered, still rubbing light back into his eyes.

The two soldiers continued their fervent digging, but to no avail. Sand was all that they uncovered, and now, it was beginning to slide back inside their thigh-deep hole. But still, they dug as if their very lives depended upon it, occasionally glancing back at Motah and Lakat, hoping that they would allow an end to come to this obvious waste of time.

From behind Lakat, another voice broke the sound of the two soldiers scratching away in their deepening sand hole. "Your presence here is not welcomed. Please remove yourselves and your riding beasts that soil the grounds of our humble village," the voice said softly, almost pleading.

Immediately, Motah attacked the voice that spoke from within the scraggly limbs and leaf-bare branches of a waist-tall sandbush tree. He slashed his own sword across the base of the tree, severing it from its supporting root structure and toppling the sandbush tree down upon the sands.

From beneath the sand and from within the remaining severed

roots the voice spoke again. "Your efforts to destroy that which you do not understand can never prove fruitful, even for the followers of Ra-Tanox. Now, be gone from our homes and leave our lives or the one which your minds can never see and never understand will serve as witness to your destruction."

Motah drove the blade of his sword deep into the sand, stabbing it into the roots of the fallen sandbush tree. As with Lakat's lance, Motah's blade struck something solid and lodged itself tight. As he struggled to retrieve his hand weapon, it began transforming its iron blade to black glass just as Lakat's blade had been changed. As the transformation quickly moved up the blade to the handle that Motah held, he tried to release himself from his weapon, but his hand was stuck fast and solidly to its jewel-encrusted grip. As he watched in panicked horror, his hand, then his arm, changed to glass, as did the remainder of his body.

"You have allowed yourself to be taken by the vile magic of these weak and deceptive villagefellows, you worthless groveling follower," Lakat raved. He slashed his own sword across the chest of his metamorphosed lieutenant, shattering his entire body into the tiniest and sharpest shards of black glass. Slowly, cautiously, Lakat backed away from the broken pile of his lieutenant until he reached his horse whose reins were being held by another mounted soldier. Lakat rubbed the last of the poisonous effects from his eyes. "We will burn this village, burn it into molten sand," he said, slowly, softly, so quietly that only the nearest of his soldiers could hear the quiver voice.

* * *

PEarlOch sat his tall, lanky body down to rest beneath the rocky overhang that launched the great Falls of Kelto tumbling over the cliff ledge above him. Exhausted, he soaked his sore and blistered feet allowing the cool, clear water to swirl around his bony and callused toes. He welcomed the fine water mist that filled the air and sprayed its cold relief across his face. PEarlOch dipped his head beneath the water and shook away the grimy trail dirt. He raised his head allowing the icy waters to flow down his hairy neck, back and chest, wetting his furred goatskin shirt and pants.

PEarlOch was looking up, admiring the rainbow that shimmered out across the cascading water, when a dark object the size of a milk calf skated down through the falling liquid from the cliff above. It tumbled onto a rock that jutted into the path of the falling water and shattered into three pieces that floated down through the thick, hanging mist and into the cold, blue pool just steps below him. The first and smallest piece floated past his dangling feet, but it was the second and largest remaining portion, the one with the small branches still attached to it, that caught his attention. From within the broken log's hollowed space the tiniest naked hand jutted out, splashing wildly at the cold water. Quickly PEarlOch waded into the pool, nearly to his neck, and grabbed the broken log, dragged it the water's edge, then struggled to pull it up onto the sandy shore beneath the overhanging rock where he had been sitting.

"Only in my dreams would such a thing occur, and seldom would I remember such a dream by morning's first light," PEarlOch said out loud and to himself. "Such a thing should not be happening, not to one so poor and unlucky as myself."

PEarlOch carefully removed the small infant, now only partially hidden within the hollowed log, its head and arm bruised, but otherwise unhurt.

"Oooweee," cried PEarlOch. "Now, it is my confusion that must first be answered." The child began to cry, further frustrating PEarlOch. "Oh," he whimpered softly, "what can I do to care for such a tiny and helpless being. One as young and small as this must have parents and villagefellow support to bring meaning and usefulness to his life. To my village he must come, if only I am able to find my way back." PEarlOch quickly replaced his shoe wraps, properly snugging the leather laces. Ready now, he picked up the crying child and stuffed him into a small back sling he quickly and expertly fashioned from nearby river reeds.

The child was small and nearly weightless, sapping only minimal energy as PEarlOch carried it along. PEarlOch hurried down the narrow and winding animal trail that followed beside the meandering river. This remained a strange land to him, and since his memory had become truer, he was reminded that his village had been destroyed by the sorcerer and his soldiers. Now, PEarlOch was unsure of where he could go. PEarlOch, not knowing where the river trail would take him and his newly acquired ward, turned eastward, hoping to pass far away from the land of Ra-Tanox, perhaps to find a welcoming village for himself and this child.

* * *

Behind Zennan and Meeshannette, Wun and Wuntu followed, saddened by Meeshannette's loss, knowing that little chance existed for finding the child alive. Zennan led the way, truly hoping that he would not discover the child he knew must perish. It was several days later that he and Meeshannette came upon the place at the base of the Falls of Kelto where PEarlOch had most recently been, but had since departed. Meeshannette was the first to find the two remaining broken pieces of the log inside of which she had so carefully hidden her child. She sat beneath the same rocky overhang where PEarlOch had sat cooling his feet while watching rainbows form inside the sprays thrown off by the overhead cascading waters. But Meeshannette did not find her child nor did she see rainbow colors dancing across the face of the water cascades. She found no sign of that for which she searched, only the imprint of a large animal track in the soft sand.

"I fear that the child did not survive the fall from above," Zennan offered, with true sadness in his voice, but measured relief in his mind. He pointed to the animal tracks. "It would appear that had the child managed to avoid such a fatal journey over the falls, then the wild creatures that roam these lands during this time of darkness would certainly have ended any additional hope of life."

Meeshannette sat down upon the sands, next to the largest piece of broken log and hung her head in her hands, resting both elbows upon her knees. Silently she cried, spilling tears of sorrow through her slender fingers, wetting the sands beside the River Kelto. Zennan stood silently behind Meeshannette, knowing that he could only wait until the last of her grief washed from her heart.

Later, as a bright moon rose, lighting the darkness that had fallen across the riverbank's shore, Zennan reached around the simmering coals of his warming fire and placed his hand upon Meeshannette's shoulder and gently squeezed. He moved his hand across her lips and silenced her words as she awakened. "Ssshhh," he whispered. "Unwelcome visitors have joined us here upon this soft sand shore."

Meeshannette's eyes opened wide, and through the moon-brightened darkness, her vision fell upon a knee-tall creature that strode easily out of the water and across the damp sand. Its long snout suddenly pointed upward and twitched as it snorted the drifting scent of an unknown intruder trespassing within its misty domain.

"I believe that what we see here is what greeted the helplessness of your fallen child, dearest Meeshannette," Zennan said. He moved slowly, picking up the smaller piece of log, then slung it hard at the unknown beast that was slowly slithering toward them. The water beast yelped a wild and shrill cry when the sodden wood chunk thumped into its large, exposed chest. Zennan leaped to his feet, with Meeshannette immediately behind him. Together they ran directly at the unwelcomed creature, chasing its long and limbless body back into the river's dark, cold waters.

Safe from such strange and treacherous beasts, Zennan held Meeshannette tightly as they returned to the glowing warmth of their fire. The night's air remained cool, even here in the mist that drizzled down upon the shore from the river's waterfall.

"We should leave at the first hint of sunlight," Meeshannette said, huddling herself tighter to Zennan's body warmth. "I fear that the reason we have come this far out of our way is certainly gone forever," she said, sadness heavy upon her voice.

"Destiny has a way of taking care of itself," Zennan offered as consolation. "We should not mourn too long that which we have no control over." He allowed her to meld her snuggling closer into him and there they sat in silence, awaiting destiny's next moment.

It was already light when they finally awoke together, much too late to depart the river trail at the time Meeshannette had originally desired. But nothing had been lost except time, and time for

Zennan was immortal. It always was and always would be, and it was nothing he could control. "Come, sweet Meeshannette, we must meet the coming darkness and fill its deepest corners with the light from within ourselves." He stood and then reached down and took Meeshannette's outstretched hands. Their eyes locked for a moment as she smiled and allowed Zennan to pull her up to her feet.

"You are right about what we must do," she said, then paused for a moment. "I have a debt to repay to those creatures that have been cast into the deepest and darkest chambers of the Castle Krog for longer than we shall ever know."

"And how shall this debt be repaid by you who has nothing?" Zennan inquired.

"I vowed to myself that I would return and free them from their chains of darkness and despair."

"Chains are made strong to resist the greatest of intentions and the most strenuous efforts to defeat them."

"I thought that you believed that time could conquer even the strongest of enemies," she answered.

Zennan smiled. "Yes, but time does not take sides in any battle. The one who wins the battle of time is the one who best understands and accepts both its limits and its power."

"Agreed," Meeshannette said, then smiled. "Let us begin using time to our favor, and not let it be wasted in idle conversation and meaningless mind wanderings."

"Agreed," Zennan repeated. "Let us begin our journey toward our destiny." He picked up his small and nearly empty sling pack as Meeshannette did the same with her meager belongings.

They headed down the river trail, each alternating the lead position as the trail was much too narrow for walking abreast. After a short distance Meeshannette hesitated in her lead for only the shortest of moments, secure in knowing that her quick and certain decision at a faint fork in the trail was the right way to continue. She chose the trail that left the river's meandering yet guiding course, and they headed upward through the thick and tangled river reeds and willows. The new trail she trampled lightly beneath her feet quickly turned to sharp zigs and sharper zags, making her vision absent of the following Zennan as the reeds grew in especially dense walls and the tules to especially tall heights.

At a triple trail fork, each no more discernible that the other, she turned back for agreement from Zennan, but he was not within sight. She waited for time to allow his steps to catch up with hers. But instead of Zennan, Wun and Wuntu pattered up the trail behind her. They stopped a short distance from her feet showing neither surprise nor concern by her presence and Zennan's absence.

"From where have you two come and to where has Zennan disappeared?" she asked her two new and uninvited, though not unwelcomed, traveling companions.

Wuntu shrugged. "We have come from where we were."

"And we go to where we are going," Wun added in much seriousness.

"But as far as Zennan's location or destination," Wuntu said.

"We really are at a loss to say," Wun finished.

Meeshannette took several paces back down the trail, stepping gingerly around Wun and Wuntu, then yelled, "Zennan, Zennan, where is it you have gone?" She awaited a reply that didn't arrive. "Do not play games, dear Zennan; time is not in our favor at this point in our journey." Again, she waited, but heard only the sound of a slight and hollow wind rustling the reeds and tules.

"It would be best if we continue forward on the chosen path," Wun suggested.

"And whose chosen path is it that we should so diligently follow?" she inquired, frustration entering her voice.

"Yours, of course," Wuntu said.

"Certainly one can only follow one's own path," Wun confirmed.

Meeshannette frowned at her two friends, knowing they were correct as usual, but she did not like their truth, nor the truth she now faced. She was alone again, yet deep inside herself she knew that she would never again be truly alone. She turned around and headed back past Wun and Wuntu but stopped suddenly as she witnessed an intense flash of blue light in the near distance.

* * *

Zennan stopped for a moment and listened. The River Kelto

no longer flowed near his path, its slapping and gurgling water sounds now silenced by the wall of lush green thickness that surrounded him. Only the sounds of the wind rustling through the tules and reeds along the path flowed to his ears. Ahead, the trail straightened, but Meeshannette was not to his front. Zennan shook his head in confused wonderment, knowing that conflicting light and shadow often played odd tricks on minds and eyes not accustomed to seeing past such arguing and contrasting lines. He hurried forward, thinking that Meeshannette would stop her journey when she became aware that he was not following within sight and sound of her. He continued, passing many crossing paths that over time had diverted their animal travelers to differing destinations.

Zennan hurried his pace even more, knowing that he must catch Meeshannette and be with her should she in some manner discover her child alive, which he didn't think possible. Yet much of what she had accomplished so far was not possible. As he stepped upon a knee-high log of an ancient and crumbling willow tree, a sudden and cold wind swept up the path, striking him in the face. Zennan stood upon the log attempting to look over the tops of the blowing tules, yet his improved vision was quickly limited by the dark clouds that suddenly swirled in low, pressing their rain-sodden fingers down into the tall tules and reeds. Thin threads of blue light arced across the tips of the tallest reeds, doing no harm as they streaked from point to point.

"It has been a long time, wondrous wizard of blue light and dark omens," Zennan voiced in his most melodious of tones, knowing that this visitor of power and mystery would soon show himself.

"You have become confident in your travels and wise in your decisions," the wizard said.

Zennan turned around to face the wizard, but remained standing upon the rotting log. "You have not chosen to come to my aid in a very long time, Wizard," Zennan said, pushing his long-grown and wind-blown hair from in front of his eyes. "It appears that much of what we anticipated has not occurred and much that we did not foresee has crossed our paths and become unwelcomed neighbors." Zennan waited now in silence and watched as the wizard put his hand to his chin while thinking his silent and unknown thoughts.

The wizard strode quickly closer to Zennan, and Zennan involuntarily stepped backward, down off the log. Now it was the wizard who stood upon the rotting log, his long flowing gown drifting and twisting in the swirling winds created by his own presence.

"The power that was created within Meeshannette," the wizard said, then hesitated again, but only for a moment before continuing. "The power that was created within Meeshannette, it is a power that continues to breathe the strength of our air and draw sustenance from the breast of mother earth."

"I saw the crushed vessel of certain death cast upon the rocks at the base of the great and powerful falls of the River Kelto," Zennan answered. Then he understood, as the past words from the wizard and wishtongue and others came into his mind. "You are right, certainly," Zennan said slowly. "It was only an empty case that I found, a case that just as well could have served as protection against the crushing waters and smashing stones of the fall. Perhaps, the hope that Meeshannette holds for finding her child is not a hope born of wishful thinking and plightful actions."

The wizard consciously pressed himself still closer to Zennan, and this time the warrior did not step away, but instead looked directly into the crystalline eyes of the blue one and waited. Zennan could feel the wizard's cold, dry breath pushing upon his face as the welcomed visitor spoke once again.

"There is a great weight that presses itself against you in your struggle to bring the forces of light to the evil darkness that pervades these ancient lands," the wizard said.

Casually, yet purposefully, Zennan looked at the dark clouds that had gathered around him since the coming of the wizard. "Perhaps it is not this one called Ra-Tanox who alone brings darkness to these ancient lands," Zennan said, his voice almost mocking, yet maintaining a necessary air of respect for one so ancient and powerful.

The blue wizard raised his arms and instantly the clouds above began to twist in an ever-tightening circle as the arcing threads of thin, blue light grew larger and more powerful. In the instant it took Zennan to blink away the final raindrops squeezed from the shrinking clouds, the mass of darkness disappeared in a flash of bright, blue vapor, allowing the blinding light of the high noon sun to spear past the weeping willows through reeds and tules.

"Your tricks are well known to me, as you will probably remember," Zennan said. "Perhaps the darkness that accompanied you here indicates your true faith, Wizard."

"Perhaps you are correct, yet if such would be so, why would I continue to visit you in times of great need? I could easily have arranged for your failure by not having come to you so long ago, when your quest began," the blue wizard explained, knowing in truth that he owed no explanation.

Zennan thought to himself for a moment. "So, tell me, why have you decided to return? And be quick with your explanation. Your light-filled tricks and confusing talk are keeping me from that which needs my attention."

"The child awaits its future, a future you must not allow it to see," the wizard said plainly.

"The child has passed over the falls, and is unlikely to have survived. If indeed this child lives, where may I find him?" Zennan inquired.

"Such things even I cannot say for sure." The wizard raised his arms skyward, sending blue threads of lightening from his fingers, dancing them again lightly across the tips of the tallest reeds. "There is a key that you must discover if success is to be yours."

"A key, Wizard?"

"A key that will allow you to open the door that holds the darkest powers of evil. A key that will allow you to lay bare and bright the truths that must be unlocked." The wizard lowered his arms and prepared himself to again leave Zennan with himself.

"Then I shall take my leave," Zennan said. "You have allowed Meeshannette to get much too far beyond what may be my ability to successfully find her again." Zennan turned away from the wizard who at that same moment stepped down from the log. "I shall leave now, unless you have something to say that is more worthy of my time and thought, such as where exactly this key or the child that I must seek may be found."

"Go," said the wizard. "The key to your plight and that of your people will be obvious enough when you have discovered it. For now, you will find that Meeshannette has not traveled far from your sight." As the wizard's blue lights suddenly streamed back around him, Zennan's vision of him began to fade, but in its last flash of brightness, the wizard's voice echoed through the willows and reeds, bending them over with its power. "The key is yours to find, or it is yours to lose, just as the light is yours to find or yours to lose. The direction you choose and the places you search are yours and yours alone to determine." Then he was gone.

Zennan headed down the faint trail, and as he rounded the first bend, past an especially old and knottily twisted willow tree, he saw Meeshannette, Wun and Wuntu. They sat quietly in a small grassy meadow whose boundary struggled to hold back the surrounding wall of head-high reeds and tules.

CHAPTER THIRTEEN

Across the gabled stone huts huddled against the interior walls of the Castle Krog, imagined notions had become whispered rumors among those allowed to live within the black stone edifice. Always the great Ra-Tanox had appeared standing upon his raised stone portico from where he admonished the masses each new moon as they gathered upon the cobbled yard. Yet, for a very great time he had not shown his face, nor echoed the evil powers of his voice commands across the minds of his squalid masses. At each new moon they had stood throughout the night, awaiting their master's appearance. His failure to appear accompanied by no words to dismiss his subjects caused them to stand waiting until the following day's sun had traveled to its highest point in the sky before gathering courage enough to disband and return to their monotonous trades and tortured lives.

As the voice of Ra-Tanox remained quiet, in the darkened evening gathering places where amber grog was shared among the cityfellows who lived within the castle's walls, their whispers turned to plain talk speculation. More sightings of strange and small creatures, whose hair hung long and voices were shrill cries through the night air, were making the fellows suspicious and curios about changes that they could feel merging around and throughout the Castle Krog.

Perched on stools at a small table in the darkest recess of the most popular of the castle's groghollows, two cityfellows spoke in whispered hushes between furtive looks about the hovel and slurps through caps of amber froth. Around them sat and stood handfuls of other shaggily dressed groups of neighbors, with never a stranger among them, tossing gossip and truths to be judged as they argued and discussed whatever came to mind. They watched each other, but never could it be noticed, for such staring at another was not regarded as natural nor right, so discretion was practiced.

"You have seen him, yourself?" Primmy asked between long slurps.

Elmof glanced over his shoulder before turning back and daring to answer. "The Grand Black Sorcerer has been seen among the willow groves along the River Kelto," he finally whispered. "His army follows, the sirocco soldiers who remain loyal to him, but only because they are not aware of his personal war against Ra-Tanox."

"And what of the shrill-voiced creatures?"

"The small beasts with their piercing, glassy green eyes, are together with us, awaiting only instructions from the yellow-eyed one." Elmof took another drink, slow and long, as his eyes stared out over the top edge of the grog flagon. As usual, the others around the groghollow appeared to ignore them.

"Have they agreed to our wishes?" Primmy continued probing.

Elmof set his empty flagon on the table and motioned to the fat and bow-legged groghollow owner for more, which he quickly tendered to the table. When the grog server had left behind refilled flagons and returned to his duties, Elmof looked back at Primmy. They both took long drinks, nearly draining the newly-filled flagons before returning to their conversation. "Such things are not agreed to without much thought and more contemplation," he said. "It may be the yellow-eyed one who becomes the binding force."

"I fear that even time may not reveal the value of my words," Primmy cautioned. "It is not destined to be the wishtongue who will lead us from the darkness of Ra-Tanox and his castle. For we now must also defeat the Grand Black Sorcerer and his rogue army, and it may take more than the power of a single wishtongue."

"The family Tanox is a battle which has awaited us always. But now the powers of Ra-Tanox have been weakened by the sorcerer's departure," Elmof reminded his co-conspirator.

Primmy set his empty flagon down on the table and looked deeply into the eyes of Elmof. "I feel it will still take more than we can create. The darkness that has filled our lives for far too long has also weakened our vision. And I fear it will require a vision, a vision as great as that seen through the eyes of an even greater visionary, to bind and unite us into a strong enough cooperative to ensure victory against such awesome and dark powers."

A hushed silence flowed across the groghollow as the door opened and a tall, hooded stranger entered and stood momentarily surveying the darkness. A hundred eyes quickly diverted their view away from the stranger, going back to their own business, but each pair remaining curious about the unknown stranger. The stranger, his hood sufficiently covering his face to maintain a reasonable sense of anonymity, shuffled across the room directly to Elmof and Primmy's private table. Primmy saw him approaching.

"Do not despair our lack of vision," Primmy said. "The one who will help us in this time of our darkest plight and brightest opportunity approaches now." He nodded his head, turning Elmof's attention toward the approaching stranger.

The stranger pointed to an empty table stool, received nodded agreement from the table's group of cityfellows, then slid it across the rough-hewn floor to the table where Primmy and Elmof sat. He bowed slightly at them, they nodded back, and the stranger sat himself down upon the wooden stool, all the time keeping his hooded head turned forward and downward.

Elmof looked quizzically at Primmy. Primmy allowed the slightest smile to twitch the right edge of his rosy lips. He looked at the stranger. "You are welcome at our table. May I offer you a flagon of amber?"

The hooded one nodded yes, and as Primmy motioned to gain the attention of the groghollow's delightfully plump owner, the stranger spoke slowly and softly, making his voice barely audible over the low and quiet din of others talking.

"Have you accomplished all that was asked of you and your companions, Primmy?" the stranger asked.

"It has not been an easy task that you have set before me," Primmy answered, sounding defensive. "These are very dark times, making trust a virtue few cityfellows can afford to possess."

The owner arrived at their table balancing a tray that held three large flagons filled with his special amber. The three grew quiet as the plump owner set the frothy liquid down upon the table before each of them, picked up the two empties and retired to continue his other duties and business.

The stranger looked at Elmof. "You are a trusted one?" he asked.

Elmof looked slightly confused, although he tried to appear otherwise. "I have been a trusted friend and partner of Primmy since before the times of our children. There is little, and certainly nothing of consequence, that either Primmy or myself has done or thought about that the other is not privileged to know and be a part of," he assured the stranger.

"Such is truly the case, and I believe it would not be otherwise," the stranger said, stopping his words for a moment to tip his flagon up and drink of the amber brew.

Elmof took the opportunity to do the same, but as he did so, he thought that he caught the slightest flash of bright and piercing yellow light reflect across the amberish froth that floated above the lip of the stranger's raised flagon. Elmof blinked quickly at what he thought might be an imagined illusion, but by the time his eyes opened and focused, the yellow light, if that is what it had been, was gone from sight. But he knew what he had seen, and if stories told by others were true, then he knew who was sharing the special amber brewgrog with he and his friend Primmy.

The stranger set his half-empty flagon down upon the table and looked up at Elmof. Suddenly, two yellow eyes blazed from out of the darkness within his hood, followed by a voice now absent its softness, instead hard-edged with great meaning. "A mission awaits you, a mission of more and greater importance than anything you have ever before thought about or gone about doing."

Elmof looked at Primmy. "You knew of this? That is why you suggested we spend this evening here?" he asked.

Primmy shrugged his shoulders, his lips again twitched, showing a slightly more obvious smile.

"Do not feel harshly about your friend, Elmof," the yellow-eyed wishtongue pronounced. "It is I who commanded that he keep my coming here secret from all, including his most trusted friend. Be angry instead with me if it is anger you must spill toward anyone."

"I feel neither anger nor betrayal," Elmof said slowly, taking a quick sip from his brew flagon. "During these darkest of times, much of what we have felt and the ways in which we have acted must make way for changes that often seem harsh and always feel strange."

"Then you will accept the challenge that I will place before you tonight?" the wishtongue queried.

"My only desire is to fulfill your wished need, if it is such that helps rid our world of Ra-Tanox and the evil that resides within his reviled Principles and the darkness of his followers, especially the Grand Black Sorcerer," Elmof said, certainty and loathing filling his voice.

The wishtongue quickly surveyed the darkened groghollow. Eyes that may have been cast upon the group of three huddled in their far corner were quickly averted as his yellow streams of sight flashed around the room, then quickly returned to the interior of his hood, angled so that only Elmof could see them.

Behind the three of them, darkness filled the far side of the groghollow as the entry door opened revealing a tall and darkly clad second stranger who quickly and silently entered, then drew up the lone and last stool at the bar.

At Elmof and Primmy's table the wishtongue again turned his attention to Elmof. "There is an infant male child who has been lost and who must be found," the wishtongue explained, this time with seriousness accompanying his drinking of amber.

"It is such that I can accomplish this search task in the morning, first thing. May I be trusted with this child's name?" Elmof asked, his voice penetrating the stale air with overtly boisterous confidence.

"His name is unknown and his whereabouts a mystery, for only his presence is felt among those who feel such things," the wishtongue explained for Elmof's sake and Primmy's understanding. But understanding came to neither of the two cityfellows.

Elmof scratched his head for a moment. "Perhaps I should inquire of those who are here in the groghollow and those I may know and trust about the Castle Krog, and also among those who have been chosen to live in the outlying villages, about whether or not a child who is unknown to them resides among them," Elmof said, mockingness entering his words.

"Serious consequences await those who fail in fulfilling the responsibilities directed to them," the yellow-eyed wishtongue warned. "You are a fine and noble fellow, so I know that you will do that which needs to be done, and do it well," he added.

"I do not wish to do anything less than my best," Elmof said, recanting his attitude. "The mourning mother must have her child found and returned to her breast," he said.

The wishtongue set his emptied flagon back down on the table and pulled his hood farther forward to better cover his unseen face. Still, from beneath the rough loden covering the yellow glow of his eyes periodically escaped. "If the child is found, he must not be returned to his mother. You will inform me, and no one else," the wishtongue said, with much force and seriousness coming from deep within his voice's tone.

"I do not understand," Elmof replied.

"And neither do I," Primmy added, his mouth immediately taking refuge behind the edge of his partially emptied flagon.

"Understanding what must be done is not necessary to the task being successfully completed," the wishtongue informed the two of them. "I will provide understanding as you are able and ready to accept and act upon it."

From the stool at the end of the bar the second stranger, still sitting alone, turned from his seat and looked upon the table where Primmy, Elmof and the wishtongue sat. The stranger picked up his flagon and rested his eyes upon the wishtongue and his two friends. When he witnessed the three drinking companions become aware of his casted view, the stranger tipped his drink in respectful acknowledgement. Primmy and Elmof, seeing the stranger's unwelcomed and unrequested action, grew nervous and turned to the wishtongue to see what thoughts and actions he might have. The wishtongue nodded and tipped his own flagon, empty as it was, toward the stranger.

"It is not good to make such notions of acknowledgement toward strangers, even here in this place of hushed friendships," Primmy advised.

"Perhaps I will invite the unknown stranger to our table and make it so he is no longer such," the wishtongue offered his two companions.

"I think it better if Elmof and myself make our way from the groghollow so that we may put into action those words which we have spoken and the words that you have spoken to us this evening," Primmy said. He stood up from his stool and motioned that Elmof should accompany him. Elmof obliged his friend's words and wants. The wishtongue nodded at the two as they walked past him on their way to leaving.

"Remember my thoughts and abide my words. The child must be brought to me if we are to succeed in our quest," the wishtongue reminded them as they departed.

Immediately after Primmy and Elmof allowed the groghollow's doors to close behind them as they departed for the relative quiet of their own stone hovels, the second stranger approached the table where the wishtongue remained sitting, patiently waiting. The stranger sat on Primmy's abandoned stool, without any overt acknowledgement from the table's lone remaining occupant.

The wishtongue motioned for the grogtender to refill his flagon and to bring one for the stranger, whose rough-hewn face of ageless sunskin and wrapped, cling-cloth clothing set him apart from the others in this place of darkened solace. Yet, others inside and around the tables and across the bar did not take obvious notice of one so different. They knew that such was not their business, thus the stranger, certainly one not appearing to harbor danger, best be left alone and unknown.

With their amber before them and once again alone in the darkened corner, the stranger lapped the leftover foam from his lips.

"You sit with those who should not be included in things that should not be spoken of," the stranger said.

"And you come to places where your presence is never requested and not welcomed," the wishtongue countered.

"I come here to speak with you and you alone."

"And so you shall speak with me and me alone," the wishtongue allowed, casually drinking his amber.

The stranger looked quickly but carefully around the darkness to ensure himself that they were to be alone with their words. Reasonably assured, he continued, "The time for you to fulfill your portion of our bargain has come."

A quickly passed flash of yellow light scattered from the wishtongue's hood. "I am not here to act as your source of knowledge for those things which you do not know, but wish knowledge of," he said.

"You have had no choice in your actions since that time long ago when you first betrayed your wishtongue fellows and crossed into the darkness of the Tanox throne," the stranger said.

Within the groghollow the quiet pall grew more intense than normal. The wishtongue looked around fearing that those who would not have been knowledgeable of his long-time treachery had heard the softly spoken words of the stranger. The stranger ignored the momentary silence and the accompanying eyes that discreetly passed across his back.

"You will bring the child to me, or Commander Lakat will have my head, but only after he has boiled yours in a vat of horse soup," the stranger threatened.

"Threats are for those without the power to act upon the wishes of their own minds."

"Still, my threat will be your guiding light through the darkness that hangs before you."

"And, my two lately departed, amber-drinking fellows have been given what is needed to track and recapture that which your commander seeks," the wayward wishtongue advised, tiring of his verbal banter with a messenger from someone so utterly contemptible. "Take my message to your master and warn him to leave me to my own devices or he will be without his bridge to that which lies beyond the beginning of the end of light."

The stranger bowed his head ever so slightly, then quickly savored the last remnant drops of his amber grog before walking from the groghollow and leaving the errant wishtongue to contemplate his next action.

*** * * ***

Endlessly tracing his trampled steps across the roughened and stained floor of the Chamber of Voices, Ra-Tanox mumbled unintelligible utterings. Alone with himself and his obligation to his family's heritage, he no longer knew what he could do to ensure the continued control of his reign. Hushed rumors had continued to reach him about the traitorous adventures of his Grand Black Sorcerer, rumors that were often as exaggerated by the givers as they were misinterpreted by Ra-Tanox. Finally, he stopped his pacing and turned his creviced and rapidly aged face toward the heavy barred door to this dark place of torture and death.

"You, soldier," Ra-Tanox mouthed only slightly louder than a whisper. "You will find Commander Lakat and bring him to me, do you understand? Bring him to me at once, or you will find your head festooning my Chamber of Horrors."

Outside the closed door, the rustle of several teams of feet scampered off in terror down the darkened hallway in a desperate search for their only salvation from Ra-Tanox's threat. Their frantic search ended quickly and successfully for once, as Lakat's early return to the Castle Krog brought him into the Grand Hall at the same moment when the panicked soldiers entered hoping to learn some sign of their commander's location. Lakat's often slow gait was hurried by the frenetic pleadings of the soldiers. He strode quickly to the Chamber of Voices and entered.

"Ah, my worthless soldier-guards have finally done something which I have commanded," Ra-Tanox said, as he moved toward his commander's face. "What have you discovered regarding my missing seed prodigy?" he demanded.

Lakat bowed low to his honored master, his intentions and feelings still fastly loyal. Raising his body, but keeping his head lowered, he spoke softly. "If my sources are to be trusted, and I believe they are, the Grand Black Sorcerer recently discovered the living place of the escaped village girl."

"Ah ha," proclaimed Ra-Tanox. "And my birthed seed was captured by the traitorous sorcerer?"

"There was no sign of a child, my master," Lakat answered. "Apparently, the village girl known as Meeshannette has gained an ally in the form of a powerful and brave stranger who easily diverted the charge of the sorcerer's sirocco soldiers. Together, the two of them escaped, and we can only assume that they escaped with the child."

Ra-Tanox turned and paced his trail once again over the chamber's floor, silently thinking about what, Lakat cared not to imagine.

Lakat cleared his throat and continued, his bowed head rising slowly to discretely peer at his master, but never directly into his eyes. "I have placed many spies among the sorcerer's sirocco soldiers and out among the cityfellows who gather during dark nights in the local groghollows. One infiltrator of special skills, and the one most loyal to me, has spoken directly to and gained the offered powers of a wishtongue," he said proudly.

A shiver shot through the whole of Ra-Tanox. "A wishtongue? A wishtongue?" he repeated. His voice became loud, but strained with fear. "It is the power of the wishtongues that has invaded the innermost sanctuaries of my personal domain. Wishtongues are to be destroyed, not trusted with the fortunes and future of my empire."

Lakat stood nervously, his head again bowed low as he tried to decide about how he might best respond. He hadn't anticipated such a strong and negative response from Ra-Tanox about something that surely would prove rewarding. Finally, Lakat's words came slow and sparingly as he tried to put confidence into his voice.

"If I have misjudged, I truly regret my actions, although they were taken with the best and most loyal interests of the Principles and of the Family of Tanox," Lakat offered. "But, I have placed my life into the hands of this person on many occasions during my long and healthful existence, and I would willingly do it again."

"That is exactly what you have done, Commander Lakat, you have placed your very life in the hands of this spy. If his quest ends in failure, so shall your life," Ra-Tanox wailed. Lakat remained silent as Ra-Tanox continued. "Wishtongues, they are harbingers of death for the family Tanox. They are never to be trusted and always to be feared," he added, trepidation filling his voice.

"Ah, such is true, with all but this one particular wishtongue," Lakat offered. "He once betrayed his own kind, and since, he has been an outcast walking the nights alone, sleeping by himself during the days."

"If he has betrayed his own kind, what prevents this wishtongue from betraying those who aren't of his kind?" Ra-Tanox inquired of his commander.

Again, Lakat thought silently for a moment. "Your wisdom is well given, Master. I shall guarantee that my infiltrating wishtongue will not possess any thoughts or entertain any actions that can possibly bring harm or danger to you and the continuing reign of the Family Tanox."

Ra-Tanox spun around, turning his back to Lakat. "I find it increasingly difficult to trust anything or anyone. Across my castle grounds, even my most loyal soldiers allow the fur creatures, that for eternities were held securely in the deepest holes of my dungeon, to run loose during the night. Once, the name Tanox struck terror in the minds of all those who inhabited my lands, and it did so even in those who lived upon lands that lie where light attempts to extinguish my darkness, where my boundaries touch the end of the beginning of light. If you and your soldiers cannot control such worthless and pitiful creatures, how will you, your spies and soldiers—my soldiers," he emphasized, "control a wishtongue, let alone an army of wishtongues and their followers?" Ra-Tanox spun around on his heels and faced Lakat. "Do my words come to you with proper and adequate understanding, Commander Lakat?"

Lakat bowed as he backed toward the door. "Master, your words have burned an indelible mark deep within my mind. Yours are words that shall be heeded and never forgotten." He continued backing out the door, turning away only when finally out of sight of Ra-Tanox.

The fire in the eyes of Ra-Tanox glowed cold. His desire to be free of those who challenged him was overcoming the arrogance that once spewed from his heart and mind. He hurried to another of the lower levels of his castle, entering through the tall arch doors that led to the belching fires of the Inferno of Tanox. Once inside, and with the thick and heavy rock doors closed tightly and secured behind him, Ra-Tanox approached carefully, yet purposely to stand before the translucent black stone pedestal. Since before the beginning of darkness, the great hearth had held fast the Fire Ruby of Molock. Ra-Tanox stood in reverent silence and abject loneliness before the great red jewel. Slowly, he reached out with his right hand, but pulled it back before touching its deep crimson brilliance. He rubbed his hand on the side of his flowing, velvet paneled robe, then again reached slowly, hesitantly, for the ruby. This time he continued until he gently caressed the ruby's scarlet power, and as he did, the Inferno of Tanox transported its power to the ruby. Ra-Tanox absorbed the gem's power as its flames rose higher, scorching his hands as dark and deeply as the blackness that filled his heart.

A sudden and unannounced return of the cold, swirling wind caused Ra-Tanox to scream his terror. "No, no, you cannot enter the sacred house of fire and quell the Inferno of Tanox. The Principles allow only myself and the souls of my great and glorious ancestors to enter this place of honor," he screamed, as his shrieking voice turned to sobs.

First, above Ra-Tanox, then quickly all around him, the cold, blue whirlwind swirled tighter and closer, knocking his breath away, blurring his mind, clouding his vision. He panicked and ripped his black-scorched hands away from the burning ruby. Ra-Tanox flailed his arms wildly at the nothingness that was attacking his sanctuary. When the blue wind grew stronger still, Ra-Tanox again grabbed for the great ruby that hadn't been removed from its place above the forming fires since Aa-Tanox first set it in place. He squeezed the scarlet jewel and again the flames of Tanox screamed upward and surrounded the Fire Ruby of Molock. He forced all of his thoughts and power into lifting the ruby from its stone-forged pedestal but the translucent crystal refused to release its tight hold on its ancient resting place. Higher, still higher, the flames shrieked their power of resistance. Ra-Tanox screamed his physical agony and mental anguish at the blue swirl as it continued above and around him, dancing its antagonism at the screaming leader.

As suddenly as it had appeared the blue-lighted wind vanished from the sacred chamber. Ra-Tanox again screamed his frustration as he continued his futile effort to remove the great ruby. Ra-Tanox had once before tried to remove the crown jewel from its flame-shrouded pedestal, knowing that with the Fire Ruby of Molock held strong in his grasp he could finally destroy any who might oppose his power. But with the blue wind now gone, also absent was the threat that would provide him the needed strength to remove the weapon. Quickly, and against the screams and threats he spewed, Ra-Tanox could feel the ruby reset itself even tighter atop its inferno-seared stone pedestal.

With the strength of Ra-Tanox wasted to nothingness, he removed his grip from the jewel as strings of fire-blackened hand skin remained firmly attached to their translucent scarlet surface.

Again, he screamed in agony and defeat, knowing now that he was not to be the one who could control the ruby's fabled powers of battle. For one last moment the Inferno of Tanox belched its victory flames around and high above the jewel, turning Ra-Tanox's skin remnants to seared black powder. The blackened skin shot upward on the rising wave of the fire's own heat, leaving the jewel sparkling in its original brilliance. Ra-Tanox screamed once more, racing from the chamber as his long robe flowed behind him, its wide and full sleeve ends still smoldering. Outside, two soldiers watched in horror as Ra-Tanox disappeared down the long, dark corridor.

CHAPTER FOURTEEN

Time had passed quickly for Zennan and Meeshannette in this strange land. The icy, cold fingers of winter were now eagerly scratching away at autumn's crimson needles and golden leaves of papold vines and greenspar trees. Each day's light became shorter as a cold and evil darkness known only in stories and fables of ancient times settled across the lands. Huddled together in a cave as old as the one in which he had last spoken to Greshem, Zennan and Meeshannette spoke of times known only from stories rarely repeated and then told only by the eldest of talltalists. As their words filtered through the cave's damp air, echoing from the curved stone walls, an earthy wind pushed its way into the empty space that surrounded the two travelers.

Meeshannette stirred the soupcurdle that nearly overflowed the ragged edge of the rusted iron pot that warmed in the glowing fire coals. She looked around as the infiltrating wind stirred the glowing ambers.

"It is nothing to fear," Zennan said, as he slowly stood up from his crouched squat. He looked around, watching as the wind worked its way wide around them. "This is not the blue wind that has met me in my travels," he said. "This one is different, yet it seems peaceful enough.

"Peace, I fear, is something we and our future child will never know," Meeshannette answered. She stopped stirring long enough to sniff at the air. "Perhaps we should not remain in this place any longer. This is not where people should live, hiding in the darkness, avoiding the light that could lead us to our goal."

Zennan looked down at Meeshannette. "Do not speak of leaving, not at this time," he said softly. "There is a messenger who must come and speak of the secrets of the power that fuels the Castle Krog and the darkness of Ra-Tanox."

"Perhaps your messenger shall arrive soon and will bring you that knowledge which you seek," she said, hopefully.

"The knowledge I seek, I fear it comes not from any single messenger, for there is too much which is needed to take us from this cave and through to the light that lies beyond the darkness of Tanox." Zennan watched as Meeshannette filled the hollowed gourd bowl and handed it to him. He cautiously pushed the steamy liquid to his lips and slurped its warmth into this body. His eyes moved away from the bowl as the wind once again pushed itself around the cave, then just as quickly subsided.

Meeshannette looked kindly at Zennan. "I can feel your newly planted seed growing each day. Our child will surely be strong and able," she said.

"Perhaps it would be better for our child if we did not continue toward the darkness of the great castle," Zennan offered. "Your first child was lost beneath the darkness of the castle. I do not wish ours to become another victim of the powers of Tanox."

Meeshannette did not drop her head in sadness, but instead kept her head raised high. "Saddened I certainly am, and always will be. But that child was created by evil and died by the hand of evil." A slight smile came across her face, but still the sadness showed. "More important than the two of us, or of my lost child," she continued, "is our coming child. I do not wish for him to live under the wall of darkness that has suffocated our people for an eternity. All will surely die if the chains of darkness are not removed," Meeshannette said, solemnness filling her voice. "Already we have delayed our return by many passing moons as we await the arrival of our child."

"You are certainly right. I have been delayed by events from seeking my ultimate destiny." He looked directly into Meeshannette's eyes. "Then we continue now, rather than wait until after our son's birth as we had planned?" Zennan asked.

"We must. Our child is still small enough inside me that our son-to-be will remain safe as he grows strong and wise." She gently rubbed the small bump of her stomach. Meeshannette smiled, touching Zennan's outstretched hand. She then filled a bowl with the bubbling soupcurdle for herself.

Zennan continued to smile, appreciating the strength and determination that weaved its way deep throughout Meeshannette's sinew, but the smile remained only on the outside. Inside he knew that without the messengers that Wun and Wuntu had promised would come, their lives would not be long and healthful. He placed his hand gently on Meeshannette's shoulder, and she tilted her head to rub her cheek across the strength that held her. "We have remained this cave's captive for too long," he said. We shall depart the darkness of this prison-cave at daybreak."

"Yes," she answered. "I will happily leave this depressing place for whatever destiny's fate shall place before us."

* * *

The sun's faltering light spread westward and the eastern shadows became increasingly longer, finally encompassing the darkness of night. The moon did not shine the first night of winter as the clouds drifted through the darkening sky, high above the open courtyard of the Castle Krog. Safely hidden by the night's darkness, the first of the fur creatures popped out of the well and scampered across the black courtyard of cobbles, stopping behind the wall of the groghollow. More followed and soon whispers passed among them as they squatted beneath the open window listening to the soft sounds of conversation that drifted through the tattered curtains and across the courtyard. A quick and successive round of agreeable nods sent one of the three climbing upon the shoulders of his two friends, where he teetered momentarily until catching his balance against the windowless window's sill. Carefully and slowly the smallish fur creature pushed the curtain aside very slightly and poked his snub nose through so his sensitive night eyes could peer into the darkened gathering place.

Inside, four dozen cityfellows sat about the scattered tables and stools, slurping and sipping from their brew flagons, their eyes cast down in furtive conversations of whimsy and warnings. The groghollow tender was the first to see the squinting eyes reflected in the dim light of the burning candles and flickering glow from the lanterns filled with papold vine oil. Quickly, he looked around and saw what he had hoped to see, that no one else had yet noticed the strange fur intruder. Casually, he raised a tray of filled and foam-dripping flagons over his head and wandered to the table nearest the window. The table's cityfellows looked up quickly from their game of doms long enough to welcome the replacement of their dry flagons.

"It is good that you return to our table," the youngest of the stool sitters said to the tender.

"Tonight is a night of much talk and more drinking," the tender said. "I work myself much too hard for such little appreciation from the likes of you." He laughed and they laughed with him. "Perhaps you should be home with your wives and children rather than spending your nights here with the likes of me?" The tender glanced quickly at the window in time to see the fur creature's finger stick itself through the curtain and motion for him to come outside. The tender finished setting the flagons before the cityfellows, and then slowly meandered his way around the other tables. At the doorway, he placed the tray on an empty table and quickly stepped outside allowing the door to close behind him.

What the tender hadn't noticed was the stranger whose head lay upon a wooden table top, but whose partially opened eyes had followed his movements. The stranger moaned a low groan and slowly raised his head, then stood, bracing himself on the bench for a short moment before heading to the doorway himself. Before he could reach it though, he was surprised by an initially unseen long arm that reached out and grabbed his sleeve. The stranger instinctively pulled away from the unexpected grasp, but the hand that held him had expected such a movement and was easily strong enough to maintain its grip.

"Who are you who dares hold the arm of a stranger?" the stranger demanded of his captor.

"You should not impose yourself in matters best left to others," demanded the deep voice from beneath the dark-caped hood.

"I am not one who is accustomed to being ordered about by pitiful cityfellows such as yourself," the stranger replied, again unsuccessfully attempting to pull his arm out of the caped one's grasp.

The caped one stood from his stool, towering over the stranger. The stranger reacted by stopping his efforts to pull himself free of the caped one's grasp.

"You were heading outside," the caped one said. "If you should continue on your way, I think it best that I accompany you."

"If you knew who I was, you would not be so free with your demands," the stranger said, adding needed authority to his voice.

The caped one released his grasp on the stranger's arm. "As you wish. Certainly I did not mean to anger one so powerful and important as yourself," he said, his voice laced with sarcasm. "You should continue on your way, and I should certainly apologize for my unthoughtful and unwarranted actions."

The stranger did not have time to deal with the insolence of this taller-than-normal, yet pitiful cityfellow. Following the actions of the groghollow's tender demanded his more immediate attention. "You are commanded to wait here until I return. I have words that must be said, for I am a trusted soldier and the personal confidant of Commander Lakat," the stranger said.

"Better, I will follow you outside and allow myself to remain within your view as you complete what business it is you have in the night air."

The stranger looked up at the darkness that filled the hooded covering of this cityfellow's cape. "Remain near, but not so close as to impede my needs, caped one." He opened the door and walked outside, with the hooded one following several paces behind him.

At the window, the fur creature had remained long enough to watch for unwanted followers. He witnessed the two strangers and watched as they left through the groghollow's front door. He dropped to the ground when the tender rounded the outside corner where the three fur creatures stood.

Shaking his stubby finger at the fur creatures, the tender strode quickly to them, his words coming even more rapidly. "I have warned you not to poke your pug noses into my business. What if someone saw you? Then what am I to do? Surely no cityfellow would drink my brewgrog if they thought for even an instant that creatures such as yourselves were lurking about."

The fur creature who had been looking in the window spoke. "I believe, yes I do, that if you were seen speaking directly to any of our kind that your place of gathering and brewgrog drinking would suffer an even more dramatic loss of face and cityfellows."

"Certainly it would," the groghollow tender agreed, satisfied that he had made his point so clearly.

"Then perhaps we should speak our business quickly," the creature said, as his two companions remained silent, partially hiding themselves behind the one more bold. "But," he continued, "so as not to let the stranger see us together, a stranger who is no stranger to us, but the confident of Commander Lakat, and who is about to come around that corner, I suggest that we quickly conclude our business."

"I have told you before and I will tell you the same again, I have no business with you and your kind. Now, be gone and do not return."

"We have need of your premises after you close."

"No, you cannot tonight."

"We will be here soon after your last customer staggers away, and we will have friends who must not be seen, even by yourself."

The tender stubbornly put his hands to his hips. "I said, no."

"So we ask that you leave your door open and only two small candles burning when you depart for your sleeping chambers," the creature continued, not listening to the tender's refusals. "Now the stranger approaches, so we will be gone, until tonight, good sir." And they disappeared.

"Ahhhh," groaned the tender. "I should not allow myself to be played the fool by such pitiful creatures."

"And what creatures are playing you for a fool, groghollow tender?" came the voice of the stranger as he stepped around the corner.

Startled, the tender nervously reached for several pieces of cut greenspar tree that lay stacked upon a large pile of fuel. "I . . . I . . . ," he stuttered. "I am referring to those cityfellows who expect me to pour them more brewgrog than they wish to pay for, and demand that I keep the hollow warmer than they are able to keep their own living places."

"Are you certain that is what you were mumbling about to yourself? Or do I detect the faint stench of those crude fur creatures that have suddenly discovered passages from their ancient dungeon prison?"

The tender sniffed the air, and he too could smell the scent of the creatures. "I have no nose for such odors as you speak. Fur creatures are found only in the imaginations of cityfellows who have come under the spell of my better and more potent brews."

The stranger looked carefully into the darkness, but it was already too late. The fur creatures had tumbled their way down the well and back to their dungeon, awaiting the night's later hour that would again bring them and others of similar interests safely from their hiding places. "You should return to your customers before they make themselves more at home and help one another to free flagons of your liquid ambers and golds."

"Thus, I shall." The tender hesitated a moment, then added: "Will you honor me and my place of business and be my guest for a house drink for your kindness and concern over my safety, dear stranger?" the tender asked.

"Perhaps I will avail myself of your hospitality on another night," the stranger said, much to the tender's relief. "Now I have my own business which I must complete, so it is a good night that I must offer to you, tender."

"And also to you, a good night, stranger," the tender said, as he started to head back around to the front the groghollow.

The stranger stopped his own retreat for a moment. "You said that you came back here to get fuel for your fireplace."

The tender was caught off guard, but thought quickly. "Yes, yes, that is what I said. But I have decided to let those inside drink more of my brew if they wish to stay warm, rather than me burning my precious fuel to keep their blood flowing," he answered, hoping his voice held a convincing edge.

"Such is the way of our people," the stranger said. He turned back and continued on his way, quickly disappearing into the darkest shadows where the second stranger had remained, out of sight.

"Whew," the tender mouthed, then continued on inside, no longer thinking about the stranger's words.

Throughout the remainder of the night, the tender worked nervously, knowing that he would have to allow the fur creatures inside once the last of his customers had departed. And, they possessed an uncanny ability to know when that time came. It was something that the tender had always wondered about, ever since the first time he inadvertently returned inside his groghollow after closing one night and found the creatures frolicking and cavorting all around. They were not drinking his brewgrog, much to the tender's relief. It was that first night, not long after the escape of Meeshannette from the grasp of the Grand Black Sorcerer and his soldiers, that the creatures first appeared in his hollow. The fierce appearance that the creatures were able to produce on command frightened the tender into ignoring them and their activities, especially since they were doing neither himself nor his groghollow harm. As happened that first night, each time the creatures had chosen to use the groghollow for whatever business it was that they occasionally conducted, in the morning everything was cleaner and neater than the tender could make it himself. So, he chose to ignore them again this night, although the stranger's sudden interest and suspicion made him nervous.

Later than normal, the groghollow's door closed behind the last two cityfellows as they stumbled out into the night's darkness. Even before the tender could gather his bag and blow out the candles and lamps, the first of the fur creatures emerged from a dark corner, surprising the tender. "Leave but two candles burning."

"How did you get in here so quickly and quietly," he asked the intruder.

"There are always more ways than one knows for solving a puzzle," said a voice behind the tender. Startled, the tender turned around and flinched backward. Standing on his bar was Wun, a strange creature the tender had never before heard or seen.

"It is only by asking that one is able to discern alternatives to the way we have become accustomed to viewing all that surrounds us," came a second and similar voice.

Again, the tender turned toward the strange voice, this time to face Wuntu sitting atop an unopened barrelkeg of brewgrog. The tender put his hands over his eyes. "I do not wish to know who you are, creatures of the night. Each moon change seems to drag new and different strangers into my groghollow, and each time they seem to grow more different from the cityfellows I have known all my life."

"Such is the way of time," Wuntu said.

"And such is the way of life. Always, it is time that brings to our lives those changes that we least expect or desire," Wun added in agreement.

"And ultimately, it is time that we battle because it is time that brings change. I fear it is a perpetual battle that none can ever hope to win," Wuntu said.

With his hand partially covering his eyes, the tender backed away from the visitors. Before he could escape to the small hovel room located behind his brewhollow where he lived his life, more fur creatures appeared, he knew not how. "I am taking my leave now and trust that when I appear in the late morn to begin my new day, that you and your signs will not be here and that I can continue as if you never existed," the tender pleaded.

Wuntu hopped down from the keg and joined Wun atop the bar. "Maybe we should tell him," Wuntu said.

"Maybe that is not wise at this time," Wun responded.

Wuntu scrumpled his nose in sudden contemplation. "Maybe," he agreed, but without complete commitment.

"Maybe not?" Wun inquired, noting his uncertainty.

The tender's curiosity was now properly piqued. "You will be gone and never return, all of you," he demanded. "I have had enough of your activities. If the soldiers of Ra-Tanox were to suspect or even think about suspecting me of harboring such creatures as yourselves, I would spend the remainder of my very short life in the rumored Chamber of Voices."

"The Chamber of Voices?" Wun queried.

"A place that is not known to us, I'm afraid," Wuntu said, picking up a half empty flagon and sniffing, then sipping the amber liquid it held.

"I'm afraid that we know little or nothing about such a place," the tender explained. "When family, friends and others are taken inside the inner castle, only rumors return."

Finally, the fur creature, still sitting quietly in the dark corner, spoke, bringing all attention to himself. "The chamber exists," he said simply.

"Such a fact confirmed is not surprising," the tender said, finally dropping his hands from his eyes, no longer attempting to separate himself from the strangers who were slowly filling his groghollow. "It is my own brother who once, it was untruthfully said, spoke forbidden words about Ra-Tanox. He was dragged in chains into the castle, never again to return." The tender lowered his saddened eyes for a moment in thoughtful contemplation and remembrance of this lost brother. When finally he looked up, the tender had a special gleam in his eyes. "If there is something that I may do that will aid your plans, I am willing to do that and more," he said having a complete change of heart.

"Such are the feelings of many when they finally recall the hard memories that they have unsuccessfully driven from their minds," Wuntu explained.

"Perhaps we shall only visit the fabled and feared chamber under much different circumstances, circumstances more to our own liking," Wun said.

"It is time to begin to set forth our hopes and plans," the small fur creature suggested.

Wun reached for the flagon that Wuntu had picked up and still held, and sipped the last remaining droplets of liquid from the clay goblet. The tender smiled a knowing smile at the two.

"The fur creatures never drink my amber brewgrog when they come here, the very best of the special ambers brewed in this land, but I see that you two have a special taste for that which temporarily fogs the lives of those who are so often experiencing personal anguish and perpetual pain," the tender said.

"It is sad that what we must discuss here tonight does not lend itself to the happiness that your brewgrog should be allowed to bring," Wun said.

"But happiness is what we shall return to our land and our people, so there is little reason not to taste the smallest bit of the happiness that we seek," Wuntu pleaded, holding the empty flagon out to the tender.

The tender laughed as he took the flagon, quickly filled it and returned it to Wuntu. "I think that maybe one who is happy can better plan the future of our land," he said, fully believing his words. He looked around the room where at least a dozen more fur creatures had silently and surreptitiously entered and quietly settled into the darker corners, not fully illuminated by the two lone candles that remained burning on each end of the long center table. The tender, realizing finally that the entry door was partially open, raced around two tables and pushed it closed, dropping the locking bar into place.

Everyone present gathered around the longest of the carved wooden tables in the groghollow, some sitting on the short benches, others on small stools, and still a few perched atop the table's well-worn surface. Before even one word was spoken among them, there was a quick and loud series of crashes against the outside door. The tender's face flashed panic, but he was the only one of the gathering creatures who reacted. All others seemed to have expected the late arriving visitor. Quietly, a single fur creature walked to the door and carefully raised the locking bar and slowly opened the door a small crack. He squinted into the outside darkness, but saw nothing. Opening the door wider so he could push his entire head outside, the fur creature looked down both sides of the building and again saw nothing, so he closed the door and dropped the locking bar across its inside face. Shrugging his shoulders to the others, he scampered back across the room and quickly perched himself on the empty stool at the head of the table.

Again, before anyone could speak, there was a repetitive crashing on the front door. Even before the fur creature could hop down and again check the door, a violent wind swept through the room, startling the gathered fur creatures who quickly scampered around, most ending up under the table, others beneath the bar and one above in the ceiling rafters. Several of the extinguished candles suddenly burst into flames, casting their yellow-orange glow across the room. The wind's force increased, then as suddenly as it came, its whirling vanished. The quiet revealed a hooded wishtongue, the yellow glow from his eyes piercing the dim candle glow, as he emerged slowly from the tender's back storage room, a place where more times than not the tender spent his night sleeping rather than returning to his adjacent home.

"Ah, he comes," Wun said, having not moved from his perch.

"Ah, finally," Wuntu added as emphasis. He motioned at the tender. "Please, do not fear this hooded apparition that is gracing our company. Bring your best brewgrog for all."

The tender looked upon the wishtongue, a site he had never before witnessed. Fright was quickly becoming the tender's regular and unwelcome partner. The yellow-eyed wishtongue stood between himself and the perceived safety of the tender's occasional sleeping quarters. Reluctantly the tender heeded Wuntu's request for brew and began pouring several flagons overflowing with his special amber.

"Whoa, hold it, friend," Wuntu said. "Only Wun, our yellow-eyed wishtongue friend and myself can drink of your hospitality."

"Oh, yes," Wun said, hopping over and grabbing two filled flagons from the bar. "I'm afraid that if our fur creature friends here were to drink the drink that you so graciously offer to us, they would be uncontrollable."

"Oh, yes, yes, I'm afraid Wun is correct. So we will have to be sure that only the two of us help ourselves," Wuntu reassured the tender.

"And, perhaps our special guest," Wun said.

The wishtongue silently moved his way to the far end of the table and stood, waiting patiently for everyone to return to their seats. "I believe that what I must say to you tonight are not words that you had hoped would greet your ears," the wishtongue advised.

Quickly, Wun, Wuntu and the fur creatures settled down ready to listen intently to their honored guest. The tender, tentative in his movements, walked cautiously around the table and set a flagon before the wishtongue. The wishtongue, his face still protected by the veil of darkness cast by the overhanging hood, raised the amber and drank long from the flagon before setting it down hard upon the table. He looked around allowing his covered eyes to stab deeply into the minds of each of those who gathered around the table.

"I have requested your presence here tonight so that I might properly and honorably warn you of treachery that lurks around the many corners of the castle's darkness and to ask for your aid and assistance in a battle that will be only the first of many that are sure to follow," the wishtongue said in a low and ever-so-slightly melodious tone. He stood in silence for a moment as the fur creatures around the table babbled seemingly unintelligible squeals back and forth among themselves. Wun and Wuntu, already knowledgeable of the words that the wishtongue was about to share with the others, sat in silence, sipping themselves tipsy quickly and silently from their flagons.

The wishtongue drank again from his flagon before continuing his words. "I can tell you little that you don't already know," he said. "It is more that I don't tell you, or what I can't tell you, that is to be a concern for all of us." He again sat quietly awaiting assurance that he held everyone's complete attention and interest. Quickly and adequately assured, he continued: "Two great and ancient evils now battle one another for the power required to maintain the darkness that surrounds and invades our very existence. There is light, potentially a very bright light of hope, but it resides now as only a candle, a candle that unfortunately stands without the wick needed to sustain its flame."

The tender's eyes watched the creatures as they nodded their scraggle heads in accorded unison, while he himself understood none of the wishtongue's riddled meaning. He decided his best role was to refill the empty flagons that sat before the wishtongue, Wun and Wuntu. He moved quickly to do so, as smiles followed his steps.

The yellow-eyed wishtongue drank again, tugging slightly on his hood to be sure it continued to adequately shield his face. Then more words slipped slowly from his unseen lips. "Two outsiders will come here soon to free us from our chains, but they hold as their only weapon, the wickless candle. Deep within the blackness that fills the Castle Krog, there breathes the Inferno of Tanox, a fire that burns upward from the very bowels of the earth. It holds within its flames a brilliant red gemstone, a gem captured from the earth's soul, a gem possessing such powers that mortal man has thus far been unable to control its fire for his own purposes."

More hushed mumblings rippled around the table. Even the tender understood enough to know that this was not a conversation that he wished to continue hearing, yet the wishtongue's words held such compelling power that he was unable to retreat to the silenced safety of his storeroom. So, he stood silently.

A crash came again on the door. Each and every creature glanced nervously at the wishtongue as he purposely ignored the intrusion and continued his words. "The following words I say to you and wish only for your concurred agreement to provide the aid that my friend coming from a strange and far away land will need to assure success in his mighty venture."

Another crash shook the door, only this time its power was larger than before, causing the door to creak on its hinges for a moment before swinging open to reveal a second wishtongue. The fur creatures scrambled to the far side of the table and hid behind its thickness, while the tender simply allowed his weakened legs to collapse and slip him safely out of sight behind the bar. Even Wun and Wuntu took refuge behind the brewgrog kegs stacked at the end of the bar. The new wishtongue ambled inside, alone. One of the fur creatures quietly slipped behind the wishtongue and closed the entry then quickly and quietly slipped around behind the bar.

The seated, yellow-eyed wishtongue stood to meet the newly arrived wishtongue. But they did not clasp hands in the ancient ritual manner of meeting wishtongues. Instead, they merely paced around in a half circle, face to face, their eyes locked as tightly as their minds.

"What say you?" the first wishtongue asked. "Why should one such as yourself join us here tonight?"

"It is my right, as it is properly word-written in the middle verses of the Wishtongue Parables, to avail my services to an ElderOne Wishtongue as adequate atonement for transgressions committed during the youthful times of my life," the second wishtongue explained.

The yellow-eyed wishtongue deliberately moved around behind the newly arrived wishtongue who remained still. "You have committed more than simple errors of omission and disobedience, Claydore Wishtongue. Your transgressions cost our kind much. Youth is not an excuse that a wishtongue may use for betraying our kind."

Claydore Wishtongue did not turn to face his elder. "Yet no sterner penance is prescribed, so I declare my life's allegiance to you, ElderOne, and thusly invoke forgiveness by all wishtongues."

The ElderOne moved quickly now to put himself face-to-face, hood-to-hood, with Claydore Wishtongue. The yellow brightness from his eyes flashed in anger for a long moment before he finally spoke. "The great word parables were written in an age before such treachery as yours was either known or suspected," he said with angered sadness creeping into his voice. Fur creature heads began to pop up from their hiding places to view the encounter. "Yet, I, unlike you, am bound by the ancient parables as they were originally written. Therefore, your services are accepted and your past transgressions will be forever removed from the pages of our written and unwritten chronicles."

Claydore Wishtongue pushed the hood back slightly from his head, but not far enough to show his face clearly in the darkness. "I will serve your purposes well, ElderOne of the great yellow eyes." He bowed slightly, then turned and walked to the door.

"Where is it you go, Claydore Wishtongue?" the ElderOne demanded, the power of his voice sending the fur creatures scampering back into their hiding places.

Claydore Wishtongue hesitated before answering. "I must return to my abode for a moment of thankful meditation, then move forward," he said. "I feel there is much that I will be doing for you as you attempt to end the reign of Ra-Tanox."

"It is strange that you would answer with words that describe that which has not been discussed in your presence," the ElderOne replied.

"I must take leave." Claydore said hurriedly. "Others await my company." Quickly, he opened the door and retreated into the perceived safety of the outside darkness.

The ElderOne allowed the glow from his hooded eyes to subside slightly as he returned to sit at the table stool. Slowly, cautiously, the fur creatures emerged from their many hiding places, joined by Wun and Wuntu, as the tender remained behind the bar, allowing only his nose and eyes to be exposed as he watched in dismay.

Wuntu approached and slowly tugged on the arm of the ElderOne's sleeve. The wishtongue's yellow eyes flashed their light from beneath his hooded cape. Wun, now standing beside his friend, pulled Wuntu's hand back from the wishtongue's sleeve.

"This is a time that I fear will become darker than anytime we have ever before witnessed or recorded," the ElderOne wishtongue said.

Wun pushed himself in front of Wuntu. "If we have the aid of such others as the wishtongue you called Claydore, I do not see that such darkness is destined to invade our future."

"The one called Claydore is not one who can be trusted," the ElderOne replied. "His words remain hollow and volatile as the mouth of a volcano."

The leader of the fur creatures also came forward. "We must unify our actions if we are to succeed in our fight," he said. "We have heard from our cousins who live outside the walls of the Castle Krog. They have seen the ones called Meeshannette and Zennan."

"Oh, yes," Wuntu said. "We too, have been with Meeshannette and Zennan, and we continue to see them as they move toward the castle."

"And they are soon to be with another child, one which will possess the powers that will ensure our advantage over the darkness that surrounds our lives," Wun added.

A combined rush of excitement rose from the fur creatures. They moved in closer around the table so as not to miss any of these words of good and promising news. Their leader hopped up on the table facing Wuntu, Wun and the yellow-eyed wishtongue.

"We have heard such stories before, just as our grandfathers and their grandfathers heard stories during their darkest times," the fur creature said. "But each of those times, the promises held within such rumored stories were as fleeting as the very tiniest and lightest of flyseeds in the strongest of wind storms."

The wishtongue ElderOne bowed his head, then raised himself from his stool to stand at the head of the table before all those gathered, wanting to hear more than simple words. He waited the appropriate time before speaking in order to assure that all attention was focused upon him.

"The words I speak to you this night are not the promises borne on the crest of a passing windfront," the wishtongue explained solemnly. With both his hands raised to his head, he pushed the hood back revealing a hairless head, the scalp adorned with blue, purple and red circles tattooed around great bolts of blue and gold lightning. To the staring fur creatures, the wishtongue's tattooed swirls and bolts of color appeared to run down his neck, disappearing deep into his robe.

Even Wun and Wuntu stepped back in surprise, having never seen the face and head of a wishtongue.

"Eeii," Wun said softly.

Wuntu echoed Wun's cry, quickly placing his hands across his eyes. "Eeii, I do not think it is good for anyone to witness what we are seeing," he said.

"The vision before you is not one to fear," the wishtongue assured them. "These are ancient and honorable patterns that within the wishtongue world are highly respected. Each of the symbols, the colors and the manner in which they blend, depicts a particular facet of both my past deeds and of my ancestors' past deeds."

"Your past is not what interests us now. It would be better for all if you knew our future, Wishtongue," the fur creature offered as his numerous friends chattered their agreement to his words.

"As my earlier words voiced, our future lies in the hands of one who is not yet among us, a seed that grows where its protectors suspect nothing of its powers-to-be."

Wuntu's look of curiosity crossed his face and passed to Wun. "Wun and I will again find Zennan and Meeshannette and inform them of the power that they have created between them."

"Yes," Wun agreed. "We will travel to advise our friend and his companion Meeshannette the treasure they carry. We will then help assure the new child's safety from the darkness that is certain to be its greatest danger."

"And our greatest danger," Wuntu added.

The wishtongue extended his hand toward Wun and Wuntu indicating for them to stop their words. "Your words, though well intended and always true to your thoughts, are best kept to yourselves on this particular occasion." He began to move slowly to the door. "I shall leave because it must be me who offers the needed guidance to the seed carrier who will bear their prodigy.

CHAPTER FIFTEEN

The Grand Black Sorcerer raised his eyes skyward:

*"Darkness fills hollows
created in minds
its completeness held fast
by the vice of time
Black ravens fly high
their futures unsure
wings casting long shadows
over hearts once pure
Eternity holds time
a captive of fate
its mindless face sinking
deeper into hate."*

The Grand Black Sorcerer's screamed words trailed off into momentary silence, his eyes crimson in their visceral hatred, as he pounded his spurs unmercifully deep into the bloodied flanks of his great white stallion. Crashing through the border reeds and into the swirling stream waters, the sorcerer drove his beast down upon the scrambling, dodging, running, terrified PEarlOch. But he missed. PEarlOch stumbled into a cascade that pushed him over a rounded stone and into an undercurrent that trapped and tumbled him down beneath the stream long enough to escape the crushing black hooves. Uncertain of what was suddenly happening and unsure of his most immediate fate, PEarlOch twisted his body straight under the water and pushed himself away from a water-swirled subsurface rock hard with his arms.

"This miserable creature holds the secret we seek," screamed the sorcerer. He pulled hard on his reins and turned the beast around, ready to charge back across the track he'd already trampled. All around him, his soldiers' horses blasted their way through the stream, shooting green tangling fans of water all around and over their heads creating confusion and chaos where calmness and serenity had moments before graced. But PEarlOch needed a breath, and as he surfaced, two of the sorcerer's soldiers sat upon their horses directly above him. When his closed eyes and open mouth reached air, the momentarily startled soldiers quickly recovered and grabbed the frantically flailing intruder. Holding him suspended between the two of them, they raced their mounts through the stream stopping before the Grand Black Sorcerer.

"You will be rewarded for your quick actions, my soldiers," the sorcerer announced for all his remaining army to hear. He spurred his horse slowly forward, stopping when his beast's hot breath broke across the gangly prisoner's frightened face. While the soldiers still held the struggling prisoner in midair, the sorcerer pulled his black onyx scimitar from its scabbard and pressed its icy cold point against PEarlOch's heaving chest. "There was a child set afloat upon the waters of the upper Kelto River," the sorcerer's hard voice explained. "Tell me where that child is and I may allow you to continue breathing my air. Lie to me and your future will be consumed in the eternal fires of darkness."

PEarlOch spewed swallowed water from his mouth and nose. His aimless and useless struggles against the grip of the two soldiers quickly exhausted him and he sank into a limp and hanging weight. He tried to speak, but his voice squeaked only babbled sounds.

"Let words of sense run from your mouth, squeaky one," the sorcerer prodded, sticking the point of his weapon deeper into PEarlOch's chest, forcing the first trickle of blood to run down its ebony shaft.

"The child, the child, the child," stuttered PEarlOch finally, his eyes growing wider as he sucked his chest away from the sorcerer's blade. "The child, it was but an infant, for which I could not properly care, oh great sir," he mutter in panic. "I left it with a poor and lonely, yet thankful villagefellow family, though strange they were."

"Ahhhchh," the sorcerer screamed in frustration. "And where

is this strange villagefellow, pitiful one? Tell me now or feel the coldness of my weapon as it enters your pitiful body."

"Up river, up river," PEarlOch squeaked out. "Up river, near where the great oxen bow bend nearly circles the great waters back upon themselves."

The sorcerer pulled his scimitar back from PEarlOch for a moment. "I know of no such place. And if indeed such a place does exist, why would you leave a child there alone." He placed his blade against the side of PEarlOch's exposed neck. PEarlOch tried to pull back from the slicing pressure of the blade, but the two soldiers holding him allowed no room for movement. "Enough of your useless priddle," the sorcerer cried. "I warn you, I quickly tire of those who fail to provide what I command."

At this moment, as the Grand Black Sorcerer was readying to remove PEarlOch's head from its resting place, the loudest of screams pierced the air. PEarlOch's eyes opened even wider than before as he pointed to the hillside on the bank behind the sorcerer.

"No, please, there," PEarlOch screamed, his voice now clear and concise. He pointed to what appeared to be a villagefellow dressed in strings of circling stones. "There, they appear now, the rock dwellers. They live near the villagefellow who now has the child you seek."

The blade pulled away from PEarlOch as the sorcerer turned to face the offending scream behind him. His soldiers responded similarly, even the two holding PEarlOch. They released their hold on PEarlOch in order to focus their attention and their drawn weapons on the unknown foe who approached.

"Eeiiii," each of the approaching rock dwellers screamed in high-pitched unison.

PEarlOch clasped his hands hard over his ears to escape the offending sounds, but he was too frightened to scramble away from his captors.

"Eeiiii," the lead rock dweller screamed, this time alone with his anguished cry. "We come to you, to you, to you," he rambled in the lowest and deepest of voices, in complete contrast with his shrill scream. "We have what you seek, what you seek we have, we do, we have, we do."

A slight smile spread across the sorcerer's face. "Bring my prize to me and I will allow you and your strange followers to live."

"Eeiiii." The rock dweller's scream was accompanied by a prancing, twisting, hopping dance. He stopped his voicing after the briefest moment and slithered himself slightly closer to the sorcerer, the grey stones circling his body rattling as they danced off one another. "We have what you wish to give us already, already we have life, life we have, you cannot give what we have," his voice rattled, as if the stones themselves were talking.

Immediately two of the soldiers started to charge the offending creature, but the sorcerer commanded them to stop. "Then it is your lives I will take. You have less than a breath of time left in your bodies, if you step another step closer to me," the sorcerer threatened.

Instantly the lead creature screamed and jumped back into his strange dance, still moving closer to the sorcerer. His tall, languid body was splotched in brown stains beneath the stone clothing. From a small spot on the back of his head dozens of long and braided strands of dark hair cascaded down his back and over his shoulders and down his chest.

The sorcerer dropped his raised hand and the two soldiers crashed across the last bit of stream water and attacked the aggressor. Without apparent thought, the rock dweller screamed his scream and danced his dance and expertly and effortlessly pranced wide of the charging sirocco horse soldiers' path. As they angrily wheeled their horses around to charge once more, the rock dweller stopped his dance long enough to speak.

"I have what you wish to have but have no wish to give," he said. "Try to steal and a price you must pay, pay a price you must, a price you'll pay."

The sorcerer flashed his great black scimitar, cutting it smoothly through the air. "You are wrong, indecent and foolish one," he screamed. "It is you who will pay with your pitiful life." He pointed his shimmering black blade at his soldiers. "Destroy them. Destroy them now, I command you!" He yanked his reins to keep his nervously prancing mount facing toward his newly-found enemies.

Behind the sorcerer and now free, PEarlOch crept back into the river's waters, ready to depend upon his swimming skills to remove him safely from the sorcerer's grasp. But he moved only out to where a small boulder stood overlooking the swirling deep waters beyond. From atop the modest promontory his curiosity made him remain to watch the play that unfolded before him, secure in the knowledge that from such a position he could easily escape the soldiers as their horses could not safely penetrate the deep waters beyond the boulder.

As the sirocco soldiers charged the rock dwellers, each identical, but each uniquely different, they magically danced away from danger, each separately, yet together, screaming their ear-piercing screams. Atop the boulder, PEarlOch covered his ears, hoping against hope that these weaponless creatures would remain safe. He soon realized that it was not the rock-dwelling creatures who were in danger. As the frustrated soldiers charged again and again, striking only empty air with their swords, the Grand Black Sorcerer spewed his crushing threats at them, pushing each forward again and again with faster, frantic-slashing, crashing attacks. As the rock dwellers danced, the soldiers' frustrations grew with their continued inability to destroy such defenseless and useless creatures.

Even PEarlOch began to laugh as the rock dwellers' shrill screams turned to haunting laughter, sending shivers of infuriation through to the very soul of the sorcerer. Finally, he commanded his soldiers to stop their useless attacks and they did so, nearly collapsing from their mounts in exhaustion. Then the sorcerer turned to the rock dwellers.

"Who are you?" the sorcerer commanded. "I must know who you are."

Behind him a rock dweller instantly appeared, and his voice boomed out so loud and deep as though a thousand stones tumbled from a mountain side. The sorcerer's white horse was startled into an almost overpowering nervousness. "I am but one of many, many make one," the lead creature said.

"One of many? Then where is it that so many of you live?" he asked.

"Where we live, we live, alive we are, and that is what you cannot give."

"Stop this useless rambling." Quickly the sorcerer's voice went from frantic screams to soft coercion. "Provide me with the child I seek and I shall provide you with wealth beyond your mind's thoughts," he offered.

"A child you seek, yet for what purpose do you seek a child not yours?" the rock dweller asked in return.

"This child has been lost. Its mother merely seeks its return to the warmth and safety of her breast."

"Such a worthy mission, a mission quite worthy, for a worthy purpose, your worthy mission," the rock dweller responded.

Without notice the Grand Black Sorcerer was now surrounded by the seven rock dwellers. Before he knew what to do, each rock dweller had placed his arms and twisting, clicking fingers around the sorcerer's horse. Realizing his exposed position, the sorcerer reared his horse, attempting to crash its powerful hooves down through the creatures. But the iron-clad hooves bounded harmlessly from what sounded to the still-watching eyes and listening ears of PEarlOch, as nothing different than solid stone. The sorcerer screamed more threats at the surrounding rock dwellers, but even as he did so, the stone clothing circling their bodies grew larger, their braided hair lengthening and hopelessly tangling with each of their neighbor's. Legs grew stouter and bodies taller, all turning to the gray and black of speckled stone. The sorcerer slashed his scimitar across the growing stones but the small chips he was able to remove quickly repaired themselves with thick scabs of new stone. Within moments the rock dwellers had grown so thick and close together that the Grand Black Sorcerer and his white stallion were no longer visible.

From PEarlOch's view, almost as quickly as he could draw and hold another breath, the Grand Black Sorcerer and his horse had completely disappeared, enclosed in the ever-growing, ever-strengthening, living stone prison. Even the Grand Black Sorcerer's frantic, screamed threats became muffled echoes and then strangely silent as the rock dwellers had merged into a single rock-encrusted creature, taller, wider, stronger than what they had been separately.

The Grand Black Sorcerer's sirocco soldiers, in chaotic panic, crashed away in all directions, escaping into the safety of the wilds beyond. Never had they seen or heard of such powers as these that could swallow one so powerful. Now, as smaller stones split off from the new rock that sat solidly upon the ground, PEarlOch decided it was time for him to leave. He waded back to the near shore from his boulder and quickened his pace away from the rock dwellers, back to the far village where he hoped to find the child.

* * *

Meeshannette and Zennan rounded a bend along the narrow cliff face and stopped their foot-travel in stunned silence. Before them stood the great black fortress of the Castle Krog. Instantly Meeshannette doubled over, allowing a muffled cry to escape from her lungs. Zennan's heart sank when he turned and saw Meeshannette on her knees upon the damp ground, her arms wrapped tightly around her stomach.

"What pains are causing you harm," Zennan asked as he reached for her. He placed his hands gently upon her shoulders, and slowly she looked up, her tear-filled eyes looking deeply into Zennan's.

"I fear our child is not happy with our long journey," she said, her voice remaining strong in spite of the pain she felt deep within her. She held tightly her growing belly as she tried to stand, but winced as pain shot its protest through her body.

"We will stay near here for as long as is needed," he said.

"No, we can't," she answered. "I feel that our child is repulsed by the sight that lies before our eyes. The castle's evil penetrates far beyond its black walls." Again she tried to stand, and with Zennan's careful help managed her way back to her feet.

"You are right, dear Meeshannette. The castle home of Ra-Tanox is not an appropriate first view to imprint upon our new unborn son's mind's eye," Zennan agreed. "Back along our trail, perhaps a long day of travel, there was a small spot beside the river where the bend in its water's course offers a sanctuary as beautiful and as safe as any we have visited."

Meeshannette smiled, pushing as much of the pain as she could to the back of her mind. "Yes, that is what we shall do, and our son will be better for our efforts."

Zennan looked down admiringly at Meeshannette, his arm still offering support around her shoulders. "Already the seed quickly grows large inside you," he said.

Together they turned their backs to the castle and retraced their path, yet both of their minds remained on the edge of the cliff. They traveled their earlier trail back toward the river's edge, a slow, although relatively pleasant journey, as an unseasonably warm wind blew down from the south. When finally Zennan and Meeshannette reached the Kelto River, their crossing was easy to the far side where safety more likely resided. With the new winter's rains having not yet arrived, even in the far away and high mountains, the waters of the great river flowed low around the large and small boulders scattered about its shallow bottom.

* * *

Zennan and Meeshannette lived quietly along the riverbank awaiting the birth of their child. The cold winds of winter had brought with them hard and driving rains that quickly filled the river to the top of its gravelly banks. While Meeshannette waited patiently for her child's birth, Zennan spent much of his day outside their small hut gathering dry wood for their warming and cooking fire. With the firewood supply made ample, Zennan wandered about gathering the few winter mushcaprooms and the over-crusted and dried fruits from the grove of baybird shrubs that littered the wet duff floor of the surrounding forests.

"Ooohh, I see the once mighty warrior has aged into a weak gatherer of hogpig food and goat meal leftovers," the familiar voice behind him taunted.

Zennan did not bother himself to turn around and face his antagonist, knowing that such would be useless in making the bothersome creature depart. "Your words are said in the absence of knowledge," he finally answered.

"Yes, knowledge that to do anything less for your life partner and your new child would show you to be less the warrior than you profess to be," Wuntu said, as he hopped onto a sodden and fallen log resting beside Wun.

"As always, you come well aware of my most personal business," Zennan said, plucking another of the dried fruits and dropping it into his shoulder bag. He spotted a small cluster of green mushcaprooms, those with the sour flavor of the ripe summer trimons that Meeshannette so much enjoyed. He crouched low enough to pluck the ripest of the caps, leaving the remainder to mature. "Is there a reason why you two have come to bother me once again?"

"Such a word, bother," Wun said, as he hopped up on the log and stood beside Wuntu. "You should learn to choose your words more carefully," Wuntu said.

"Why does it matter? You two choose to say and do as you please as you involve yourself in things that should not concern you," Zennan said, still not choosing to look at his two friends.

Wun and Wuntu looked at each other for a moment, then together they turned back to Zennan and spoke in perfect unison. "Our concerns are the concerns of the world," they squeaked.

Wuntu strolled down the length of the log following Zennan who walked through the damp needle duff searching for a last bit of food he would need for the evening meal. "We offer our assistance because alone we are individuals," he advised.

Zennan stopped and looked over at Wuntu. "And together?" Zennan queried him. "Together we are more?"

"No, together we are one," Wun said.

"And as one we are stronger," Wuntu added.

"And as one can we hope to fight the powers of two so evil as Ra-Tanox and his Grand Black Sorcerer?" Zennan asked. He hitched his filled carrybag up higher on his shoulder and headed back toward the hut where Meeshannette waited. As he passed through the last trees before reaching the small opening where the hut stood, a sharp scream escaped from inside the hut.

"The time is now," Wuntu said.

"Hurry you must," Wun added.

"You two aren't amusing. Meeshannette's time is still much in the future," Zennan said, knowing his words were true.

"Then amused you shall be with your newly born daughter," Wuntu chirped.

The words stopped Zennan outside the closed door to his hut. His look of surprise was unimaginable. "Daughter?" he asked, turning slowly to face his two followers. "I am the heir to great Throne of Light, upon the death of my good friend and lifelong advisor,

Greshem. It is a son that must be born of me and Meeshannette. It can be no other way," Zennan proclaimed. Another scream from inside the hut sent Zennan hurrying inside.

Chuckles of soft laughter fell from Wun and Wuntu as Zennan swung open the small wood door and was greeted by the infant cry of his new child and the strained but happy smile upon Meeshannette's face.

"It is a healthy and happy daughter we have, though much before her time," she said, holding the tiny child out to her father. "Please, take her. I'm feeling quite tired, as this child did not enter its new world as easily as the first." A quick and passing look of sadness crossed her face.

"A daughter?" Zennan mumbled.

"Yes, a daughter, strong and healthy," Meeshannette said.

Wun poked his head inside the hut. "Yes, a daughter."

"Strong and healthy," Wuntu said as his head popped inside next to Wun's.

Zennan took the child, holding her gently. "She is much smaller than . . . ," he began to say, but stopped. He looked down, into Meeshannette's eyes. "I will take our daughter to the river and bath her." The slightest hint of disappointment was carried in his voice.

"Things happen, whether they be for good or for bad, because they are destined to do such," Meeshannette said, a small wince of pain shooting through her body.

Zennan noticed the anguished look upon Meeshannette's face. "You are not well?" he asked. "Is there something I may do that will ease your pain?"

"Such pain is probably nothing more than a response by my body giving up my child earlier than was originally planned. Please, bathe our new daughter in the cleansing waters of the river, and when you return, we will choose a name that befits the daughter of a great warrior," Meeshannette said pridefully.

"And the daughter of a great queen," Zennan added. He left Meeshannette in the hut and carried his first child to the river's edge, followed closely by Wun and Wuntu. As he gently lowered the infant girl to the water's surface, a crashing beast of an unknown kind tore through the towering reeds adjacent to where he, Wun and Wuntu stood. Before Zennan could do anything, PEarlOch emerged from the brush spewing and coughing.

"Ahiee, it is the creatures who travel in darkness," PEarlOch howled when he finally looked up and saw Wun and Wuntu. His initial fear subsided but did not vanish the moment he realized that it was Zennan who stooped at the river's edge, behind the two creatures. "Zennan, my friend," he said. "It is luck and fortune that I have found you."

"Luck?" Wuntu asked.

"Fate, I believe," Wun said.

"Yes, it returns to haunt us," Wuntu responded.

"It must be fate that makes me feel that it is good to see you again," Zennan said. "Much has passed since you left our company." He set the infant into the water, and she screamed the moment the icy liquid splashed across her naked body.

Those infant screams caused PEarlOch to finally realized that it was a child Zennan held in the water. "Indeed, such be the truth," he exclaimed, confusion lacing his voice. He looked closer. "Oh, surely this is not Meeshannette's son-child." He looked closer at the child. "He is a daughter! Dear Meeshannette now has a daughter?" he questioned. "A child should not be reared in a life of wandering and adventure. And now two children?"

Zennan quickly washed the child as he answered. "PEarlOch, you have returned. It is good to see you again, but I feel saddened that you must hear such news as that which I must share."

"I see both sadness and relief in your eyes, Zennan," PEarlOch said.

Zennan tried to subdue his hidden relief that PEarlOch so easily witnessed. If PEarlOch could see his true feelings about the fortunate loss of the first child, then so might Meeshannette, thought Zennan. It would not be right for her to know the truth, at least not now. "My sadness lies in the loss of Meeshannette's first child. The joy that I feel and you see is not for the loss, but for the birth a new child moments ago, the arrival of our own . . ." he hesitated a moment, "daughter." He hesitated again before speaking his truth. "It was a son that I had hoped for; a son that would continue the Zennan family name."

"And your daughter, you feel she cannot wear your name

proudly?"

"A daughter is not a proper warrior," he said with finality. Zennan pulled his daughter from the cold river water, and instantly her screaming stopped as he quickly wrapped a small and softly woven blanket around her tiny body.

PEarlOch looked around. "Zennan, where have your two friends disappeared, although I must say that they are not missed, at least not by me."

"Ignore their comings and goings as I do, or your mind will evolve into a mash of confusion and frustration." Zennan headed back to the hut with the child. "Come, food would do you well," he said.

When the door swung open and Zennan entered, Meeshannette was lying on the straw that formed a narrow bed in the far corner of the one room. A small fire was still burning in the opposite corner in the stone circle fireplace. PEarlOch crowded in behind Zennan and quickly headed to the fire where he warmed his hands.

"Meeshannette, look who has returned."

PEarlOch waved to Meeshannette. "It is so good to see you," he said, then noticed that she didn't move. "Oohh, but you don't look so well."

Still standing near the entry door, Zennan looked more closely at Meeshannette's face. It was ashen colored, and she lay still and quiet.

Zennan stepped quickly to where his guest stood. "PEarlOch, please hold my child." Zennan pushed the infant girl into PEarlOch's chest even before he could answer, then rushed to Meeshannette's side. "Meeshannette, what is it that makes you so weak?" he asked.

She did not respond, except for a short wheezing sound that escaped through her clenched lips. Zennan slipped his hand under her head and raised it slightly. Still, she did not move. He looked down at the straw on the floor next to Meeshannette. A small pool of blood had formed and a quick trickle continued to swirl it larger.

"No," Zennan yelled. "Do not let it be so." He pulled the roughly woven blanket back from Meeshannette. Birthing blood still spilled from her ashen body. One last gasp left her lips, and she was quiet. Only the soft whimpering cry of her daughter broke the silence that filled the hut.

"Sadly, it is so," Wun murmured as he and Wuntu appeared together standing next to the fire.

"Sadly, yes," Wuntu agreed.

"Tis a sad, sad day, it is," PEarlOch added, no longer showing fear and disgust for the two creatures. He turned and walked from the shanty hut, followed by Wun and Wuntu. Wuntu closed the door, leaving Zennan, Meeshannette and their newborn daughter alone.

As darkness began to fall, Wuntu, Wun and PEarlOch sat together near the edge of the river watching the fading light trace its last footsteps of the day as reflections across the rippling water. PEarlOch thought he was the first to notice it, but both Wun and Wuntu had already been aware of the orange light flickering dimly through the twist of branches and reeds.

"The hut, it is ablaze," PEarlOch said, as he leaped up from his rock seat and pointed.

It was only a short moment later that Zennan emerged from the hut, his body silhouetted by the hut-fueled flames that suddenly shot high into the air. He carried his new daughter with him, walking slowly, silently past his three witnesses.

The night moved slowly, purposely delaying room for dawn's light. It was near the first light of dawn that PEarlOch made the suggestion, but Wun and Wuntu would not agree that they should view the remnants of the hut.

"Peering curiously at the ashes of one such as Meeshannette is not a responsible way to show our respect for one so brave," Wuntu said. He turned his back to the slight hint of smoke that still rose from the hut's ashes.

"We must turn our backs to show respect for the deceased," Wun said.

"And we must not dwell upon that which has already passed, but move forward to reach our ultimate destiny." Zennan's voice sounded strong and clear coming from the direction of the cindered hut. He walked toward his three friends, carrying his small child. "For the past we cannot change; it is the future that awaits our actions." He stood now, surrounded by Wuntu, Wun and PEarlOch. "It is time that I name my daughter. It must be a name that reflects the wisdom and bravery of her mother," he said.

"Yes, a name worthy of a mother so great will be difficult to find," PEarlOch thought out loud.

"And a name befitting her mother's wondrous beauty," Wuntu insisted.

"And a name befitting the child's own wondrous beauty," Wun said.

"And her great spirit," Wuntu said.

"And her spirit, of course," Wun agreed.

Zennan stood alone, his friends around him, listening to the soft breathing of his daughter as she slipped into a light sleep. In a voice as quiet as the morning air, he spoke. "The spirit of Meeshannette lives in her daughter."

"Then Spirit she should be," Wun offered.

"Spirit," would be a name appropriate," Wuntu purred.

Spirit opened her eyes, slightly at first then wide-eyed as her father gently touched her nose. Zennan looked deeply into the sparkle that shone from his daughter's turquoise eyes. "Yes," he said. "Spirit is truly a name that would serve my daughter well and remind me equally of her mother's quality, beauty and spirit."

PEarlOch smiled his best smile. "Yes," he said while looking at the infant in Zennan's powerful arms. "It is spirit that moves all that is worth moving." He caught Zennan's eye for a moment. "Perhaps it is best if Spirit lives with those who are better able to care for her," he said.

Now Zennan's full attention turned to PEarlOch, but it wasn't a favored look that passed his eyes. It was one of irritation and one that PEarlOch immediately sensed.

"You are right, of course," Zennan said reluctantly, although the look on his face did not leave. "It is my spirit which must serve to protect my Spirit," he said. "I cannot provide that which must be provided for one so young and helpless while seeking the light which our kind has for too long awaited and justly deserved." Now Zennan looked kindly upon PEarlOch. "You, my friend, are thinking of only the best for Spirit. It is necessary that she be protected."

"Perhaps there will be a time when Spirit is not the one who will need to be protected," Wuntu said.

"Her spirit will one day grow even stronger than Meeshannette's," Wun said.

"So it will be," Wuntu said.

Zennan kissed Spirit on her forehead then pushed her gently to PEarlOch. "My friend, you must take Spirit safely to the home of Faro, her grandfather, the father of Meeshannette. Then they can properly mourn for their daughter while basking in the light created by Meeshannette's Spirit."

PEarlOch bowed his head as he took Spirit into his own arms. She whimpered slightly, then smiled as her tiny hands reached for his protruding nose. He teased her for a moment moving his face back and forth before letting her grasping fingers touch his face.

"I will do as you ask as though your wishes were commands that I as your servant soldier must carry out without hesitation," PEarlOch whispered confidently. "Already I have placed another lost infant with a wanting family."

"Your intentions are true and your word I trust," Zennan answered. "Go now, before the clear thoughts that now course through my mind are changed to less thoughtful wishes absent of wisdom."

As PEarlOch turned to leave with his entrusted treasure, he was suddenly stopped by Zennan's powerful command.

"Stop, my friend! You say you have placed another infant? How could this be so?"

"So true sir. I found a tiny and bruised child floating in a broken log below the Falls of Kelto, not yet nursed from its missing mother.

"No!" screamed Zennan. "This cannot be so!"

Fear covered PEarlOch's face, not knowing why his friend was so angered. "Was it wrong to save such an innocent creature?"

Zennan slowly softened his face of pained anguish. "No, such an act is never wrong," he assured his friend. "May I ask what became of this lost child?"

"As with your daughter Spirit, I could not care for a child so tiny and needy of a mother's breast. I discovered a lonely villagefellow family living near a band of very strange rock creatures who happily took the child as their own." PEarlOch wished to begin his journey with Spirit, but waited patiently as Zennan thought about what he must do.

"Where is it that this village family lives, my friend?"

"That is the same question that the evil sorcerer asked of me. It is near the river's great ox bow."

"You visited a sorcerer?" Fear now crossed Zennan's entire being.

"Sir, he came upon a great white horse with his soldiers. He threatened to remove my head from its current place of honor if I did not share with him this information."

"And he now has this child?"

"No my friend, as far as I know the child is safe. The sorcerer attacked those very strange rock creatures and they easily defeated him and his soldiers. They turned him to stone, both the sorcerer and his horse, while his soldiers fled in fear."

"And of this you are certain, my trusted friend?"

"Of this I am as certain as I stand here breathing."

Zennan waved to PEarlOch. "Then take your leave my friend and ensure the safety of my daughter, Spirit."

PEarlOch nodded and quickly departed for the village of Faro.

CHAPTER SIXTEEN

Zennan found the bluff where he and Meeshannette had last viewed the Castle Krog. Here, quietly and alone, he sat with his back to a small warming fire, staring hard into the still darkness that encircled him. Above his head small dingerbats darted through the blackness, spearing flying night insects that dove toward the flickering scratches of light created by his fire's tiny flames. Through an oval opening in the distant castle's center tower Zennan saw another light flicker for a moment. It subsided quickly then reflashed its power several times as Zennan continued his observation. Following the fifth and final flash of light from inside the tower Zennan felt a force appear suddenly behind him. Although he knew it was there, he did not react, knowing that its power was benign, at least regarding him.

"Ah, Wishtongue, your timing is as it always is," Zennan said, without moving his eyes from the castle below.

"It was only as I promised you in your age melding ceremony," the ElderOne Wishtongue explained. "I come and stand before you bearing a warning that must be given, if success is to accompany your journey to the castle of Ra-Tanox."

"Your words I have awaited for a lifetime, Wishtongue."

"As the ElderOne Wishtongue, it has been a lifetime filled with the joys of life and a time filled with the tragedies of life," he replied.

Finally, Zennan turned to face the ElderOne Wishtongue, knowing that he must grasp the true meaning of the words that were to be spoken and spoken only once. "I was never certain, but always suspected that you were the ElderOne Wishtongue. I shall not wonder why you have waited so long to share with me awareness of your esteemed social status, but I now especially await the welcome sounds of your wisdom, ElderOne," he said, truthfully.

The ElderOne walked closer to the fire. "As the ElderOne, my life is a life wrought with signs, signs that must be constantly watched for their ever-changing meanings and those meanings debated until their truths are discovered," he said, as Zennan listened intently. "One of those signs was visited upon us by the fringed wisp of the blue wizard's passing cape. His words told of a power that once lived where the light of life shined down upon all the peoples of our world. But," he quickly added, "that was a time that existed long before you or your remembered ancestors lived."

Zennan looked thoughtfully at the ElderOne, yet hesitation was discernible in his voice. "Many of these same words I have heard from others, from lesser wishtongues and talltalists who still lurk in the dark corners of our homeland, maintaining the word histories that so many of my people now perceive as mere hollow stories without meaning."

"And you? Are your thoughts also filled with doubt about the words of those shadow characters who live without living?"

"Perhaps, but less so than many of those who retold their stories to me ever doubted."

"Your hesitation . . ."

"Is not uncertainty," Zennan finished, his voice now assured, "but concern for where you may decide to place yourself within my plans to restore light where darkness supports only death." Zennan thought for a moment, as the ElderOne remained silent. Finally, "The Blue Wizard, he came to me occasionally upon my leaving, but the seasons have changed many times since he last chose to emerge from his own secret darkness. And even when he did appear early in my quest, he chose to remain mostly obscured behind the changing winds and flickering lights of his riddled words," Zennan said.

"He is one who chooses his own time and place," the ElderOne explained. "Your two friends, those you call Wun and Wuntu, have the power to transfer the thoughts and desires of the Blue Wizard to you, as they have done on many occasions."

"Tis true," Wun said, suddenly appearing in the small opening through the scrag trees.

"Tis more than true," Wuntu chimed happily, also stepping from the shadowed trees.

"We are with you," Wun said.

"Only at the personal request of the one you call the blue wizard," Wuntu said.

Wun scratched his chin. "Though his true name be more noteworthy than simply the Blue Wizard."

"And we now have become one with you and your mission," Wuntu said.

A broad smile came across Zennan's face, and his voice returned to its melodic tone for the first time in a very long while. "I welcome you, Wun and Wuntu, into my family. I should have done so a great while ago, as your wisdom was greater than mine and your sharing of such knowledge was always done without need for personal gain."

"Yet, our mutual friends and I did indeed gain much from you and your actions, as did all those who remain dependent upon you to retrieve the Fire Ruby of Molock from its forged stone pedestal," the ElderOne explained.

Zennan looked confused, and his melodic voice tones ended as quickly as they had begun. "Of all the words said to me throughout my life by talltalists and others, none ever mentioned or even whispered words about a Fire Ruby of Molock."

"Oh, yes, the Fire Ruby," Wuntu chirped.

"Yes, yes, Molock, of course. Such words could not have been said then because then we did not know such words existed," Wun said.

"It is only most recently that we have discovered its existence," Wuntu added.

"And still more recently that we discovered where it lay hidden," Wun said.

The ElderOne grew more serious. "The strange and small fur creatures freed by Meeshannette revealed to her that they had discovered the secret power that the Tanox dynasty had kept hidden deep within the Castle Krog since the very beginning of the darkness."

"Meeshannette?" Zennan questioned. "She told me very little about her capture and escape. She is the one responsible for revealing such a long lost power?"

"Oh, yes," Wuntu said.

"Oh, yes, oh yes," Wun echoed.

Zennan kicked at his small warming fire, stirring its remaining coals back into a sudden but short-lived flame. He looked at his friends, thinking, waiting, as flickering light momentarily illuminated their bespectacled and furry faces, then quickly returned to shadowed darkness. "Always before, if I didn't understand the words of one of the learned ones, I could ask another to interpret for me and thus they would not suspect my ignorance." Zennan hesitated. "But now, my ignorance does not allow me the luxury of waiting to discover from others in another time what I must know now."

"Ask your question, Zennan," the ElderOne advised. "In those inquiring days of your youth, we often found amusement in trying to confuse your thoughts by providing only the smallest pieces of a puzzle, our way of testing your mind, developing your intuition, pushing your imagination."

Zennan appeared slightly surprised. "So, it was trickery then? Your trickery? And now?"

"Now there exists an absence of our need to trick, confuse and expand your mind. The ways of our past must change, as we all must change before the power of the Fire Ruby."

"Surely, it is true that the power of a great warrior's sword might transfer its strength into the arms of another worthy of its power. But what is it that the Fire Ruby of Molock possesses that could change the structure of our world?"

"Ooohh, my, he asks questions never before asked," Wuntu whispered to his furry friend.

"My, yes," Wun answered. "A question that demands an answer, but an answer as yet undiscovered."

Zennan eyed the ElderOne suspiciously. "Is there truth in the words of these two annoying, but worthy creatures of insight?"

"Although one's own truth may indeed be true, one's truth is not necessarily another's truth," the ElderOne acknowledged.

"Then the power that is suspected of this mysterious Fire Ruby, does it necessarily exist?"

"Oh, exist it does," the ElderOne assured him. "Exist, yes, it surely does exist, but it is a power not fully understood. Not by Ra-Tanox nor by his ancestors, all of whom failed to fully grasp and control its forces, or certainly it would have been used against us long before now."

Wun and Wuntu stepped into the dim flicker of light released by the glowing coals and pushed several dry branches into the fire. Soon, flames had again flared as the newly sacrificed wood fodder ignited.

Zennan eyed his two small friends and their work for a moment, allowing his eyes to follow several of the brightest sparks as they spiraled skyward, and then he looked back at the ElderOne. "And how shall I use this Fire Ruby, if I should choose to set it free and I am successful in removing this gem from the darkness that has obscured it since before our earliest time?"

"Once freed from the dungeon of darkness it is said that its light will guide your actions," the ElderOne explained. "Only be sure that the power of the light that shines from the Fire Ruby shines its color true."

"Mystical words of warning? Why do you speak in riddles, ElderOne?"

"My words are heard by you as riddles only because the answers are not as easily forthcoming as the questions that are asked."

"And your questions?"

The ElderOne lowered his head, his mind temporarily lost deep in thought. His eyes closed as he raised his head again. "My questions are the same as yours, my friend." He opened his eyes to peer deeply into Zennan's. "The path to winning the Fire Ruby of Molock, and thus forever ending the power of the Principles of Tanox, is a path strewn with danger and laced with peril."

"Such as been my way since leaving the cave of Greshem."

"That was a lifetime ago," the ElderOne said.

"Two lifetimes ago," Zennan corrected, sadness entering his eyes. "My journey cost Meeshannette her life, and our child is being taken to a place far from me and far from my home."

"It was necessary that your daughter be carried to a place of safety where she may be allowed to grow and learn, much as you did during your early years. For she is the one spirit possessing powers that are destined to exceed all others. For if you should fail in your journey to free the Fire Ruby of Molock, then such a task shall someday be your daughter's task." The ElderOne did not blink his eyes, just as Zennan did not remove his stare from the ElderOne.

"My daughter, Spirit, certainly possesses powers that coalesced and amplified themselves as a result of the joining of Meeshannette and myself," Zennan said. "But, it is not my wish nor my intention that she should be hobbled with the responsibility of doing what her father might possibly be unable to accomplish." Zennan's voice again grew melodic in tone. "It is my intention to accomplish all that needs to be accomplished, free that which needs to be freed, relight the light that must be reignited."

"Warnings," Wuntu said.

"Oh yes, warnings and cautions," Wun said.

"Yes, I nearly forgot the cautions," Wuntu added. He and Wun looked to the ElderOne for a response.

"It is not a warning that I am able to give," the ElderOne said.

"Then it will be we who shall offer such warnings," Wun said.

"Yes, we are not chained to such ancient structures of order," Wuntu said, not wishing to anger or disappoint the ElderOne.

The light flashed once again through the window of the distant castle, catching Zennan's eye. He allowed his thoughts to gather for a moment before looking back at the ElderOne. "What special warning is it that you cannot tell me about?" he asked.

The ElderOne turned away from Zennan and began to walk slowly toward the nearest shadows. As he did, Wun tugged on Zennan's arm to garner his attention. Zennan looked down at his friend. "Are you going to reveal this secret so dreaded that even the ElderOne is unable to speak or hear what must be revealed?" Zennan asked Wun.

"We reveal only what we know," Wuntu said.

"Yes, only what we know," Wun agreed. He looked at Wuntu, who nodded his affirmation. "So," Wun continued, "we . . ."

"But," Zennan interrupted, "there is the one known as the Grand Black Sorcerer, the one who originally kidnapped Meeshannette and still pursues us."

"Oh, no," Wun chuckled. "He no longer is a concern. Been gobbled by rock dwellers."

"Oh, yes, the sorcerer is the permanent guest of the earth's stones. No longer a bothersome creature of darkness."

"Then it is true what my friend PEarlOch has said," Zennan said under his breath.

"Oh, yes, tis true, but still there is one called Claydore," Wun revealed.

"A wishtongue whose early days were days and nights filled with deceit," Wuntu said.

"Deceitful lies," Wun continued, "many lies, compounded by additional lies."

"A wishtongue with thoughts and actions filled with evil?" Zennan asked. "I did not believe that such could be true."

At the edge of the shadows the ElderOne Wishtongue stopped and turned back toward Zennan. His shoulders slumped and his eyes showed sadness as he nodded affirmation. "But our ancient ways demand that Claydore be given a second chance if he should request it."

"No matter his transgression?" Zennan asked.

"No matter his transgression," the ElderOne reluctantly declared.

"And he's requested such consideration?"

"Yes, even though I believe that his request itself harbors more evil than he has ever before been guilty of," the ElderOne explained.

"So, beware of his intentions should they include you," Wun advised.

"Yes, beware and be cautious," Wuntu said.

Zennan looked carefully at his three friends. "I see no reason why I should ever meet this one named Claydore, but should such ever occur, I will watch my back as closely as I watch my words to him." He turned away from them and looked across the distance to the tiny window in the Castle Krog. The intermittent flash that earlier had shot from the tower window's opening had been replaced by a steady glow of reddish golden rays.

Once again standing close behind Zennan, the ElderOne pointed to the castle. "The light that shines before you is the light of the Fire Ruby of Molock. It lies in the deepest bowels of the castle, and Ra-Tanox continues as its guardian, though he does not control its power."

"I shall defeat the one named Ra-Tanox," Zennan said, his eyes still fixed on the distant light. "Then I shall take from him that which has never been his and never will be."

"We shall call a gathering of all those you will need for success," Wuntu announced.

"Ah yes, a gathering is needed," Wun said, rubbing his hands together in happy anticipation.

Zennan turned back to Wun and Wuntu. "There will be no gathering," he stated.

"No gathering?" Wun queried.

"No gathering?" Wuntu repeated.

"It will take stealth and secrecy to enter the black castle and discover the hiding place of the Fire Ruby," Zennan said. "I must move like the owl upon the crest of the night wind, swift and focused, silent and deadly, my eye trained only on its prey."

"I see," Wun said.

"Quite right," Wuntu said, as he scratched his head.

Wun looked at his friend. "Scritch scratch?"

"Again, yes," Wuntu acknowledged.

The ElderOne ignored Wun and Wuntu, looking only at Zennan. "You are quite right, of course," he said, nodding his head in agreement. "A gathering would be sure to include potential undesirables, or at the very least, those who might warn Ra-Tanox of your coming."

Zennan looked toward the distant horizon. The first glimmer of dawn's light warmed the top edges of the far mountain beyond the Castle Krog. "I will leave upon this new day's end, as its fading light lowers the curtain of darkness across this land of Ra-Tanox. I will use the safety that darkness affords in order to defeat the evil that darkness protects."

* * *

"Keep those torches held high and be complete and thorough in your searches," Lakat ordered the dozen soldiers who creeped slowly ahead of him. "Those creatures of darkness have interfered with our operations for the last time." He raised his voice. "The one of you who impales the first creature will be rewarded beyond your dreams," then added, "fail and you all will pay a price you never dreamed possible."

The soldiers did not turn to look into Lakat's eyes to see if his words were true. They knew that Lakat would not allow them to settle for failure. They raised their burning torches higher above their heads and doubled their pace, knowing that the creatures they sought could be only paces in front of their sweep through the deep dungeon halls beneath the Castle Krog.

Since the time Meeshannette had released the night creatures from their ancient prison, they had filled the soldiers of Ra-Tanox with fear. Each night they came to the castle's surface courtyard to meet and plan with cityfellows and others, always bringing death and havoc to encountered soldiers. Now the creatures had circled behind and quietly stalked their hunters, staying far enough from sight so that the light from the torches did not sear their sensitive eyes.

Lakat's rage increased as did his threats against his soldiers for their failure to corner and snare even a single one of these pitiful and nearly sightless creatures. The soldiers responded by increasing their pace, now nearly running. But the soldiers' thoughts were quickly turning from anticipation of success in finding their prey to escaping Lakat's saber tongue and his equally sharp and hungry sword.

The lead creature stepped out ahead of his followers, tracking closer to Lakat's back. The moment that Lakat's torch-carrying soldiers rounded a corner, momentarily leaving him in darkness, the creature slipped his body around and in front of the commander. Lakat immediately stumbled over the crouching night creature and fell hard to the stone floor.

Still unaware of what caused his fall, Lakat become more angered because his soldiers and the torches they carried were quickly disappearing, leaving him in total blackness. Lakat slammed the broad edge of his sword's blade on the floor's ancient stone. Quickly, he tried to pick himself up, but before he could get back to his feet he felt a sharp stabbing pain drive deeply into his left thigh. Instinctively he swatted the butt of his sword quickly at the pain, striking the night creature in his head. The creature yelped in pain at the same time that Lakat screamed his own pain-filled warning to his soldiers. But his soldiers weren't listening. They had again increased their pace and had disappeared around still another distant corner. Now only the blackness of stone walls and the muffled sound of scratching foot claws surrounded Lakat.

"Creatures of the night, I will see you burn and your ashes scattered in these dark halls of death," Lakat screamed. He slashed his sword in a large arc, slicing the hand off the lead creature in the attacking horde and gashing the head of another. Before he could bring the blade back in the opposite direction, six creatures simultaneously buried their dagger teeth into Lakat's body, one paralyzing his arm. The sword dropped to the floor, the clang of its metal echoing off into the darkness. A moment later, Lakat spit out his last screaming breath and then lay silent. The creatures quickly disappeared, trailing after the fleeing soldiers and their flickering yellow-orange torch flames that still reflected ever so faintly off the cold stone walls.

The soldiers, now hopelessly lost in the corridor maze, and with their torches burning near their ends, stopped their pursuit of emptiness where the corridor split into three new tunnels and stood nervously arguing among themselves. Indecision, anger and fear cried out as the soldiers splintered into competing groups, each as seemingly destined to failure as the others.

A soldier called Prioton whose loyalty to the Grand Black Sorcerer and Ra-Tanox had never been questioned, stepped forward grabbing two of the closest torches from soldiers too feeble and frightened to argue the loss of their light sources. "You are not soldiers of Ra-Tanox!" he screamed at them. "You are cowards, all of you!" He swung the burning torches around surveying the defeated army. "You will follow me, and we shall escape these darkest bonds of hopelessness."

"Prioton, so you have anointed yourself our new leader?" inquired the largest and oldest of the following soldiers.

Prioton moved his torches being certain that he could see into the eyes of the one who was questioning his intentions. "Would you care to choose the avenue that sends these soldiers to their deaths?" Prioton asked.

There was an immediate rise in the chatter among the gaggle of soldiers stranded deep beneath the castle, but it subsided when Prioton raised and slowly waved his two torches. Again, the old soldier answered for the others.

"And you can guarantee our deliverance from this black hole of death?"

Prioton smiled ever so slightly. "I guarantee only that my way offers more of a chance than either of the three doorways that stand before you."

The old soldier laughed. A few of the others did the same, but nervousness laced their verbal smiles of hope. "And if one of these three ways is not your way, then I suppose you can magically wish us into the castle's courtyard?"

Prioton spoke quietly, certain of his words. "What pursues us from behind will be our future," he said. "We must turn to face our fears if we are to live beyond this moment."

"We cannot fight that which we can't see," one of the soldiers cried.

"My desire to battle them has long passed. My proposal is that we join them in their search for light."

More quickly now, the light from their torches dimmed as two more burned to their ends. Behind Prioton there was a swishing, scratching across the stone floor of the primary corridor. Suddenly the glistening reflections of dozens of green eyes appeared.

Prioton turned to face the fur creatures. "Behold my truth as I speak it to you," he said, his voice sharp with confidence. "We understand the evil that has visited your kind for as long as the great halls of the Castle Krog have existed. We wish to end the wrongs that have destroyed your lives and your kind."

The sounds of shuffling claws stopped. Now only the hisses of a hundred breathing creatures filtered through the long and dark tunnel. A couple quick snorts to Prioton's left pulled his unseeing eyes in that direction as still another of the fire torches died, leaving but one remaining.

A soft, yet menacing voice came from where the snorts had emerged. "You, Prioton, are a strange one to talk of righting wrongs."

"You know my name?" came Prioton's startled reply. He slowly reached for the hilt of his scabbard-held sword, but thought wisely that such was not a useful gesture. He lowered his hands and the remaining torch.

"We know much more about you and your kind than you obviously do about us, but then, knowing us was never a thing of importance to you, was it, Prioton?" the anonymous fur creature advised.

The last of the torches died. In the blackness there was a quick and sudden movement by the fur creatures, causing several whimpered cries to leave the mouths of the soldiers standing behind Prioton.

"Quiet, you pitiful excuses. We have nothing to fear here, as I will demonstrate," Prioton declared. He stared hard into the blackness, seeing nothing, but was able to feel the air movements as the creatures shuffled about. "What say you, creatures of darkness, what commands do you give to us, your newest allies in the search for light?"

Following snorts, shrieks and a few groans, finally the elder fur creature placed his hand upon the arm of Prioton. "Your words offer hope, yet we listen to our hearts, which demand retribution."

"No, you are wrong, as wrong as the Tanox family was treating you as they have done," Prioton insisted. "I and my soldiers await only your word of acceptance and your command to serve, and our services will be yours." He placed his opposite hand over the soft hair of the fur creature's paw-like hand, but the creature of darkness pulled away.

"We will discuss your fate among our learned ones and then make a decision," the elder fur creature announced, his voice soft and serious.

As Prioton and his soldiers began their impatient wait to learn their fate, the noises that had accompanied the gathering fur creatures grew silent, the quickly fading stench only a frightful reminder of their recent presence. It was at this moment that Prioton realized that he and his soldiers were alone with the blackness that surrounded them.

"We are lost and alone," one of his soldiers whimpered into the darkness, hoping that one of his companions was near enough to hear.

"We are alive," came a reply.

"But for how long?" asked another voice.

"Quiet you fools," Prioton commanded. "We will stay together and escape this black prison that those pitiful fur creatures have apparently sentenced us to for eternity. Everyone touch another. Here, one of you move toward me and touch my arm. We will guide ourselves from this miserable stench."

The soldiers gathered, each reaching out to touch another, and the huddled mass followed the commands of Prioton as he felt his way through the corridor's blackness, guessing at which passage might take them one step closer to light. Behind them, two fur creatures ambled along, watching, hovering, knowing that for these followers of Ra-Tanox escape was impossible, even if they happened into the correct tunnels of darkness. As the group shuffled along, the two creatures, one balanced upon the shoulders of the other, moved up closely behind the last soldier in line. Silently, the top creature placed his hand over the soldier's mouth and whispered in his ear, "Do not scream out if you wish to ever again enjoy light during your lifetime."

At the same moment the bottom creature grabbed the startled man's arm. Together the creatures quickly pulled the soldier backward, away from the main body, pushing him down a side tunnel that led back to the cages that the creatures had only and always known as their home. As the first two creatures pulled their soldier away, two new fur creatures did the same to the next soldier, and the process was repeated until only Prioton shuffled along, shouting panicked commands to those who no longer existed. He suddenly swung his arm in a backward arc assuming he would touch the nearest of his subordinates, the one who had accidently let go of his arm, but he swatted only air. He turned to face what he thought was the direction he had just traversed, the slightest feeling of panic beginning to infiltrate his mind.

"Loyal soldiers of Ra-Tanox, believers in the Principles, protectors of all that is ours, answer my call," Prioton commanded, waiting for an answer. When none responded, his voice cracked as fear pressed its heavy foot upon his chest. "Where have you gone? Why do you choose to go by yourselves into the darkness that surrounds us?" He pulled his sword and began swinging it wildly all about him, turning, twisting, dodging imagined sword thrusts from enemies, losing what little sense of direction he had held.

Around him, remaining safely outside his sword's swing, a

dozen fur creatures watched in amused silence until Prioton finally collapsed to his knees, his shoulders slumped, exhausted beyond any ability to defend himself.

The elder fur creature stepped up to Prioton and pulled away his sword, letting it clatter to the stone floor. "You have not fared well, Prioton, and it has been only a very short time. What will you do as the days and nights pass?"

Prioton raised his lowered head and squinted hard at the voice, hoping to see even the slightest hint of form. He saw none. "Please, I have offered my services and those of my soldiers if only you allow us to escape from this place of infinite darkness."

No response came from the fur creatures. Silently they had melted deep into the tunnels, leaving Prioton by himself.

"Do not leave me here alone," Prioton screamed. "I do not deserve to live like this. I have done nothing to any of you." His voice lapsed into sobs. Slowly he stood and began moving through the blackness, feeling, probing, hoping.

CHAPTER SEVENTEEN

Snowflakes, sodden heavy with moisture and frozen into tiny spiked balls, tumbled down from the bottomless sky. They clung to the first surface they touched, most awaiting only the next slight wisp of wind to be pushed and twisted to their final place of frozen rest, their blanket of white concealing the castle's black stones. Zennan's footsteps pressed deeply into the piled snow as he trudged closer to his destination. Behind him his trail pointed toward the tall cliffs where he and Meeshannette together had first viewed the black monolith that now stood within his arm's reach. He could feel the cold grow more frigid as he traced his way around the great black outer stone walls of the Castle Krog.

"It is a meeting we have set for you," Wun's familiar voice piped.

"Tis a meeting of some importance," Wuntu added.

Zennan, tired already from trudging through the thick white blanket, stopped and turned to face the two friends who had suddenly popped up behind him. He knew better than to be surprised by anything he saw, but still he remained curious about why his footsteps alone revealed themselves in the deep snow. Surely, he thought, even smallish creatures such a Wun and Wuntu would leave marks of passage in such a soft and yielding substance. He knew it was futile to allow his thoughts to linger.

"I would prefer not to meet with anyone at this time, just as I told you and the ElderOne." Zennan placed his hands on his hips awaiting their expected argument. They simply stared back and said nothing.

"You need not concern yourselves with my actions beyond the gate and into the castle. Such creatures as yourselves would surely bring only additional and unwelcomed attention to our mutual goals," Zennan reasoned out loud.

"We are not concerned with your concerns," Wun answered.

"Not concerned at all, no, not at all concerned about your concerns," Wuntu said, scratching his back as far up as he could reach with his left hand, then switching to his right hand, which he stretched back around his neck.

"Claydore must see you," Wun said. "He awaits you in the castle ground's most distant brewgrog hollow."

Wuntu simply nodded his agreement, remaining silent for once.

"I would certainly welcome an amber or golden running down my throat. It has been a time longer than I can remember since I last felt such pleasure." He watched as Wun and Wuntu quickly slipped back the way he had come, carefully, yet quickly, stepping in his deep steps. Zennan nodded to himself, knowingly. "If this untrustworthy one named Claydore should be in the place where they serve the brewgrog, and he wishes to speak to me, why should I listen?" he asked of his two friends. Without slowing or turning, Wun waved his hand quickly in acknowledgement, with Wuntu imitating the movement.

Another dozen steps and Zennan stood at the final corner before reaching the castle's primary gate. He stood quietly behind the protruding rocks that extended out several paces beyond the base of the towering wall. He crouched down and pulled his hood over his head, allowing the whiteness of the clinging snow to further hide him from any probing eyes that might search the area. Zennan needn't have worried as he quickly discovered. Those few cityfellow travelers who passed in and out of the castle's open gateway did not look up from their chosen paths. Their eyes remained downward cast, as their shuffling feet carried them onward, each step closer to their awaiting concerns.

When finally the first hint of darkness cast its shadow across the already dusky gray of the low hanging snow clouds, the passing of cityfellows became even more intermittent. In a smooth and seamless movement, Zennan slipped from behind his rock hiding place and leaped up to the worn and deeply cut pathway that led to and from the castle's gate. If one of the cityfellows saw him, none was willing to make any obvious notice. Each silently continued along his chosen way as Zennan took up their same slow, shuffled gait, blending himself well, only the slightly larger size of his hunched body making him stand out. As he passed through the open gateway, Zennan noticed the series of relatively small rollers that were set on the ground beneath two massive, translucent black stone gates, each resting on opposite sides of the expansive and open entry. Although he knew that it was not wise to stare too long, it was obvious to Zennan that the two walls could be rolled together in order to fully and securely block entry. But he thought that it would take far too many of the strongest soldiers to push the great gates closed. He continued on, careful not to pass too closely to the slump-walking villagefellows ahead of him.

Now in the open courtyard, many more cityfellows scurried around like confused mice seeking a meal they did not know where to find, hoping only to avoid the crushing hand of the soldiers of Ra-Tanox. But, the soldiers were few, and those who remained stayed deep within the Grand Palace. Before Zennan lay the entry to the Grand Palace, but he turned away from its approach and instead headed to the most distant of the groghollows within the castle's walls. Zennan kept his head down as he walked, and as he came closer he was joined by others whose destination was also the groghollow. One of the cityfellows, the one taller by a full head than the others, moved up closely behind Zennan as he entered the door into the darkened interior of the busy establishment. Zennan stood for a moment and cautiously surveyed his new surroundings. Those inside returned his look, but without conspicuously moving their heads or shifting their eyes away from their own business.

Seeing nothing that threatened or should be feared, Zennan seated himself at an empty table. The head-taller stranger who had hovered close behind him also had not gone unnoticed by those inside. The stranger stepped up behind the seated Zennan.

"You are not one who I am anxious to meet," Zennan said without turning to face the stranger. The old groghollow tender moved steadily from table to table. Zennan nodded as the tender scuffled by before heading off to fill his largest flagon for the huge visitor, noticing, but refusing to acknowledge the stranger standing at Zennan's back. "Should I turn to face you?" he asked the stranger. "Is your presence a threat that should concern me, Claydore?"

"Me, a threat?" Claydore asked, the surprise in his voice at being known by name only partially masked. "If you know who I am, you would know that I wish only to help you in your quest."

"Come, sit," the sense of command obvious in Zennan's voice. "Join me this evening and we will see if you will indeed be useful to my endeavors."

Claydore grabbed an empty stool and scooted it up to Zennan's table and sat down. He raised his hand high and garnered the tender's attention. The tender nodded and quickly returned to Zennan's table with two filled flagons, their foamy amber heads oozing over the sides and spilling out onto the table. The tender quickly swiped a damp rag across the tabletop's loose liquid, then left the two visitors as he attended to lighting several more candles and lanterns filled with papold vine oil. Soon the thickly sweet scent of the oil lanterns spread through the groghollow.

Claydore took a quick drink of his amber, savoring its sweet bitterness. "What is it that you wish from me?" he asked.

"What makes you think that it is I who needs anything from you?"

"Ra-Tanox still possesses a strength that can smother life from even the strongest of adversaries," Claydore said. "I wish to assist you in stealing the power that fuels the strength of Ra-Tanox."

Now it was Zennan's turn to drink his amber, keeping his eyes focused on Claydore as he did. Finally, "What is this power that you speak of?" he asked.

Claydore smiled, thinking that he had so quickly captured this traveling warrior's mind. "It is said that there is a power that only the family Tanox has controlled since the beginning of time. A power such that even the greatest of enemies is powerless to defeat."

"You say there is a power possessed by this one called Ra-Tanox, the ruler of this castle and all its domain, a power such that it ensures his power to last an eternity?" Zennan feigned ignorance and concern for a moment as he drank again from his flagon.

Claydore looked around the darkened room and noticed that many eyes were upon him, though none stared directly. He looked back at Zennan. "We must find a place of more solitude and privacy if I am to give you the information that you will need for success."

"You assume that there is some great and dangerous quest that awaits me," Zennan said. "Perhaps what I seek is all that I have already found, a quiet place in which to enjoy this delightful amber." Claydore stood and motioned for Zennan to follow him outside. Zennan sat, thinking, but quickly decided that it was best if he listened to this one called Claydore. He slugged down the remainder of his amber grog, then followed Claydore. The tender watched them leave, then hurried into the groghollow's back room.

Outside, Claydore directed Zennan to the darkest of the shadows. He looked around to be sure that all was clear.

"I have come to lead you to the lower chambers of the castle," Claydore whispered.

"Why should I trust you, one who has already deceived his own kind?"

Claydore was uneasy about Zennan knowing so much about his past, but decided after a moment of contemplation to use it to his advantage. "Yes, it is true that past youthful indiscretions led me away from the true course of a wishtongue. And for that I have paid dearly, losing all of the powers and intellect that are part of even the lowest of wishtongues."

Zennan smiled. "So, a wishtongue who is a mere mortal? How sad for you and those you have failed." He waited for a response from Claydore, but the failed wishtongue remained silent. "Why should I trust you now? Why should the success or failure of my entire quest be put into your hands?" Zennan asked.

"Our laws allow that if I do all that the ElderOne requests of me, I may once earn the return of my powers."

Zennan thought for a moment, looking through the darkness, attempting to see Claydore's eyes. He didn't believe the failed wishtongue's words, but his way was the fastest way into the bowels of the castle, a place he must ultimately seek. "I will go with you, but I warn you, treachery will end your life, mere mortal."

"I understand," Claydore said, as he motioned for Zennan to follow him to a nearby entry door that had been left partly open.

* * *

The creature scampered out of the groghollow's backroom window and easily slipped past the two soldiers standing half-asleep near the well. Over the well's short stone wall, down the rope, a quick swing and it was running along the same low and lightless tunnel that Meeshannette had traveled down, so long ago. When finally the creature of darkness stopped running, it stood before the gaggle of its own kind. It slid in next to the leader and whispered silently into his ear.

"He comes to us soon," the creature said, slightly panting.

"Ummm," grunted his leader.

"The grog tender," the small creature of darkness said, "he watched them leave together. The traitor called Claydore has led the seeker of light into a treachery bred by the evil of Ra-Tanox." The creature looked around him, finally noticing that his companions were still standing in motionless silence. "Why do we stand together in such a quiet manner?" he asked.

The answer to his question came to him and the others before anyone could speak. In the center of the open cell a glow pierced the blackness, bright and blue, at first pulsating, then slowly turning to a steady stream of multi-fragmented beams. The small creature's mouth fell open as he and all his companions squinted their light-sensitive eyes nearly closed. The old leader was the first to notice, feeling the tortured banners of pain caused by the bright light leave his senses untouched. He carefully opened his eyes fully to take in the view of the apparition that stood before him. The blue light wizard smiled a slight smile as he nodded his acknowledgement to the old leader of the creatures of the dark tunnels.

"Now is the time for you and your faithful to open your eyes wide to the evil that the family Tanox has spread heavy across these lands since before any of our memories can recall," the blue wizard announced, his voice soft with compassion, yet strong in conviction.

"The one called Zennan has entered the castle grounds," the leader said.

"And the one called Claydore now accompanies him," the blue wizard added.

"That we know is true, wizard."

"The one called Claydore seeks to mislead and betray Zennan, yet Claydore is not capable of deceiving this one who has traveled from beyond the beginning of the end of light."

Now, the other creatures were realizing that the light that had pained their eyes since the beginning of all they knew, no longer hindered their seeing beyond darkness. The young creature who had just returned from his meeting with the brewgrog tender stared wide-eyed at the blue wizard. He turned to his leader once more and nudged him slightly.

"If I knew what it was that my eyes were seeing, I might ask a question that would lessen my uneasiness about such a vision," he mumbled, his voice barely audible to the leader and unheard by the others of his kind.

The leader placed his hand on the young one's shoulder. "The fear that you feel burning inside you is merely the ignorance pressed upon us since the eternal darkness began," he said.

The blue wizard raised his voice for all to hear. "Be brave, creatures of darkness. I have lifted the veiled shadow that has darkened your lives. Use this opportunity to help seize the power that Ra-Tanox holds."

"And how shall we, ones who have lived our lives in darkness, recognize the direction that the new light points?" asked the leader of the creatures of darkness. "What shall we do to ensure success?"

The blue wizard slowly, yet instantly, made eye contact with each of the individual creatures who stood before him. And each creature, in turn, nodded to acknowledge the vision that the blue wizard projected into each of their minds. The leader understood even more than his followers, yet his understanding did not bring comfort to his mind.

"What you ask is perhaps too great a request of ones so long trapped and terrorized by the powers that live above us," the creature leader stated.

"The power that controls, controls only those who allow it go on unquestioned by knowledge and unchallenged by time," the blue wizard countered. "You will know which way to turn when your time comes, and it is then that you will once again gain control of your own destinies."

The leader nodded, and as he did, the vision of the blue wizard grew brighter, quickly turning into a brilliant luminescence that reflected the black cave into cascading shades of blue-white. Then the wizard flashed an explosion of blue spears of light and disappeared.

The young creature of darkness looked up at his leader waiting for direction. Without uttering a word, the leader nodded to his young follower, turned toward the open doorway that led past their old cells and to the first set of stairs, and shuffled off. The youngster motioned for the others to join, and together, the entire tightly huddled gaggle of creatures began their journey to light.

* * *

The great and flowing robe of fine black silk flew back from his shoulders, revealing a thin and boney bared chest, covered only with its swirl of tattoos. Driven by the madness that careened through his mind, Ra-Tanox flew down the stone steps, taking three with each leap. His breaths came in heaving gasps, and his heart pounded.

When Ra-Tanox reached the heavy double doors guarding the entrance to the Inferno of Tanox and the eternal guardian of the Fire Ruby of Molock, the two soldiers immediately retreated down the darkened tunnel, fearing for their lives. Ra-Tanox ignored the two soldiers, instead crashing his right shoulder into the sacred chamber's doors. The door remained closed. He screamed an agony-filled howl that echoed its way after his retreating soldiers. Another crash of his shoulder into the door and it creaked open enough for him to slip through.

The two scrambling, escaping soldiers rounded the first corner, and in the darkness they collided with two strangers. The soldiers stumbled backward into the sliver shaft of light that escaped through the entry and into the sacred chamber. Surprised and shaken they regained their balance just as Zennan and Claydore stepped into the same stream of light. Frightened and confused, the two soldiers attempted to scream, but couldn't. They stumbled away from the two strangers, finally managing to turn around and run once again, darting back past the great doors, down the corridor and up the stairs from where Ra-Tanox had just come.

"This way," Claydore encouraged. "The prize we seek will be found just beyond those two doors." He pointed to the slight opening in the great guarding doorway.

Zennan stepped ahead of Claydore and quickly approached

the slightly opened door. Claydore stayed close behind. Suddenly, Claydore put his own shoulder down and charged himself into the unsuspecting Zennan, driving him into the sacred chamber. Zennan stumbled as he passed through the door and landed, sprawled on the floor and staring up at the back of Ra-Tanox, who faced the forged stone pedestal that held the great Fire Ruby.

Without turning to face Zennan, Ra-Tanox spoke. "You have traveled a great distance in order to meet your death."

Zennan, still lying on the cold, black floor, looked up to see the once unarmed Claydore, standing over him, now holding a massive, yet sleek and glistening iron sword above his head, ready to strike. Ra-Tanox turned to face Zennan.

"I have only to command the end to your pitiful life, and you will be but a sad and short memory in the minds of your people, whoever and wherever they may be," Ra-Tanox said.

Zennan noted the absence of honest strength that betrayed the threatening and ominous words of Ra-Tanox. Ra-Tanox's voice was not as certain and powerful as it should have been in such a situation. Zennan's next words came slowly, but they emerged from the deepest part of his being.

"You are a power whose time has ended," Zennan started, causing Claydore's face to tense and his muscles to ripple in readiness as he brought his sword to its highest apex. Before he could drive the iron blade into its intended victim, Ra-Tanox raised his hand.

"No, not yet," Ra-Tanox said. "Let the stranger finish his words, then you may quench your sword's thirst for blood." He looked back down at Zennan. "You, intruder, tell me what I wish to know and I will guarantee you a quick and relatively painless death. Fail to speak the truth and your blood will boil slowly in the great fires that burn before us." Suddenly the Inferno of Tanox roared its flames around the Fire Ruby and then up toward the ceiling of the chamber behind Ra-Tanox, disappearing in the lofty heights above, finally escaping through a small ceiling port.

"There is little I could tell you that you don't already know," Zennan answered, still remaining in his disadvantaged position on the cold stone floor.

"There was an infant, a boy child who was born to a young yet pitiful village creature whose name was Meeshannette," Ra-Tanox began. "Tell me if you have seen them in your travels, and where they are at this time." He moved close to Zennan, allowing the black, silk cape to flow out around him when he stopped, its bottom edge nearly touching the prone prisoner.

Zennan suppressed the look of surprise quickly followed by anger that fell across his face. He took a deep breath before answering, hoping the slight delay would allow him to fill his voice with the neutral tone needed to keep Ra-Tanox from commanding Claydore's hovering sword to fall. "A child, you say? And its mother whose name is as strange as this question that you ask of me?"

Ra-Tanox screeched, "Do not play games with me. My once-trusted sorcerer told me that one who appears as you, traveled with Meeshannette." He squatted down placing his face only inches from the face of Zennan. "I have little patience for you. Tell me what I wish to know or suffer the consequences, which I can assure you will not be pleasantly endured." Ra-Tanox gleefully kicked Zennan in his ribs, forcing him to roll over onto his stomach.

As Zennan's spoke his next words, he slowly moved his hands under his chest and flat against the floor. "Yes, yes, I have indeed seen the one you call Meeshannette, although I did not know her name. I saw her running along the river, her belly filled with the swollen form of a new child. She hesitated at the edge of the precipice of a great and powerful waterfall, but before I could get to her, she leaped from its edge and disappeared into the foam and cold at the bottom of the falls."

"Lies, lies!" Ra-Tanox screamed, moving his face within a breath's of Zennan's. "She was seen with the child already born," he raged. "You will pay dearly for your lies." Just as Ra-Tanox motioned for Claydore to strike the stranger dead, Zennan reached out with his right hand and grabbed Ra-Tanox's spindly neck and pulled him down across his own back. The iron blade fell, and before Claydore could reverse his strike, Ra-Tanox shrieked in agony and horror as his right arm lay severed and bleeding on the floor beside them. Claydore panicked and his lungs heaved to a stop as fear gripped his heart. He stood looking down at his master and Zennan. Zennan quickly pushed Ra-Tanox off him, rolling him over the bloody, twitching arm. Without thinking another thought, Zennan kicked upward striking Claydore under the chin, instantly snapping his neck. Claydore dropped to the cold floor, the back of his head striking hard against the black stone.

"Mere mortal! I warned you about such treachery!" Ra-Tanox again screamed in horror. He attempted to fight his way to his feet, failed, then crawl-slid on three points, finally rolling to a stop with his back pressed hard against the stone pedestal holding the Fire Ruby. He looked at his stub-arm spewing blood from its severed arteries, then pushed his head up and back staring at the glimmering edge of the Fire Ruby. The heat from the inferno behind the pedestal flared momentarily causing Ra-Tanox to draw back from its searing heat. With his remaining arm, he reached upward, stretching his long fingers near, but not quite touching the ruby.

Halfway across the chamber Zennan's immediate thoughts focused on Claydore, being certain that his body remained lifeless. Quickly Zennan's eyes moved to Ra-Tanox as he watched the evil one's second failed attempt to reach for the ruby. Zennan swept up Claydore's fallen sword and spoke to Ra-Tanox, and for the first time in a very long while his voice flowed in its ancient melodic tone. "You have stretched far beyond what your reach will allow you to grasp. The prize you seek is not yours to possess." Zennan moved to within striking distance of the fallen, one-armed leader and looked down upon him, pity or sorrow absent from his eyes. "It was never yours, and without it you are nothing more than the wind of a fearful and lingering storm that ultimately passes."

"You will not have it," Ra-Tanox screamed. He suddenly tucked his leg up under himself and leaped upward, his outstretched fingers reaching the Fire Ruby and wrapping themselves tightly around it. The flames shrieked out from their darkest depth and swirled their burning fires around his fist that clenched the unmovable gem. Ra-Tanox screamed again, this time his agony filled the chamber.

Zennan raised the sword but stopped and watched. He stood ready to slash its blade through Ra-Tanox's remaining arm as the leader of darkness struggled to pull the Fire Ruby from its mount. Just as every muscle in Zennan's arms tightened to strike, the Fire Ruby exploded shooting bolts of red light through Ra-Tanox's hand, piercing jagged holes through his flesh, leaving only a blackened cage of finger bones grasping the glowing stone. Still, Zennan did not drop the sword's blade through Ra-Tanox's bone and flesh. He only watched, transfixed at what he was witnessing.

Slowly, the bones surrounding the Fire Ruby tightened their grip as Ra-Tanox ignored the searing light and charring flames and attempted to wrench the crystal from it resting place atop the stone pedestal. From deep within his body a low growl began to emerge, quickly growing into a high-pitched howl as his mouth opened wide, exposing long and ragged teeth, now stained and streaked black. As the scream reached its highest crescendo, Ra-Tanox lunged his entire body into the pedestal, and for the first time in untold centuries the pedestal began to teeter. Still grasping the jewel, Ra-Tanox sent a final and still more powerful lunge into the pedestal, toppling the stone edifice onto its side. At that same moment, Zennan slashed his sword downward at the outstretched arm of Ra-Tanox. The sword missed its intended target, slicing instead through Ra-Tanox's upper left leg. Ra-Tanox shrieked, not from the pain, but because the falling pedestal pulled his fingers free from the Fire Ruby. When the pedestal crashed to its resting place, the Fire Ruby cracked loose from its ancient fixture and shot across the floor's stone surface. As Zennan raised the sword for a second blow, Ra-Tanox struggled to chase after the prize, dragging himself across the floor, now slick with his own spilled blood. His arm stretched outward, the remnant bones of his reaching fingers straining toward the fallen jewel of power.

Before Ra-Tanox could again capture the prize he had sought his entire life, Zennan let the great sword fall, this time finishing its intended work. As the life forces heaved their way from the body of Ra-Tanox, the great Inferno of Tanox screamed, swirling its flames and heat upward and around the fallen leader.

Quickly and in one smooth motion, Zennan dropped the sword and leaped forward toward the Fire Ruby. Just as he did, the great door to the chamber swung open. A moment later he grasped the mystical crystal and pulled it close to his chest as the creatures of darkness flooded into the room. Zennan looked at them as he held the stone. The creatures parted and allowed the blue wizard to also enter the chamber.

At the sight of the blue wizard, Zennan smiled, but it was a smile that lasted only a moment. Zennan's hand began to feel the heat as the Fire Ruby pulsated to life, sending shards of blue flame through his fingers. Instead of trying to throw the jewel to the ground and free himself from its uncontrolled energies, he squeezed it tighter, then wrapped his other hand around the first that held the prize of power. Still, the heat intensified and the odor of seared flesh filled the nostrils of all those present.

"Aggghhh, I will not allow that for which I have searched for so long and sacrificed so much, to defeat me now in my time of victory," Zennan said, his voice only slightly louder than a normal tone, and equally without fear or loathing.

"Aaeeeaaiii," the chorus of frightened and shrill voices cried out. The creatures of darkness reeled backward, then slowly, one by one, they relaxed. Before them, as the ruby cooled its interior fire in the grasp of Zennan's hands, long and twisting shards of sharp-edged red-turning-to-blue light shot outward, circled near the top of the tall ceiling, then crashed straight down, slicing and burning into the chest of Ra-Tanox.

"Aaeeeaaiii," came a second chorus of screams from the creatures of darkness. It was then that the heart of Ra-Tanox exploded from his chest as his disfigured body and its severed parts burst into orange and blue flames, crackling hot flames that consumed the flesh, the bone and the departing soul of Ra-Tanox.

"Tis a mess you have made," a familiar voice said.

"Tis truly a mess that you have made," the second and equally familiar voice of Wun added.

Zennan, aware that the Fire Ruby he held had removed its vengeance and ended its searing heat, now turned his attention to the two smallish creatures who emerged from the darkness. They had not come from where all of the others, including himself and Ra-Tanox, had entered the chamber. Instead, they stood behind him in the dark shadows near the precipice edge of the suddenly mellowed flames of the Inferno of Tanox.

"Your presence, as is your usual custom, does not come at an unwelcomed time, although its timing could have been earlier," Zennan said.

"Timing is not always a matter of choice," Wun said.

"Yes, truly a choice of time is not always controlled by us," Wuntu added.

"We control only our actions," Wun explained to the uncomprehending Zennan.

"Which in turn destiny's time controls," Wuntu concluded in explanation.

Zennan shook his head slowly. "I appreciate all that you bring." He motioned to the blue wizard, but still spoke to Wun and Wuntu. "I have learned to assume nothing, and sometimes suspected that you two are acquainted with the blue wizard who has been an occasional, though not unwelcomed visitor to my night dreams."

The blue wizard nodded his acknowledgement toward the two smallish creatures. "My friends here invited me tonight, explaining your needs," he said.

"Perhaps it would be good if either you or they explained to me what my needs are," Zennan said, the slightest fragment of sarcasm tracing its way into the sound of his words.

"There can be only one answer," Wun responded. He walked up to Zennan who still stood only a short distance from where the image of Ra-Tanox lay burned into the stone floor.

"Truly only one answer," Wuntu chimed, following in Wun's footsteps and stopping at his heels.

"For all the times that I have been acquainted with you, I have never known either of you to hold only one answer to anything, at least any single answer that could be understood to be only one answer," Zennan said. He turned his attention back to the dimmed Fire Ruby he held in his hands. Cold as ice now, its searing light escaped, though its sharp brilliance remaining unblemished. He held it out before him and looked to the blue wizard for words that might guide him.

"You have offered me welcomed wisdom when through ignorance none was desired by me," Zennan began. "Now that I hold in my hand what seems to be the final quest of my journey, you must tell me what it means."

"Your wings have grown much during your journey. The wind that once pressed your face, now bends at your beckoning call, Zennan. The flames that fired the Inferno of Tanox have been quenched of their maelstrom anger." The blue wizard raised his arms and motioned to all the creatures of darkness who stood around him. "They are with us now, having witnessed the final demise and destruction of the power that for more than ten eternities has held in bondage all who sought the sight and gift of light."

Zennan lowered his hand that held the Fire Ruby. "I do not understand how such a power could have existed. The family Tanox, which has pressed light into darkness during all this time, why could they not physically possess the Fire Ruby? Why did they allow it to remain atop its ancient pedestal?"

"The weakness of Ra-Tanox lay not in his ability or inability to possess the Fire Ruby. Indeed, he and his ancestors have always controlled the stone that rested upon its equally ancient pedestal," the blue wizard said. He walked up to Zennan and pointed his crooked forefinger at the crimson jewel that Zennan held. "But none of the family Tanox fully understood that the stone's power lay, not in possessing the stone itself. The power, as it always has been, lay deep within the master who controls it. Ra-Tanox, just as his did predecessors, could not look deeply enough into himself for the power that could be created and possessed only from within himself. All expected the power to come from deep within the bowels of the Inferno of Tanox, transmitted through the Fire Ruby to its holder."

Once again Zennan held the fisted Fire Ruby out before him and slowly opened his hand. As he did, the jewel took on a dim but powerful glow that slowly pulsated, passing its light chards harmlessly through all those who stood before him. All except the blue wizard.

"I fear that I have much to learn about the power of the Fire Ruby," Zennan said.

"Do not fear what you do not yet understand. Seek only the knowledge and strength that will be needed to allow the sacred jewel's light to penetrate all those who will now bow before you and your power and wisdom," the wizard responded, his voice hard, yet solemn.

"Yes," Wuntu said, perching himself atop the empty Fire Ruby's fallen pedestal. "Do not fear."

"Certainly, not now," Wun agreed, scrambling to sit himself atop Wuntu's shoulders. The two teetered precariously. There was a last gasp of warm wind that pushed up from the dying inferno's belly far below them.

"You have had no fear, even when fear would have caused most of your kind to tread softly before fleeing," Wuntu chirped, again trying to settle himself more securely atop the pedestal.

The largest and oldest of the dark dwelling fur creatures stepped forward and bowed slightly to Zennan. "You are the one we have sought since before we were imprisoned in this place of darkness," he mumbled softly. "Me and mine will loyally serve you as our commitment to repay your kindness to us."

"It was not I who freed you and yours," Zennan reminded him.

The elder creature lowered his head in sadness. "We have shed many tears for the one called Meeshannette. Without her, we could not have become the one who could successfully pry loose the bands binding our feet and our minds for this eternity."

All grew quiet as time escaped, the creatures of darkness losing ancient thoughts of anger and misery from their collective minds. In the hushed quiet, the air above their heads was cut softly and silently by the wings of a bird, large and powerful, yet more sleek and swift than any that even the blue wizard had ever before witnessed. The great black bird climbed silently from the depths of the inferno, unseen and unheard until it was flying above them. As they stood in awe of this unknown beast circling above, riding the warm rising air still simmering from the inferno, it suddenly tucked its wings close to its body and became a projectile falling faster than even the burning rocks that sometime fell from the black heavens above. It aimed its powerful beak at the two who sat atop the pedestal, but its trajectory changed just a wink before it struck them, instead wheeling over, and swooping through Zennan's still outstretched hand.

So quickly was it over that Zennan did not even realize the pain from his missing hand until the great black flying beast had disappeared into the highest reaches of the tower above them and out the top port. When Zennan realized his outstretched hand and the Fire Ruby it held were both missing, he screamed, his lungs echoing both pain and frustration. Wun and Wuntu had also disappeared, as had the blue wizard. Cowering in the shadowed base of the chamber's walls, the creatures of darkness shivered in their feelings of fear as a last burst of fire and inky smoldering smoke swirled upward from the inferno.

CHAPTER EIGHTEEN

Zennan, his arm heavily bandaged, sat in the groghollow, with the cityfellows and creatures of darkness gathered around him. The grog tender passed among the silence pouring their flagons full of his amber and gold liquids. Wun sat cross-legged on the table directly in front of Zennan, while Wuntu perched himself on the top of a stack of empty brew kegs against the near wall. All their eyes ignored the door as it opened and the eldest of the Wishtongues entered, clothed in his loden, rough-weave hooded cloak. His yellow eyes glowed in the groghollow's uneven light. He tugged the hood to better cover his face.

With no word being passed between them or among others, the wishtongue ElderOne settled himself down on the remaining empty chair at Zennan's table.

"Much has passed since our first meeting in the house of Farro," Zennan said, sadness filling his voice.

"Much sadness, yes," piped Wuntu from the top of his perch. He took a long drink from his near-full flagon.

"Tis sadly true," agreed Wun, shuttling himself around to face the ElderOne.

"I know of your loss, Zennan," the ElderOne said. He paused for a moment, allowing his acknowledgement to be heard and fully understood by Zennan. "It has been said that you held the Fire Ruby of Molock in your hand." He glanced at the bandage. "But it appears you paid a very high price for temporarily possessing such a prize."

Zennan held up his bandaged stump. "Yet not a price so high as paid by Ra-Tanox."

The wishtongue pushed his hood back from his head and his yellow eyes glowed bright in the dim light. Those in the groghollow drew themselves back from the sight. He held out his closed fist. Before all those gathered to celebrate the end of Ra-Tanox and to mourn the loss of the Fire Ruby of Molock, the wishtongue slowly opened his hand, revealing the stolen jewel. Pieces of light spilled from its edges, mixing their amber cast with the golden flickerings of the groghollow's candles.

Zennan looked with uncertain trepidation upon the holder of the Fire Ruby as its light reflected its image upon his eyes. He uttered no words and made no move from his seat, choosing instead to await the wishtongue's next move.

"Your confusion awaits a straight line on which to walk its way to comprehension and completion," the wishtongue announced. "Perhaps I should explain."

"A wise man awaits the clearing of the fog bank before sailing his ship through a rocky passage," Zennan said.

"And a wiser man allows others to tread before him in such dangerous waters."

"Your point, ElderOne?"

"Impatience has not been robbed from you, I see." The wishtongue moved his chair around the table closer to Zennan, plucking a flagon of brewgrog from the tray of the tender who wandered near yet was careful to keep a respectful mind and a respectful distance from the strange visitor.

"Impatience, a weakness of such enduring strength," Wun chanted, quickly plopping himself down from his seat and onto the edge of the table. Wuntu shifted his position atop the kegs.

"Tis true, indeed," Wuntu agreed as he dug his heals into the barrel's wooden staves for added balance.

The wishtongue guided his vision around the groghollow. With all pretense of modesty or honor abandoned by those inside, all eyes were directed upon the wishtongue ElderOne, awaiting what words he might utter. The wishtongue looked hard now at Zennan. "You have traveled far and learned more than any before you," he began. "Yet there is more which you must learn if you are to successfully allow the light of the Fire Ruby to enlighten the distant lands of darkness."

Zennan nodded acknowledgement that he had heard the wishtongue's words, though not necessarily agreeing with them.

The wishtongue continued: "Ra-Tanox and those of his family before him who controlled the resting place of the Fire Ruby of Molock did not understand the power they possessed," the wishtongue explained. "What they found was confusion, believing that the sparkle of red light transmitted by the jewel that lay before them and the wealth it promised, granted to them a special power." The wishtongue took a drink of his brew, allowing a moment for his words of confusion to meld with the minds of those who surrounded him. "What they didn't realize was that the control they wished to possess could not come from a gem, brilliant though it might be, but must come from each of them. The ruby served only to confuse and hinder what were surprisingly simple, yet evil and calculating minds."

"So," said Zennan, "these same words I heard said by the blue wizard. Now you confirm that the Fire Ruby is worthless?"

"Certainly as worthless as the once touted Principles of Tanox had become to those who believed in such things," the wishtongue offered. In the beginning the Principles were offered by Aa-Tanox, the first of the Tanox rulers, as a way of placating his conquered ones, providing them with guarantees of certain freedoms and rights, outlined within reasonable limits."

"If such were true, then how did these Principles become the ropes that strangled light and life from the world as we know it?" Zennan queried.

"Just as the power of the Fire Ruby had become distorted and misunderstood," the wishtongue stated to those who listened. He took a long slow drink of his amber grog, then refocused his eyes upon Zennan. "As the evil within the family Tanox waned and expanded upon the wishes and abilities of its rulers, so too did the interpretations of the Principles. From freedoms guaranteed, to a corrupt and disfigured sense of entitlement owed its owners, further strengthened by the discovery and capture of the Fire Ruby of Molock, the Principles became the chains of enforced servitude that strangled life and light from the empire. The Principles became words, changed as required, to meet the growing and changing demands that the Tanox rulers placed upon their people."

"If the Fire Ruby is truly absent of its proclaimed power, why then did I pay for it with the loss of my hand, and Meeshannette with the loss of her life?"

"Indeed, the loss of Meeshannette was unfortunate, but the loss of your hand was merely illusionary, a false vision created by the blinding powers of the ruby," the wishtongue said. "It was the blue wizard who brought the great black bird up from the imagined depths of the inferno, not me."

"The blue wizard, as he stood before me, was responsible for the loss of my hand?" Anger welled to the surface of Zennan's face. He held high the bandaged stump at the end of his arm. "The loss of my hand, my wizened wishtongue, is not illusionary."

A brush of cold air pushed itself into the groghollow as the door quickly opened, then closed. The surrounding villagefellows moved outward from the newest intruder who now stood before them. Even Wun hopped down from the table and joined Wuntu atop the brew barrels.

The intruder nodded at Zennan. "The loss of your hand is truly as illusionary as the power of the Fire Ruby," he said. "Remove your hand's wrappings and allow light to enter where bandages of darkness now bind your mind."

Slowly, Zennan began to remove the bundle of bloodied bandages that wrapped the end of his arm. To his amazement the feeling of his hand began to return as the wrappings were removed and piled upon the floor. The last bandage dropped away revealing a strong and healthy hand.

"Ooooh, such magic is even beyond our dreams," Wuntu gasped.

"Oooh, yes, tis much beyond what we could know," Wun agreed, keeping his voice soft and unheard by any but Wuntu.

"What trickery is this that you play upon my mind? First to steal my hand, then to return it unharmed? Is it also your intention to restore the Fire Ruby to my possession?"

The blue wizard smiled ever so slightly as he looked thoughtfully at the Fire Ruby that remained in his possession and he held out for all to witness. He tossed the gem to Zennan who reacted quickly enough with his newly restored hand to catch the flying jewel before it passed him and smashed itself on the hard floor.

"Take the ruby. Its power is symbolic. The power to restore the light where darkness has been cast by the family Tanox now lies within you and you alone. Go now and spread the word that you have destroyed the power of Tanox. Let the Fire Ruby of Molock be your truth."

Zennan stood, slowly tightening his fist around the red jewel. Silence crossed his mind and he remained motionless for several moments. Finally, he looked at the wishtongue, then to the blue wizard. "You have used the magic of illusion to steal and then return both my hand and the ruby. Meeshannette was taken . . ." His voice trailed off into silence as the blue wizard raised his hand motioning a halt to Zennan's words.

"It is illusion only when I have initiated the action," the wizard said. "Meeshannette's life was not an illusion, nor, sadly, was her death." He stopped, allowing Zennan to fully grasp and understand the meaning of his words. "Yet," he continued, "there was a child."

Zennan looked at him, happiness quickly tempered by sad remembrances filling his eyes. "There were two children," he corrected. "The first a boy, his fate unknown, though he is likely filled with the anger and darkness of Ra-Tanox. The second child, a daughter we named Spirit, the joy of our love, I hope that she is safe. But I lack faith that I shall ever see her again so that I may tell her of her mother's beauty, her bravery, her enduring spirit."

"Understood, my friend," the blue wizard said, as he scrunched his brow. "What are your plans now that all is again peaceful and the sun once again sheds its light on all those who wish for darkness to be vanquished?"

Confidence filled the beginnings of the age crevices that were now making their marks upon Zennan's weathered face. For the first time in many passed seasons his voice resumed its youthful, melodic sing-song resonance: "I shall seek the daughter of my union with Meeshannette, and when I find her, she shall come to know her mother as though she has been with her always. Then, I shall enjoy my own years as an elder in our village and as the grandfather of my daughter's children.

"All appears well, then?" Wuntu asked.

"All appears well, though illusion may remain," Wun answered, knowing it was so.

"The beginning of the end?" Wuntu asked.

"Yes, the beginning, though reaching the end may prove elusive," he said.

"One final drink of my special amber," cried the grog tender as he tapped the keg upon which Wun and Wuntu sat.

"Aye," went the combined cry of the gathered cityfellows. Even the creatures of darkness who were present joined in as Wun and Wuntu offered their able assistance in pouring full the empty flagons. As the flagons were hoisted and quickly emptied, Zennan slipped out of the front door, with only the wishtongue, Wun, Wuntu and the blue wizard aware that he had gone in search of the Spirit of Meeshannette—the Spirit of One.

THE BEGINNING OF THE END OF DARKNESS...

* * *

Great young people
Doing great things for the world!

Stand Up! is the generation-defining book that focuses on the globabl youth movement like never before. This anthology features stories by 75 of the world's most dynamic young activists who share their amazing experiences and challenge readers through spirited calls to action. Today, by way of their grassroots movements and international work, these young men and women are brining their own barnd of savvy compassion and unstoppable courage to the crossroads of social entrepreneurship and activism.

Available at Amazon as both print and ebook

ISBN
978-0-9850602-9-9

Print cover price:
$16.95

E-book price
$8.99

Do you have a great teen story to share?

OMG! My Reality! For Teens

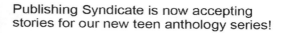

Publishing Syndicate is now accepting stories for our new teen anthology series!

This new anthology will feature a collection of personal real-life stories written by and about teens. We are looking for humorous, heart-warming and inspiring stories **written by individuals 25 years old and younger about teen life.**

If you have a story to share about a personal experience that will touch the hearts, lives and souls of teens, we would love to consider it for publication in *OMG! My Reality! For Teens*. Royalties will be paid to those whose stories make the final cut.

For more information and to read submission guidelines, please visit the website below. And tell your friends, too!

www.PublishingSyndicate.com

Proof

Made in the USA
Charleston, SC
03 September 2014